Praise for Owl Goingback's
Bram Stoker Award–winning novel

CROTA

Also by Owl Goingback
CROTA

DARKER THAN NIGHT

Owl Goingback

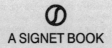

A SIGNET BOOK

SIGNET
Published by New American Library, a division of
Penguin Putnam Inc., 375 Hudson Street,
New York, New York 10014, U.S.A.
Penguin Books Ltd, 27 Wrights Lane,
London W8 5TZ, England
Penguin Books Australia Ltd, Ringwood,
Victoria, Australia
Penguin Books Canada Ltd, 10 Alcorn Avenue,
Toronto, Ontario, Canada M4V 3B2
Penguin Books (N.Z.) Ltd, 182–190 Wairau Road,
Auckland 10, New Zealand

Penguin Books Ltd, Registered Offices:
Harmondsworth, Middlesex, England

First published by Signet, an imprint of New American Library,
a division of Penguin Putnam Inc.

First Printing, November 1999
10   9   8   7   6   5   4   3   2   1

Copyright © Owl Goingback, 1999

This book is for Mike Heidbrink and Bruce Chiu.

And for my good friends Tom Fourre, Ken Kiger, and Jerry Power. The three wild men of Torrejon.

Prologue

Night came once again to the countryside. It moved over the land like a hungry beast, chasing away the fading embers of a setting sun. It filled the forest and covered the road with darkness, scurrying up the driveway to press its cold black nose against the windows of an old farmhouse.

Vivian Martin stepped back from her living room window, fearful of the night that pressed against the glass. Afraid of what dangers the darkness might contain. She stood in the center of a room where lamps and candles burned brightly, pushing back the night with their bright amber glow. It was a room painted a hideous dark green by those who did not fear the darkness as she did, preferring instead to ridicule an old woman rather than help her.

She turned away from the window and looked around. Somewhere in the living room were a sofa and two chairs, but they lay hidden beneath a cluttering of boxes and bags. The coffee table and most of the floor were also lost from view, leaving only a narrow pathway to navigate across the room from the windows to the hallway. The rest of the rooms on the lower level of the house were equally cluttered, as were those upstairs.

A month ago, or maybe it was last year, she had sorted through dozens of boxes and bags, hoping to reduce some of the mess, but she just couldn't find anything that she was willing to throw away. Certainly she could not part with her collection of old newspapers and magazines, for they might be valuable one day. And it would be foolish to throw away the bags of clothing, because the scraps would come in handy if she ever decided to make a quilt for her son.

A frown tugged at the corners of her mouth. She could not make a quilt for her son, because he was dead. He had died in a car wreck many years ago. His wife had died with him. She couldn't make a quilt for the dead; that would be foolish. People would talk.

Maybe she could make a quilt for her grandson. He was still alive. Her grandson lived in New York City, but she had not spoken to him since he was a boy. He used to live with her, but the authorities had taken him away. She lived by herself now, but she was not alone. No. Never alone. The night brought visitors. Unwelcome, dangerous visitors.

Leaning her weight against a broken rake handle for support, Vivian slowly crossed the living room and stepped into the hall. She hadn't always needed a rake handle for support, but three years ago she had slipped on a patch of ice and broken her hip. Since then it had been painful for her to walk without some extra support. Even with the handle she still had difficulty getting around, and she could no longer climb the stairs to the rooms above. Nor could she go down the basement stairs to turn on the furnace, which meant the house was always cold in the winter.

Sometimes it got so cold in the house that she couldn't feel her ears. She had to wear a stocking cap when it got that cold, and a scarf, and three pair of socks inside her rubber boots. She didn't mind the extra socks, or the scarf, but she hated wearing the stocking cap because it made it difficult to listen to the radio. Her hearing wasn't the best, and she had to hold her portable radio tightly against her left ear to hear her favorite shows. Talk shows mostly; sometimes late-night mysteries. The stocking cap always got in the way.

Maybe she should try to go down into the basement to turn on the furnace, but the steps were terribly steep. And even with the lights on, the basement was always dark. She was afraid of the dark. Very afraid.

There had been a time when Vivian did not fear the night, or the darkness it brought. As a young woman living in St. Louis, she had loved to take strolls through the parks after sunset, or sit outside and count the stars. But then she had moved to the country and things had changed.

Using the money from her late husband's estate, she had bought a piece of property for a price far cheaper than the land surrounding it. She did not pay attention to the rumors associated with the property, nor did she mind that most of her neighbors had already moved away. With the money she saved on the price of the land she could afford to build herself a nice two-story house, and a barn to go along with it. She even had enough left over to plant an apple orchard. She loved apples, and knew that she could sell what fruit she did not eat.

It had been a long time since she last visited her apple orchard. She no longer had the strength to get around much, and she was fearful of the shadows lurking beneath the trees. Her dog, Gypsy, had not been afraid of those shadows. Before she broke her hip, he had accompanied her on long walks through the orchard. Sometimes they even went into the forest together, but only during the daytime. Never at night. Not even Gypsy was brave enough to go into the forest at night. Nor would he set foot in the basement.

Vivian stopped in the hallway and picked up a revolver from where it lay on top of a box, checking to make sure it was still loaded. She had never felt the need for a gun when Gypsy was alive, but the poor old dog had died last summer. Something had killed him.

She had just picked up the revolver, when movement caught her eyes. A small shadow had darted across the hallway, disappearing into the kitchen. Vivian made no move to chase after the shadow to see what it was. Instead she turned and fired the pistol, not even bothering to aim. The bullet struck the floor near the kitchen doorway, burying itself in the floorboard.

Another shadow darted across the hallway. Vivian fired twice more, the smell of gunpowder stinging her nose. From somewhere in the kitchen came a strange whispering that sounded almost like laughter. She had started to take a step forward when the lights went out.

"Oh, no. Please, no." She looked around, terrified of the darkness that suddenly engulfed her. There were no candles in the hallway, nothing to keep the darkness at bay. There were candles in the living room, lots of them, even a few in the kitchen and bathroom, but none in the hallway. None at all.

"I must have blown a fuse," she said, her voice sounding small and timid. Supporting her weight on the rake handle, she dropped the pistol into a box and hurried down the hallway to the living room. From the darkness behind her came the strange whispering, sending chills up and down her back. She dared not stop and look around, fearful of what she might see.

She entered the living room, thankful for the friendly glow of her candles. But as she stepped across the threshold, something darted out from behind one of the boxes. Something small, black, and very fast, flowing like liquid as it crossed her path. Startled, she stepped back, landing her full weight upon her injured hip.

A cry escaped her lips as the brittle bone of her left hip snapped like a stale taco chip. She tried to catch her balance, but fell backward, crashing into the wall. A second pain shot through the left side of her body, bringing tears to her eyes. It was the fiery agony of a weak heart pushed far beyond its limits.

Vivian placed the palm of her right hand over her chest and pressed hard, praying that the pain would ease off. But the pain only grew stronger, and she knew that her heart was about to give out. From the darkness in the hallway behind her came the whispered sound of laughter. She tried to look in that direction, but the pain was too bad. She could only lie there and clutch her heart, feeling the labored beating of a dying organ.

More movement caught her attention. This time it came from above her. Lifting her gaze toward the ceiling, she looked upon the shelf that lined the far wall. On that shelf was her collection of Indian statues. As Vivian watched, those statues began to magically vibrate and move, turning around to face the wall— turning to face something that was trying to come through from the other side.

"No," She whispered, feeling the beat of her heart beginning to slow. "No. No. No."

Vivian Martin's heart give a final beat then stopped, the angel of death coming to carry her away to a place without darkness. The tiny statues that lined her shelf continued to move.

Part I

There is nothing that man fears more than the touch of the unknown. He wants to *see* what is reaching towards him, and to be able to recognize or at least classify it. Man always tends to avoid physical contact with anything strange.

—Elias Canetti

Chapter 1

They say you can never go back, but sometimes you have to. Sometimes life deals you a surprise hand, forces you to turn back the clock and take a good look at things best left forgotten. Memories once buried deep in the subconscious rise to the surface like zombies from a moonlit graveyard. Old pains begin to hurt anew. Ghosts speak.

Michael Anthony felt a shudder pass through him as he spotted the rusted road sign standing like a sentinel among the tall weeds. A shudder of fear? Nervous anticipation? Perhaps both.

Over thirty years had passed since he last resided in Hudson County, Missouri; thirty long years since he last lived at the end of the narrow, graveled lane called Sawmill Road. He had left the area long ago, a boy raised in the shadow of his grandmother. A woman who was not quite right in the head. He returned now as a man, a successful author of more than a dozen dark fantasy novels, a husband, and the father of two healthy, beautiful children. But the ghosts that waited for him did not care about his career, or his family.

"Are we almost there, Dad?" Tommy asked as his father slowed the van. "Huh, Dad? Are we?"

"Almost." Mike nodded, a smile unfolding on his face. The trip had been long and tedious for all of them, especially Tommy, who, at the ripe old age of eight, had all the nervous energy of a bag full of bumblebees. The books and pocket video games they had brought along had kept the boy occupied through most of the trip, but now they were nearing the end, and he sensed release from the confines of the vehicle as much as a horse could sense water from half a mile away.

If Megan hadn't assumed the big sister role, Tommy would probably have been bouncing off the walls by now. For several hours, the fifteen-year-old had kept her brother occupied with word games, trivia facts, and answering countless questions, giving Mike and his wife, Holly, a much needed rest.

But five miles back down the road Megan had grown tired of entertaining her younger brother. She had slipped on the headphones to her portable CD player and resorted to staring out the window at the surrounding darkness. Mike thought at first she had fallen asleep, but she would occasionally lean forward to pet Pinky, the family tomcat. The seventeen-pound yellow tabby sprawled on the floor between the two rear seats, sleeping on his favorite tattered doormat.

"How much farther, Dad?" Tommy asked, leaning forward in his seat, straining against the seat belt and shoulder harness.

"Just down the road," Mike answered, as anxious to get out of the van and stretch his legs as the boy.

"Good. I've got to pee," Tommy said.

Mike and Holly both laughed.

"You always have to pee," Megan chided, slipping the headphones down around her neck.

"Well, I do."

"I told you not to drink that orange soda," Holly said, smiling.

"But I was thirsty," argued Tommy.

"We'll be there in a few minutes, champ," Mike said, looking at his son in the rearview mirror. "Think you can hold it?"

Tommy thought about it for a moment, then nodded. "I can make it."

"That a boy."

Turning onto Sawmill Road, Mike thought about the elderly woman who had taken care of him after his parents were killed in an automobile accident, before the state of Missouri decided he would be better off living with a foster family. He didn't remember much about Vivian Martin, or about the years they had lived together. The shock of tragically losing both of his parents, and being taken from his home, had erased much of his memory of that time, leaving him with only bits and pieces, images that had long since faded with the passage of time.

The years he spent with his grandmother were now nothing more than a few dusty chapters in the filing cabinet of his life, as dusty as the house she once lived in. That house was now his, along with over forty acres of land.

Six weeks ago he had received a registered letter from an attorney in Braddock, a small town five miles east of Sawmill Road. Attached to the letter was a copy of Vivian Martin's last will, naming him as her only living heir. She had left him the house, property, and all of her worldly goods. A gift from a woman he had all but forgotten.

Mike had arranged a trip to meet with the attorney in order to sign the necessary legal documents, take possession of the house keys, and put his grandmother's affairs in order. Her funeral had taken place several days before he arrived, a simple service and burial paid for with the money left in her savings account. Pressed for time, he had done little more than give the house and grounds a quick look. The old farmhouse was still in good shape structurally, but it needed a thorough cleaning. A very thorough cleaning.

He could have refused the inheritance, or could have sold the house and property for a considerable sum of money. But he didn't need money. What he needed was an escape from New York and all the madness that went with big city living.

He used to love the city, having lived there for almost eighteen years, but during the past two years he had become painfully aware of just how crowded the Big Apple really was. Where he used to love the hustle and bustle, the throngs of people, the lights, sounds, even the traffic, he now longed for a quieter, slower way of life. Despite having a spacious apartment a few blocks north of Central Park, he felt as if he were being squeezed by the masses of humanity surrounding him.

Nor did it help that he was suddenly worried by crime in the big city, a realization nailed home when one of his best friends, also a writer, was shot and killed during a robbery late one night after a publisher's party. Mike had also been at the party, leaving just a few minutes before his friend had. It could have been him the robbers picked out, could have been his body lying dead and cold on the sidewalk in a pool of blood.

After the murder of his friend, Mike had taken to watching the evening news more than he had in the past, horrified by the number of rapes, robberies, and murders taking place on a daily basis in the city he called home. With each broadcast he felt the city closing in on him a little more, squeezing him a little tighter, making it harder to breathe.

A knot of fear had formed in his stomach. A tiny seed which blossomed and grew, gnawing at his insides like a hungry rat. He worried about his family, taking extra precautions to ensure the safety of his wife and children. His work had also suffered, as he found it almost impossible to write novels of dark fantasy and horror when the world was filled with far greater fears than those he could compose from his imagination.

Far more frightful than zombies and vampires were the crack dealers who stood on street corners, selling their poisons to children on their way home from school, or the gang members who set fire to elderly homeless men just to watch their flesh sizzle and burn.

How could you feel sorry for someone pursued by a slobbering beast in a fiction novel when thirteen-year-old girls were being forced to work as prostitutes? Robbed of their childhood dreams, they were the victims of fiends far more dangerous than any ever created in the black forests of Transylvania.

His grandmother's gift had provided an escape for Mike and his family from a city grown dark and dangerous. It was a reason to finally leave, to get away from the things he had begun to fear. A chance to start over, shake the cobwebs from his mind, and begin anew as a writer. And if a few ghosts of his past turned up in the process, then so be it.

A few ghosts never hurt anyone.

The house was not visible from the road, for it lay hidden behind a clustering of oak trees and cedar bushes. The foliage had been deliberately planted to shield the two-story farmhouse from prying eyes, even though few people lived in the area. Fewer still had reason to travel Sawmill Road, which dead-ended about half a mile past the house. Pulling into the driveway, Mike brought the van to a halt and sat staring at his family's new home.

The farmhouse sat quiet and brooding in the pale moonlight, its faded paint more gray than white. Dark green shutters framed each of the windows, and a large wooden porch ran across the front of the building.

Beyond the house was a sagging barn, and an apple grove which came to an end where the black waters of Bloodrock Creek twisted their way through the surrounding forest. According to local history, the creek had earned its name from a minor skirmish fought at the beginning of the Civil War. Men had fallen dead along the banks of the creek, had probably been buried there as well, their names forgotten with the passage of time.

Mike experienced a feeling of being watched as he sat there looking at the house. He could almost imagine his grandmother peeking at him from one of the windows, as she often had when he was just a small boy. Always watching, peering out from the safety of her home. A prison created by neurosis and fears.

Shaking off the feeling, he switched off the engine, grabbed a flashlight out of the glovebox, and climbed out of the van. He took a moment to stretch the kinks from his body before starting toward the house. Leaving Pinky in the van, his family followed him as he crossed the porch and slipped a key into the front door. No one spoke, even Tommy was quiet, which made the sounds of the night all the more noticeable. Country sounds. A nightly chorus of crickets, tree frogs, and a boisterous whippoorwill.

The door opened with a sinister creak, releasing an array of unpleasant odors into the night. Mike stepped back, coughing, as the reek of mothballs, bug spray, and Lysol assaulted his nostrils.

"Phew ... it stinks," Tommy said, wrinkling his nose. Megan also coughed, waving her hand in front of her face. Holly looked at him questioningly.

"It's not that bad," Mike replied, trying to catch his breath. "It just needs to be aired out, that's all." He remembered that his grandmother had always seemed to be spraying something. Not that she was an excessively clean woman. In fact, he didn't remember ever seeing her cleaning. Spraying yes, can after can of aerosol bug spray and Lysol, but never cleaning.

He stepped across the threshold and swept the beam of his flashlight from left to right, illuminating the foyer, hallway, staircase, and part of the living room. The house was still furnished, everything as it had been when his grandmother was still alive.

Exactly as it had been.

More memories unfolded as he gazed upon the littered disarray of boxes, stacks of old newspapers and magazines, and plastic trash bags filled with everything from old clothes to bits of twine and yarn. Nearly every available space within the house was filled, stacked high with junk and garbage, leaving only narrow pathways to navigate from one room to another.

His grandmother had been a pack rat, never throwing away anything she thought to be even remotely valuable. Items considered to be junk by others were all treasures to her. It was a phobia born during the lean days of the Depression when she and her family were often forced to live without the basic necessities of life.

Locating a light switch just inside the doorway, Mike flipped on the lights. He had arranged for the electricity to be turned on prior to their arrival, but the lights did little to push back the darkness. The fixtures were caked with years of accumulated dirt and grime. Cobwebs hung from many of them like gossamer chandeliers.

Kicking a bag of newspapers to the side, he pushed the front door all the way open. His family remained standing on the porch, staring past him with mixed expressions of awe and outright horror.

"You guys going to stay out there all night, or are you coming in?"

"I'm staying here," Megan said.

"Me too," Tommy added.

Mike forced a smile. "There's nothing to be afraid of. It's just a big old house, that's all. A little dirty, but dirt never hurt anyone."

"Spiders," Megan said.

"What about them?" Mike asked.

"There's spiders in there."

Tommy nodded. "Big ones I bet. Maybe tarantulas."

"And cockroaches," Megan added.

"And big mean rats with long sharp teeth." Tommy hooked the first two fingers of his right hand beneath his lips to represent the sharp teeth of rats.

Sensing things were about to get out of hand, Holly put her arms around Megan and Tommy, giving them a reassuring hug. She sniffed loud enough to be heard. "There's not a spider, roach, or rat tough enough to survive a night with all this bug spray and mothballs. Come on, let's go in before the mosquitoes chew us up out here."

"But . . ." Tommy stuttered.

"No buts. Let's go." She herded the children inside, leaving the door open to allow the house to air out. Mike smiled, impressed at his wife's ability to put down a potential uprising. Still he noticed Holly's mask of confidence slip a little as she looked around and saw just how big a mess they faced. A mountain of cleaning awaited the four of them. It would take days, maybe weeks, to make the house livable.

"I guess I should have warned you about the mess," he said. "If you want we can drive back into town, try to find a hotel to spend the night."

Holly shook her head. "I didn't see a hotel when we passed through town. And the children are tired, and hungry. Me too. We'll finish the grand tour and decide where to sleep: the house, or in the van. I'll bring in some of the supplies to make sandwiches, and soup." She smiled. "Things always look better on a full stomach."

"I hope so," Mike whispered under his breath, looking around at the endless mess.

The house was big, with five bedrooms and two bathrooms. The master bedroom was on the second floor, along with two other bedrooms and one of the bathrooms. The other two bedrooms were located on the lower level, at the beginning of the stairs, on opposite sides of the hallway. One of them connected to the library, so Mike claimed it as his future office. Holly claimed the other bedroom, opposite, as a studio for her artwork. Once a commercial artist, she now devoted her time to oils and acrylics of a more personal nature.

Since the bedrooms on the second floor were much bigger than those on the first level, the children had no objection to choosing rooms on the same level as the master bedroom. Megan picked the bedroom closest to the stairs, on the same side of the hall as the master bedroom. Tommy chose the back bedroom, which was closer to the bathroom and had a view of the barn, orchard, and forest. It also had two built-in cedar chests in front of the windows, perfect for storing his collection of *Star Wars* figures.

As they explored the house, Mike's grandmother's insanity became even more obvious. With the exception of the library, which had dark paneling, all of the rooms on the bottom level had been painted a hideous dark green. Floors, ceilings, and walls. Even the tiles on the kitchen floor had been painted a green so dark they were almost black. The color gave the impression that the rooms were covered with a layer of thick algae, like the slimy walls of an underwater cavern.

The hallway leading to the stairs was also painted green, the paint spread thick over peeling wallpaper. Dozens of holes had been knocked in the wall, as though someone had repeatedly struck it with a hammer. Holly stopped and fingered one of the holes, frowning.

"Maybe we have termites," Mike joked, smiling. She looked at him, but did not return his smile.

Following a narrow pathway between garbage bags and boxes, they entered the living room and then the library. A single wooden shelf ran along the walls in both of the rooms. Displayed upon the shelf were hundreds of carved wooden statues, dressed in feathers and brightly colored bits of cloth.

From past research on Native American cultures, Mike knew the wooden figures were statues of Hopi kachinas. The Hopi Indians believed the kachinas to be supernatural spirits and gods which inhabited the mountains of the American Southwest. During ceremonial dances these gods were supposed to leave their mountain homes to visit the different villages. Male dancers selected and trained for the task donned wooden masks and elaborate costumes to portray the visiting spirits.

Wooden dolls representing the kachinas were used to teach the village children about the spirits and gods inhabiting their world. There were more than one hundred different kachinas, each with a name, a distinct form, and an individual type of dress. The statues were never treated as toys, or playthings. Instead they were effigies, each thought to contain a portion of the kachina spirit's power. Once the kachina statue was presented to a child, it was treated as a valued possession and hung from a beam or wall in the house, out of harm's way.

Mike knew authentic kachina dolls were quite expensive, having priced them at several Native American gift shops back in New York City. His grandmother's collection was probably worth thousands of dollars. Oddly enough, all of the dolls in the collection were displayed facing the walls, with their backs to the occupants of the rooms.

He crossed the room to get a closer look at the collection of statues. "I kind of like the kachinas. Wouldn't mind keeping them, if that's all right with you. A collection this size has to be worth a small fortune. It must have taken her years to collect."

Several grotesque wooden masks also adorned one of the walls in the library. They were hideous caricatures of human faces with twisted grins, bulging eyes, and protruding tongues. They looked similar to the

"False Face" masks once used by the Iroquois during healing ceremonies, but there was enough of a difference in their design to make him suspect they might actually be something altogether different.

Perhaps they were tools once used by Indians in ancient magical ceremonies to ward off the evils of the encroaching white men, or maybe they were merely props to frighten small children into obeying their parents. Either way, they were enough to give nightmares to even the most stout of heart.

"I'm sorry," he said, seeing the expression of disgust on Holly's face as she stared at the masks. "I didn't know things had gotten this bad with my grandmother. She was always a little strange, even when I was a boy, but nothing like this. If you want, we can get out of here tonight. I'll call a real estate agent in the morning and tell them to put this place up for sale. We can go back home."

Her expression of disgust lasted for a few more seconds, then she shook her head. "There's nothing for us back in New York. This is our home now." She turned to him and smiled. "It's all right; the house just needs a thorough cleaning." She pointed at the wall. "You can keep the kachinas, but those masks have got to go."

Chapter 2

Dawn came all too quickly, shafts of golden light shining rudely through the yellowed curtains that hung over the windows in the master bedroom. They had all slept in the same bedroom on the second floor, pushing the boxes and stacks of newspaper out into the hallway to make room. The children had slept on the queen-sized bed, with Pinky the cat curled up by Tommy's feet. Holly and Mike had slept atop sleeping bags spread out over the wooden floor at the foot of the bed.

The smell in the room had been bad at first, nearly gagging. The windows had been sealed shut with caulking and paint, but Mike managed to force them open with a screwdriver and a lot of effort. He had also switched on the antique ceiling fan. The fan squeaked loudly at first, but after a few minutes the noise died down to a barely noticeable hum.

It had been a warm night, but there was a breeze blowing out of the northeast which helped cool the room and carry away some of the odors. Even with the fan going at full speed, and the windows open, Mike still awoke with the taste of mildew and bug spray in his mouth. A mild headache had also formed behind his eyes.

Sitting up, he stretched and attempted to work some of the knots out of his back and shoulders. Two days' worth of steady driving, and sleeping on a hard wooden floor, had left him sorer in more places than he could count. At forty years of age he was no longer a young man, could no longer spring back from physical exertion like he once could. And though he tried to keep in shape by working out twice a week, and taking long walks whenever possible, the sedentary writing life was beginning to take its toll on him. His arms no longer had the bulging biceps he once possessed when in his twenties. His belt had also been widened a notch or two over the past ten years.

Rubbing his neck, Mike pushed himself up off the floor. He staggered across the room to his suitcase, fishing around beneath his shirts and underwear for the aspirin bottle. Crunching two aspirins between his teeth, he dropped the bottle back in the case and turned around.

Holly watched him through one open eye, a smile tugging at the corners of her mouth. Slowly sitting up, she brushed a strand of reddish-blond hair out of her face and turned to look at the children. Megan and Tommy slept side by side on the bed, dead to the world. Turning back to her husband, she whispered, "Should I wake them?"

He shook his head. "No. Let them sleep. They're tired. Besides, it's still early."

Holly glanced out the window. "What time is it?"

Mike checked his wristwatch. "It's a little after seven. Time to go to work."

She groaned. "But the rooster hasn't crowed yet. This is the country, there's supposed to be a rooster."

"Rooster? We don't need no stinking roosters. Farmers rise with the sun."

"Farmer? Since when have you been a farmer? You couldn't even get your Chia Pet to sprout hair."

"Ah, but that was the old me. The new me is genuine country. I've even got dirt between my toes."

"Dirt between your ears is more like it," she laughed. "I think you've been watching too many episodes of *Green Acres*."

She stood up and stretched. Holly was three years younger than him, and in much better shape physically despite the fact that she never dieted and rarely went to the gym or worked out.

"Okay, farmer boy," she said, pulling her hair back and tying it in a ponytail. "Let's go kill us some breakfast."

Allowing the children to continue sleeping, they tiptoed out of the bedroom. They stopped at the bathroom across the hall to brush their teeth and freshen up before heading downstairs. The water that came out the tap hissed and splattered at first because of air trapped in the line, and there were tiny bits of visible sediment, but then it cleared up and settled down to a nice, steady stream. The water came from a deep well located just behind the house and had a distinct taste of minerals to it—mostly iron—but it was much more pleasant than the chemical-laced water they were used to back in New York.

Finished in the bathroom, they crept past the open doorway of the master bedroom and descended the stairway to the lower level. Even in the daylight the bottom floor was oppressively dark, the hideous green paint making everything look like it was part of a medieval dungeon. As they zigzagged through the clutter toward the kitchen, Holly flipped on the lights, and opened the curtains in the library and living room, attempting to brighten up the interior. Her efforts were only partially successful.

The four-burner gas stove in the kitchen was supplied by a large white propane tank located on the west side of the house. Since there was still gas in the tank, Holly was able to heat a pot of water for instant coffee. While she prepared the coffees, Mike grabbed a clean plate and arranged a breakfast of day-old doughnuts on it. Electing to escape the mess inside the house, they took the doughnuts and coffees out on the front porch. Grabbing a seat on the steps, they watched as the morning sun rose slowly above the treetops to the east.

It was much cooler outside the house than inside. The air had a bit of a nip to it, reminding them that the official start of autumn was only a few weeks away. The air was also noticeably cleaner than what they were used to back in the city, the wind carrying the pleasant scents of pine trees and rich black soil.

At the end of the driveway, in the shadows cast by the oak trees, a pair of rabbits frolicked in a patch of clover. The rabbits were oblivious to the red-tailed hawk circling high above them in search of a morning meal. The hawk must not have seen the rabbits, because it moved off to the south, gliding on invisible updrafts of air.

Mike watched the hawk disappear, feeling a great happiness swell in his chest at being able to observe nature in all of its simple beauty. Such sights would probably become commonplace in the days and weeks to come, but for now everything was excitingly new to him. Holly must have shared his joy for she too watched the hawk until it could no longer be seen.

Lowering his gaze, he took a sip of coffee which had cooled enough not to burn his tongue. The coffee was wonderful, flavored with just a touch of hazelnut creamer, made all the more delightful by the sights, sounds, and smells of the country. Resting the cup on his knee, he took a glazed doughnut off the plate sitting between them. Holly selected a raspberry-filled doughnut, laughing in childish delight when a glob of gooey jelly dribbled down her chin.

They each had two doughnuts apiece, and two cups of coffee, followed by an equal number of cigarettes to prolong the morning meal and put off going to work for just a few minutes longer. They were still very tired, and it took more than the normal amount of sugar, nicotine, and caffeine to get their motors running.

Knowing they could no longer put off the job facing them, Mike and Holly carried their empty cups, and the plate of doughnuts, back into the kitchen and then focused their attention on the mess at hand. The clutter inside the house seemed endless, so they decided to organize a plan of attack rather than just have a go at it. They started in the hallway, just inside the front door, making their way slowly toward the kitchen and living room.

They carried the boxes and bags outside, setting them at the side of the house. There were boxes and bags filled with old clothes, records, moldering books, magazines, and stacks of newspapers, some dating back over twenty years.

Just inside the doorway, hidden behind a stack of rubbish, they discovered two moldy mattresses leaning against the wall. Behind the mattresses was an antique

cabinet filled with broken doll parts and old phono-
graph records. Since the cabinet smelled as bad as the
mattresses, they decided it too should be carried outside. Maybe once it aired out, and after a thorough
cleaning, they would bring it back into the house, but
not before then.

It was a little after 10 AM. when the children awoke,
making their way slowly down the stairs. Neither one
of them wanted to stay in the house. Grabbing doughnuts and pouring glasses of milk from the carton in the
cooler, they sat on the porch watching as their parents
carried armloads of garbage past them. They stalled as
long as they possibly could, or as long as Holly allowed
them to. She put them to work in the living room, carrying out the smaller boxes and items that didn't smell
too bad to handle.

Shortly before noon Mike turned over the cleaning to
Holly and the children. He had to make a run into Braddock to have the telephone service connected. He also
needed to stop by the utilities department to request
the use of a trash Dumpster. Megan and Tommy both
wanted to go with him, probably to get out of work
rather than to see the town in the daylight as they claimed,
but he denied their requests. There was an awful lot of
work to do, and it wouldn't be fair to leave it all to Holly.
Ignoring their frowns and unhappy faces, he climbed
into the van and started down the gravel road.

There were no other houses along Sawmill Road, at
least none that were occupied. Mike spotted two
other farmhouses, and a small cabin, but it was obvious they had been sitting empty for years. The
farmhouses were a dull brown color, with glassless
windows that watched his passing like the empty eye
sockets of skulls. The cabin was also windowless, the

rotting logs of its outer wall partially hidden in the shadows of pine trees. All three buildings stood abandoned and unloved, a haven for spiders, snakes, and ghostly memories.

Sawmill Road connected to the blacktop lane of State Road #315, which had not been repaved in almost twenty years. Following #315 to the east, you passed through the towns of Braddock, Warrenton, and Logan, eventually connecting with Interstate #70. If you followed #315 to the west, you would probably end up lost.

Unlike on Sawmill Road, there were actually a few occupied homes along State Road #315. Not many; just a few. Farmhouses mostly, with an occasional mobile home tossed in for good measure. Mike wondered why there were so few houses in the area, but only for a moment. The countryside was remote, hilly, and heavily forested, which made it less than ideal for farming or raising a family.

The town of Braddock, Missouri, was rather small, with a population just under two thousand. It looked like a place that had been frozen in time, a page torn from the 1930s. The town had no mall or major shopping centers. Instead all of the businesses and stores were located in turn-of-the-century buildings that lined Main Street. The street ran for a little over seven blocks, ending at an intersection where hung the town's only working traffic light.

Within the seven-block stretch of Main Street were two grocery stores, an equal number of taverns, a feed and bridle store, an army-navy surplus, a couple of clothing shops, two restaurants, a barbershop, and the local billiards hall.

At the west end of the street stood the county court-house. The three-story, domed, red brick building was built just before the Civil War and housed all of the county offices, including the land management office, tax office, telephone, trash and utilities office, the mayor's office, and the courtroom. Sitting to the right of the courthouse was the county jail, a small, two-story brick building with bars on all of the upper-story windows. Behind the courthouse was the Braddock Public Library.

Mike pulled his van in between two pickup trucks, then got out and walked up the long sidewalk to the courthouse. Before entering the building, he paused briefly at the granite marker to read about how the courthouse was built in 1854 on what was known as the Booneslick Trail. According to the marker, the trail had been forged by Daniel Boone and his sons in their search for salt mines, salt being an important com-modity back in the days of old Daniel.

The marker neglected to mention that a few years later, in 1863, the trail that brought settlement and pros-perity to the region was used by the United States Gov-ernment in the forced march of the Cherokees, and other peaceful Indian tribes, to their new home in Okla-homa. Crossing the Mississippi River into Missouri, the Indians had spent a bitter winter being herded like cattle down Daniel's original salt trail. Thousands had died from sickness, starvation, and the freezing cold. Few towns wanted it known that their tiny communi-ties had played a part in the holocaust. Braddock was no exception. Mike only knew about it from the re-search he had done for one his novels. Shaking his head, he entered the courthouse.

All of the major offices were located on the first floor,

so it didn't take him long to arrange for telephone service and the temporary use of a trash Dumpster. Since he lived beyond the city limits, he didn't need any other utility service. The water supply was from a deep well, and he had to haul his own weekly trash to a collection point about a mile from his house. There was also no cable television, which meant no MTV or HBO, something neither one of his children knew about yet. Maybe later, to keep them happy, he would purchase a satellite dish antenna, if such a thing could be purchased in Braddock.

Finished with the necessary business of the day, he started to go back to his van, but his attention was drawn to the Braddock Public Library. The gray brick building was nestled in the shade of towering oak trees, appearing as an oasis of coolness in an otherwise bright and sunny day.

As he stood there, looking upon the library, a few long forgotten memories floated to the surface of his mind. The library had been one of his favorite places as a boy. A kingdom of wonder where dreams existed between the covers of leather-bound books. He wondered if it was still the same as he remembered it.

Forget the library. You need to get back home. There's work to be done. Lots of work. You can go book browsing later.

Mike frowned. He really needed to get home. It wasn't fair to leave all of the cleaning to Holly and the children. He started toward the van again, but changed his mind and cut across the grass to the library. One quick look inside wouldn't hurt.

There were no cars parked in front of the library, which made him wonder if the place was closed. But the door opened when he tried the knob, a bell jingling softly. Entering the library, he stopped just inside the doorway, allowing his eyes to adjust to the sudden change in lighting. The library was dark, and as cool as a cave, filled with the wonderful aroma of ancient books.

Mike closed his eyes and inhaled, momentarily taken back to a time long ago. A much simpler time. As a boy, he had spent many hours at the library reading tales of fantasy, mystery, and science fiction. Here his love of literature had blossomed, planting the creative seed which would one day turn him into a writer.

"Air-conditioning's not free."

He opened his eyes, startled by the voice. A gray-haired woman sat behind the checkout counter watching him with an expression of stout disapproval. Embarrassed, he quickly closed the door behind him.

"Sorry," he muttered. "I guess I was daydreaming. I haven't been in here since I was a kid." He looked around, escaping the woman's gaze. "This place hasn't changed a bit."

"No reason to change things if they aren't broken." The woman's gaze softened. She smiled.

He smiled back. Stepping up to the counter, he offered his hand. "I'm Mike. . . ."

"Mike Anthony," she finished for him. "I know who you are. I'm Connie Widman. Please, call me Connie."

"You know me?" he asked, somewhat surprised.

She laughed pleasantly, the corners of her eyes wrinkling. "Of course I know you. I put the books on the shelves, don't I? Can't help looking at the backs of them sometimes. Although you do look a little different in person than you do in your pictures. And I doubt if you even smoke that pipe you always seem to be holding."

He coughed. "No. I don't smoke a pipe. Not really. I was just trying to look dignified for the photos, like what people think a writer should look like. My wife thought the pipe was a dumb idea. She said I looked goofy."

"Next time listen to your wife. Women have a knack for knowing what looks good in a photo and what doesn't." She laughed. "Still, you don't look any more goofy in your photos than you looked as a boy."

"You knew me when I was a kid?" he asked.

"You and your grandmother used to come in on Saturdays. Your were a skinny thing back then, bony, all elbows and knees. Had a mess of freckles too, if I remember right. And you were very shy. I used to think you were scared of your own shadow. Made me want to yell 'boo' just to see what would happen. You probably would have peed your pants."

Mike frowned. "Was I that bad?"

Connie nodded. "I don't think I ever heard you speak. Not a word. Your grandmother used to bring you in on Saturday, regular as clockwork. She would read the newspapers, check out a mystery novel now and then. You spent most of your time in the science fiction section. I used to think you were an odd child for reading that sort of stuff, but I guess you weren't nearly as odd as your grandmother."

Mike lowered his gaze.

"I'm sorry," Connie said quietly. "I shouldn't have said that, her being passed away and all."

He raised his head. "No. It's okay. No harm done. My grandmother was odd, at least what I remember about her. I hadn't seen her since I was a kid, so I don't remember much. Just bits and pieces. A lot of my childhood memories have been lost; I guess it's because of the shock of losing my parents when I was still young."

"Your grandmother was very proud of your success.

She used to come in and show me articles in the newspapers about you. Also made sure I carried all of your books. I had them all, but a couple of the copies have disappeared over the years."

Wanting to change the subject from his grandmother, he said, "Let me know what books are missing, and I'll be happy to give you replacements. Sign them if you'd like. It's the least I can do for the library that gave me my start."

"It's a deal," smiled the librarian. "I'll make up a list for the next time you come in."

They chatted awhile longer, talking about his career as a successful author, changes in the town since he went away, and a bit of local gossip. Connie also gave him the name and phone number of a local teenage girl who baby-sat in case he and Holly ever wanted to go out.

Mike left the library feeling like a small bit of his long lost childhood had been recaptured. Another piece of his memory had floated up from the darkness of his subconscious, clicking into place in the jigsaw puzzle of his mind. But there were still a lot of pieces missing.

Chapter 3

The contractors arrived bright and early Tuesday morning, showing up in a noisy parade of four pickup trucks and one van. By then Mike, Holly, and the kids had accomplished several days' worth of cleaning, carrying out enough junk and trash to completely fill the green Dumpster sitting in front of the house. At least now the workers would be able to get into the house to make the repairs and improvements they had been hired to make.

Standing on the front porch, Mike watched as ten men climbed out of the collection of vehicles. Still clutching coffee mugs and cigarettes, they milled about waiting for their boss to arrive.

The company foreman, a Mr. Charles "Chuck" Strickland, arrived a few minutes later in a bright green Cadillac. He was a big man, probably in the neighborhood of six feet four inches tall and weighing somewhere around two hundred and sixty pounds, his skin bronzed dark by the sun, the butt of a cigar clenched between his teeth. Despite his size, he wasn't fat. Instead he gave the impression of one who had served considerable time in the Marine Corps, or maybe spent a few years as a professional wrestler.

Whereas the workers appeared sleepy and reluctant to move too quickly prior to their boss's arrival, they practically snapped to attention when he appeared on the scene. Cigarettes and coffees were quickly finished, and white coveralls donned, as they set about unloading tools and supplies from the trucks. Mike almost laughed at the sudden changes in the attitudes of the contractors. Instead he smiled and stepped off the porch to greet the foreman.

"Good morning," Mike said, approaching the Cadillac. "You guys are bright and early."

Chuck slipped out of the car and closed the door behind him. "We try to be on time," he said, shaking Mike's hand. "Although sometimes it's hard to get the boys going in the morning, especially on a project this size."

He spotted the overflowing Dumpster and nodded. "Looks like you've been busy. Did you leave us any work, or did you do it all yourself?"

Mike glanced at the Dumpster. "No. No. There's plenty of work left to do. Believe me. We just thought we would get some of the mess out of your way."

"Why, that was right considerate of you." Chuck grinned. "Now, if you would show me what all needs to be done, and where you want us to start, I'll get these guys moving before they decide another coffee break is needed."

Mike nodded and led Chuck inside, showing him where repairs needed to be made and which room got what carpeting. The carpeting, and linoleum tiles for the kitchen floor, had already been picked out and were in the van, but Mike needed to reaffirm which selection went where. Chuck went through each room carefully, jotting down notes to make sure no mistakes would be made. A work order was also produced for Mike to sign, showing the cost of labor. The price of the carpeting, tiles, and paint had already been negotiated over the phone. Walking back outside, Mike was asked to approve the carpeting and tiles before they were unloaded.

"Anything else?" Mike asked, stepping back from the van.

"Nope. That should do it," Chuck answered, re-lighting his cigar. "For now at least. There's always the unexpected that pops up during a job." He turned to look at the house. "Have you thought about having this place fumigated? A house this old is probably crawling with bugs."

Mike resisted the urge to laugh. "My grandmother was a big-time phobic about bugs. Used to spray all of the time. I doubt I'll need to fumigate anytime soon."

Chuck nodded. "Still, I'll tell the boys to keep an eye out when we tear up the carpeting. It wouldn't do to have all that work done only to find out a month later that you're infested with termites."

With that Chuck closed the back doors of the van and put his men to work, instructing them on which rooms of the house to tackle first. Mike was pleased to know the house would soon look more like an actual home instead of a pigsty. The mess was far from over, how-ever, as the crew of ten men set about installing new carpeting throughout the house, replacing the tiles in the kitchen, and repainting the rooms and hallways. Soon strips of protective plastic, rags, and scraps of old carpeting lay everywhere, making it just as hard to walk through the house as it had been when they first arrived. And though the reek of Lysol, bug spray, and mothballs was not noticeable anymore, those smells were replaced by the stench of paint, paint thinner, new carpeting, and Chuck's cheap cigars.

Holly and Mike had decided on beige carpeting throughout the lower level of the house, and light blue and green in the bedrooms upstairs. With the exception of the library, all of the rooms on the lower level were to be painted white. The painting proved to be quite a task, for it took several coats of paint to cover over the hideous dark green. The holes in the hallway also had to be patched, and the old wallpaper removed, before any painting could begin. Upstairs the painting wasn't so difficult, with the color of the bedrooms almost matching the particular shade of carpeting being installed.

It was a little after twelve when Chuck called Mike from the downstairs hallway. The foreman was having a conversation with one of his workers about the holes in the walls.

"Something wrong?" Mike asked, walking up to the two men.

Chuck shook his head. "Nothing's wrong, but we did find something a little odd."

"Oh?" Mike said. "What's that?"

"You said your grandmother lived here before you? Was she the original occupant of the house, or did she buy it from someone?"

"As far as I know she was the original occupant. I think she had it built sometime back in the 1940s. Why?"

Chuck scratched his head. "It's these holes. Most of them look to be made by a hammer, like someone decided to beat the hell out of the walls for the fun of it.

Most of them look to be made by a hammer, but not all. Larry here dug these out of the studs inside the wall."

He opened his hand to reveal three round gray pieces of metal. Mike picked one up to examine it.

"They're bullets," Mike said.

Chuck nodded. "Offhand I'd say they were fired from a .38 revolver."

Mike looked at Larry, puzzled. "You found these in the wall."

Larry nodded. "That's right. There might be more; I wasn't looking all that closely."

"It don't make sense," Chuck said. "Shooting up a perfectly good wall is not something a woman would normally do. I could understand a man doing it. A guy lives here all alone, gets a little drunk one night, and decides to shoot off his gun. What the hell, he figures. It's just a wall, won't take too much to cover over the holes. Maybe his girlfriend just dumped him and he has to let off a little steam. But a woman; they don't do stuff like that."

"Not unless she was shooting at something," Mike said, looking at the wall.

"You figure she might have been shooting at someone?" asked the foreman.

"I don't know," shrugged Mike. "Maybe."

Chuck thought about it a moment. "Could be someone broke in here one night. If so, then they had themselves one hell of a surprise."

Holly came out of the kitchen with purse in hand. She started to say something, but Mike interrupted by handing her the bullet.

"What's this?" she asked.

"What does it look like?"

"A bullet. Where did you get it?"

"Larry dug it out of the wall. It looks like my grand-mother used this place for a shooting gallery. Maybe someone broke in and she convinced them never to try it again."

"Broke in?" A nervous look crossed her face. "Are there a lot of robberies around here?"

"Never heard of any," Chuck said. "Most folks in these parts don't even bother to lock their doors at night."

"Maybe they should," Mike said.

Holly frowned. "If your grandmother owned a gun, it must still be in the house somewhere. We better look for it before one of the kids finds it."

"We've already gone through everything," Mike said. "I don't think the gun is still in the house. We probably threw it out with the other junk and didn't even know it. Still, I'll go back through everything just to make sure."

"I'll help you," Holly said.

He glanced down at the purse she held. "It looks like you were going somewhere."

Holly also glanced down at her purse, as though she had forgotten she held it. "I was going into town to do a little grocery shopping, but that can wait until after we look for the gun."

"No. You go ahead and go. It will do you good to get out of the house for a while. I'll look for the gun."

"Well, okay," she said, reluctantly giving in. "Just be careful. It might still be loaded."

"Careful? Hell, if I find that gun I'm going to shoot it." Mike grinned. "See if I can't put a few more holes in the wall before the day is over."

Holly smiled. "Just stay in the hallway. I won't tolerate any gunplay in my kitchen. Put a hole through one of my pans and there will be hell to pay."

"No gunplay in the kitchen. You got it." Mike gave Holly a quick hug, sending her off to do the shopping before she could change her mind about going. He started to hand the .38 slug back to Chuck, but decided to keep it as a souvenir. He wondered why his grandmother had kept a loaded handgun in the house, and what she could possibly have been shooting at. Burglars? Prowlers? Shadows? Chances were he would never know.

Truthfully, Holly did not need to go grocery shopping. The pantry was already well stocked with food. What she needed was to escape the chaos taking place at the house. She was tired of the noise, and the mess. She was also fed up with the smell of the cheap cigars that Chuck smoked in the house, despite her pleas to Mike to tell the man to take them outside. What she needed was a dose of temporary solace, and if it meant going to the store to do a little shopping then so be it.

She would have preferred to go alone, but Megan begged to go with her. She too had found the contractors to be crude and obnoxious, especially those who had the annoying habit of referring to her as "sweetheart" or "good-looking." Tommy, on the other hand, seemed fascinated by the work going on around him and elected to remain behind to help his father supervise the workers. The eight-year-old was all grins when one of the workers allowed him to carry his hammer.

The trip to the supermarket started out rather routine. Holly chose the Kroger store at the east end of Main Street, over the rival IGA, because it was larger and more modern. It also had a rather nice deli section, something the other store lacked.

Pushing a shopping cart before them, Holly selected an assortment of easy-to-fix items. She also replenished her stock of cleaning supplies, wondering if there would ever be an end to the scrubbing, dusting, and mopping back at their new house. She sincerely hoped so, because—despite wearing rubber gloves for most of the cleaning jobs—her hands were starting to look like something out of a really bad fright movie. How she longed for a nice manicure, a quiet dinner, and a good glass of red wine.

Stop dreaming. The good life is past. You're a hardworking country girl now. You can't buck hay bales, plow the fields, and milk the cows with manicured nails.

As they shopped, Holly developed a peculiar feeling that she and Megan were being watched. At first she thought nothing of it, attributing it to fatigue and little else, but several times while selecting a particular item from a shelf she turned to find one of the other customers watching her. Some of those she caught staring quickly averted their gazes, as though they had been caught looking at something they shouldn't. Others continued to stare openly.

"Mom, what's wrong?" Megan asked, apparently seeing the look of concern on her mother's face.

"What?" She looked at her daughter and shook her head. "Oh, nothing dear. I was just a little distracted, thinking about what to cook for dinner tonight, that's all."

"But why is everyone staring at us?"

"Staring? What do you mean?" Holly asked, looking around as though she hadn't noticed anyone was staring at them.

"They keep looking at us like they think we're going to shoplift something. And it's not just the employees. The customers are looking at us funny too."

Holly forced a laugh. "Maybe they're just looking at us because we're new in town. Or maybe they're wondering where two such absolutely beautiful women could possibly come from. I'm sure it's nothing. Just ignore them."

"It gives me the creeps."

"No harm ever came from looking at someone. And if they stare too hard, then stare back."

Megan smiled and went back to loading the shopping cart. Holly relaxed, glad to have put her daughter's mind at ease. Growing up in New York City, she was used to the strangeness of others, almost expected it at times, but that was New York. A small town in central Missouri should have been different. A little friendlier. Perhaps the locals were just curious about the new faces in town. Maybe a fairly attractive mother and daughter were worth taking a peek at. Whatever it was, by the time they got to the checkout she was starting to get spooked by all the stares they were receiving.

Placing the groceries on the counter, Holly started to write a check, but then she remembered they would probably not take a check drawn on a out-of-town bank. She had planned to open a new checking account with a bank in town, but with all of the cleaning it had completely slipped her mind. A flash of panic surged through her as she dropped the checkbook back into her purse and started searching for enough cash to pay for the groceries. It was too late to put anything back, because the cashier was already ringing up the items.

"Shoot," she said under her breath, pushing aside

her powder case to open the hidden side compartment in her bag.

"What's wrong, Mom?" Megan asked, putting down the *TV Guide* she had been glancing through.

"Oh, nothing dear. I just forgot they probably won't take an out-of-state check here. I may not have enough money to pay for everything."

"I've got some money," Megan said, opening her purse and withdrawing a wrinkled twenty-dollar bill and a couple of ones. "Will this help?'

"Yes, dear. Thank you." Holly took the bills out of her daughter's hand, suddenly aware she was the center of attention at the checkout. The stares she was receiving were open now, no attempt by anyone to hide them. She felt a flush of embarrassment warm her face as she pulled the rest of her money from her purse, adding it to what Megan had already given her. Twenty. Thirty. Thirty-five. Forty. Forty-eight dollars. More than enough to pay for the items she had purchased.

Thank God, she thought, resisting the urge to yell at the other customers to quit staring. Her face still flushed, Holly waited for the cashier to total up her bill. Handing the girl two twenties and a five, she waited for her change and the receipt. She then helped to load the bags into her cart and headed for the doors, not daring to look behind her for she still felt the penetrating gazes of the other customers on her back.

Holly felt instantly better once she got outside. It was foolish to let a few curious looks upset her, but she couldn't help it. She did not like being stared at, especially when she didn't know why everyone was staring. Had she a rip in her pants large enough to show her ass, or bright purple hair, she could have understood the looks, but there just wasn't any reason for them that she could figure out. Just to be sure, she ran her hand quickly over the back of her pants. Nope. No rip.

To the right of the double exit doors there was a newspaper bin containing the newest issue of the *Braddock Tribune,* the town's weekly newspaper. Rummaging around in her coin purse for fifty cents, Holly purchased a copy of the paper. Both she and Mike were anxious to learn more about the new community they called home, and there was no better place to start learning than in the pages of the local newspaper.

She had started to stick the newspaper into one of the grocery bags when she noticed a publicity photo of her and Mike on the back page. The photo was accompanied by an article about the best-selling author and his family moving into the area.

"Jesus. No wonder everyone was staring at us."

"Let me see," Megan said, stepping closer to see the picture. Holly tilted the paper to show her daughter the photo, then quickly read what had been written about her husband.

The article was fairly basic, nothing more than what had been written about Mike in the past. Neither she nor her husband had been contacted about the article, so she had a suspicion that most of the information had been obtained from articles written about Mike in other periodicals. The article did mention that Mike had once lived in Hudson County, and that his grandmother had been a longtime resident of the area, something no other newspaper had ever said about him, but it probably wasn't news to the locals.

"They could have at least put the photo on the front page," she said with a smile, folding the newspaper and putting it into one of the grocery bags. She turned to Megan. "How does it feel to be a celebrity?"

"It sucks," her daughter replied.

Holly laughed. "Well, get used to it. A town this small probably doesn't have too many famous people to talk about."

"Or stare at."

Casting a final glance back at the grocery store, Holly pushed the shopping cart across the parking lot. She was halfway to the van when she spotted an old man walking rapidly toward her. He was thin and dark skinned, his face wrinkled from the sun, with long gray hair that fell about his shoulders. Around his neck he wore a strand of silver beads, while turquoise rings adorned most of his fingers. His clothes were soiled and wrinkled, and it looked like he had slept in them. As he approached, the man spoke aloud to himself, making sharp gestures with his hands and head. He appeared to be a homeless derelict, perhaps an Indian, and maybe crazy. He could be dangerous.

Never taking her eyes off the approaching man, Holly pushed the cart faster, hurrying to get to the van. Still there was no way she and Megan could get the groceries loaded and drive away before he reached them.

"Shit," Holly whispered. She tossed Megan the keys. "Get inside and lock the doors."

"What? Why?" Megan hadn't seen the derelict, but turning around she did now. A look of fear crossed her face as she spotted the old man moving rapidly toward them.

"What about you, Mom?" Megan asked, looking beyond her mother to the grimy old man.

"Just do what I say."

Megan did as she was told. She unlocked the passenger door of the van, then climbed in and locked the door behind her. Knowing her daughter was safe,

Holly wheeled to face the approaching man. Her hands fumbled into one of the grocery bags in the cart beside her, searching for a weapon to defend herself if need be.

The old man stopped a few feet from her and stood staring, his head cocked slightly to one side.

"What do you want?" Holly asked him, hoping the customers inside the store could see her if anything bad happened.

"What do I want? What do I want?" the old man repeated, mocking her. He ran a grimy hand through his hair and then swiped at the air. "The question is what do they want?"

"Who?" Holly asked.

"The boogers, that's who," he answered, looking quickly behind him as though he were being followed. "What do they want? What do they always want? That's the question. It is. It is."

The old man waved his arms above his head. Holly took a step back. "You'll see. You'll see," he said. "You'll find out the question, but not the answer. Just ask Sam Tochi. He knows. Sam knows all about the boogers, but they won't believe me. Nope. Nope. But you'll see. You will. You have their house."

With that he staggered past her, leaving Holly dazed and confused. Turning, she watched him cross the parking lot and turn left at the sidewalk, continuing down the street. She watched until he disappeared from sight, and then shook her head and breathed a sigh of relief.

Braddock was proving to be quite a place. First a house filled with garbage and riddled with bullet holes, and now staring customers and a crazy old Indian talking about boogers. Insanity at its finest. There had to be something in the local water supply. Just had to be.

Looking down, Holly saw that she clutched a cucumber in her right hand for protection, although she didn't remember grabbing it out of the bag. A cucumber for protection? She laughed.

"I do believe I'm getting just as crazy as the rest of them."

Chapter 4

Their furniture arrived the following morning, the big Mayflower moving truck squeezing between the trees at the bottom of the driveway. The truck was a welcome sight, but Mike and Holly refused to get too happy, fearing that half of their household belongings had been broken or damaged during the long trip from New York.

The contractors had already finished painting and recarpeting the rooms on the bottom floor, so all of the furniture and boxes could be unloaded. They showed the movers where to put the bigger items, then lent a hand carrying boxes. The children helped too, although they only carried the boxes with their names on them. Even Pinky joined in to help, the big tomcat carefully inspecting each item as it was carried into the house. Holly shooed him a dozen times, worried he would trip one of the workers, but he kept coming back.

By noon the truck was completely unloaded, with most of the items in the rooms where they were suppose to go. Holly made sandwiches for everyone, then went back to unpacking boxes. The movers left after eating, a check for $1,200 in the driver's shirt pocket.

The spare room connected to the library was to be Mike's office. The room appeared to have ample space when empty, but now looked rather crowed with the addition of a walnut desk, computer station, four filing cabinets, typewriter stand, additional bookcases, two office chairs, and a small wooden table used to hold a coffeemaker and a fax machine. The desk and other furniture were barely visible beneath the brown cardboard boxes containing manuscripts, copies of his novels, and assorted important paperwork.

Moving two boxes from the secretarial chair, Mike sat down and looked around him, trying to get a feel for his new workplace. He had positioned the desk in front of the window that faced out the back of the house, looking over the apple orchard and forest beyond. He wondered if the view would be a distraction when he was trying to write, but decided he would rather have the view than face a blank wall. Besides, if he got to daydreaming too much, he could always close the curtains.

His Gateway 2000 computer sat in its protective cartons atop the desk. More than anything he wanted to put his system together, for his office just wasn't a real office without it. But he knew if he hooked up the computer he would have the urge to sit down and write, and there was just too much work yet to be done. Besides it would be selfish to arrange his office first while ignoring the rest of the house. Of course he knew that at that very moment, the children were upstairs concentrating on getting their rooms in order, and Holly was across the hall in the room that was to be her art studio.

He smiled. Maybe what they all needed was some

time alone in their own rooms to bring a little order back into their lives. Things had been rather hectic the past two weeks, and none of them had had much time alone. Still, he felt rather guilty about setting up his office knowing it would be a day or two before he was able to get back to his writing. Let the kids do their own things, he would start unpacking in the family rooms.

Leaving the office, he stopped across the hall to see how Holly's studio was coming. Since the room was to be used for the painting of canvases, new carpeting had not been installed over the wooden floor. It was much easier to wipe spilled oils and acrylics off of wood than to try and scrub it out of a carpet.

Stepping into the room, he saw that his wife had wasted little time in getting organized. Her workstation had already been placed against the wall opposite the window, where it would get the best natural light. The swivel lamp clamped to the wooden workstation provided illumination when Mother Nature was not at her best.

Outside of the workstation, and a few shelves to hold supplies, there really wasn't a lot more that needed to be set up. She still needed to unpack her tubes and jars of paints, pigments, and sealers, lining up the brushes and sponges in their proper places. One set of shelves would be used to hold Holly's collection of art books and magazines, while the closet would provide storage space for many of her paintings.

"Gee, it looks like you're just about ready to go."

Holly turned around and flashed him a smile. "I wish. I still have to unpack all of my supplies, and I can't remember which box is which. I knew I should have written more on the boxes than just 'art supplies' when I packed everything away."

Mike grinned. "Just think of all the fun you're going to have when you open the boxes. Not knowing what's inside makes each one of them a new surprise."

"Some surprise," she said. "How's your office? All set up and ready to write the next great novel?"

"Not hardly. I haven't even started," he said. "I'm kind of like you: I just don't know where to begin."

Holly laughed. "That's easy. You unpack the coffeemaker first. You know you can't put two words together unless you have a cup of caffeine first."

"The coffeemaker will be the first thing I unpack, but I'm not sure what to tackle after that. I thought about hooking up my computer, but that takes time and there's so much other work that needs to be done first. I think I'll leave the office alone until I get the living room and upstairs taken care of."

Holly looked around. "I'll give you a hand as soon as I get some of this stuff put away. It won't take me long."

"Take your time," he replied. "The last thing we need in this house is a fidgety artist."

"Fidgety? Who's fidgety?" She asked, wringing her hands together in a nervous motion. She smiled and gave him a quick kiss on the cheek. "I'll be there to help you in a minute."

"Sure you will." He grinned as he left the room.

Knowing if he went upstairs one of the kids would enlist his aid in putting up decorations, he decided to start working in the living room. The movers had positioned the hutch, television, and furniture where Holly wanted it, so there really wasn't much left to do but sort through the boxes, dividing them up between those that stayed downstairs and those that went upstairs.

The boxes staying in the living room were, for the most part, decorations: family pictures and portraits, paintings, Holly's crystal dragon collection, his collections of antique banks, and other assorted knickknacks and curios.

He looked around, spotting the one box that meant more to him than all the others containing living room items. The word "Stoker" adorned all sides of the box, carefully written in the heavy black letters of a Magic Marker. He held his breath as he opened the box, praying the item inside had survived its long journey without being damaged.

Mike let out a sigh of relief when he saw the trophy the box contained had come through the trip without a scratch. The Bram Stoker Award was shaped like a miniature haunted house, complete with gargoyles and other spooky effects. The brainchild of fellow writer Harlan Ellison, the award was given annually by the voting members of the Horror Writers Association. Mike's novel *Zero Hour* had won the award two years ago, beating out three other finalists. He was quite proud of winning, because the Stoker was the only literary award he had ever received.

Lifting the statue carefully out of the box, he crossed the room and set it on the hutch. He couldn't resist the urge to open the haunted house's tiny front door, although he had already done so hundreds of times in the past. The door opened to reveal a brass plaque which read:

Superior Achievement
novel
Zero Hour
by
Michael Anthony

A smile unfolded on his face as he read the plaque. Being recognized by his fellow writers of horror and dark fantasy was one of the highlights of his literary career. Too bad winning the award had no effect on the money he received for his novels. Now if he won the Nobel Peace Prize . . .

Turning away from the hutch, he was about to unpack another box when he heard a car pull into the driveway. Curious, he left the living room and headed for the front door.

Stepping out onto the porch, he saw a sheriff's patrol car pulling to a stop in front of the house. He frowned, wondering what could possibly be wrong. Could they have done something without obtaining the proper permit? He was sure they had taken all of the legal steps necessary to repair the old house.

The patrol car pulled to a stop and a tall, muscular man in a tan uniform stepped out. He was about six foot three, and looked to be in his late forties, his brown hair little longer than a crew cut. He reminded Mike of all the marine drill sergeants portrayed in Hollywood movies, a flower child's worst nightmare. The man looked around, then removed his sunglasses and turned toward Mike.

"Mr. Anthony?"

Mike stepped off the porch and approached the officer, seeing by his badge that he was a sheriff.

"I'm Mike Anthony," he replied with a nod. "Is there something wrong?"

"No, sir. Nothing's wrong," the sheriff said, looking Mike over in that funny way law enforcement officers often do, mentally sizing him up. "I'm Jody Douglas, Sheriff of Hudson County. I heard you had moved into the neighborhood, and just wanted to stop by to say howdy."

The sheriff offered his hand but did not smile, leaving Mike to wonder if it really was a friendly visit. Mike took the hand offered him, feeling a hidden strength in the sheriff's grasp. This was not someone he would ever want to get into a boxing match with. Nor did he want to arm wrestle with him.

For some reason Mike felt as if he should know the sheriff. The name was vaguely familiar. Suddenly, as he stood there shaking hands, another forgotten piece of memory clicked into place.

Jody Douglas was a name from Mike's childhood, a name that left a bad taste in the back of his mouth. The man standing before him, a person who now upheld the law, once belonged to a group of local teenagers who had delighted in tormenting Mike's grandmother.

Several times a week Jody and his cohorts would drive down Sawmill Road past the house, shouting "Crazy woman" and other derogatory things as loud as they could. Sometimes they would even pull into the driveway, daring the old woman to come outside and confront them.

Mike released the sheriff's hand and stood looking at him. He started to say something, but was interrupted by the feeling of Pinky rubbing against his leg. Jody looked down at the cat, a look of disdain clearly etched upon his face.

"That's one hell of a cat you got there, Mr. Anthony. He must weigh at least fifteen pounds."

"Seventeen," Mike answered.

"Never did care much for cats," Jody continued. "I'm a dog man myself. Got a couple of retrievers."

Almost as if he understood what the sheriff was

saying about him, Pinky looked up at Jody Douglas and hissed.

The sheriff took a step back. "That cat of yours seems a little vicious. You might want to think about putting him on a leash."

Mike almost laughed. You couldn't put a cat on a leash, especially one as independent as Pinky. "He's never attacked anyone yet," he said, bending over to rub the big cat behind the ears. "He probably just smells your dogs."

"Maybe," Jody nodded, looking suspiciously at Pinky as he wandered off in search of attention elsewhere. The sheriff watched the cat enter the house, then turned his attention back to Mike.

"There's going to be a social dance at the VFW Hall this coming Saturday night, kind of a monthly gathering of the locals. If you haven't got anything planned, you and the missus might think about stopping by. Practically the whole town will be there. You being a celebrity of sorts, I reckon a lot of people will expect you to show up. You wouldn't want to disappoint your fans. Would you?"

Mike doubted if any fans of his would be in attendance, but the dance might be just the thing to meet some of their new neighbors. Besides, he and Holly could use a little rest and relaxation after working so hard with the move.

"I'll try to squeeze it in," Mike said.

The sheriff nodded and walked slowly back to his patrol car. "I'll probably see you at the dance then," he said, opening the door and climbing behind the wheel. He nodded to Mike as he slipped his sunglasses back on and started up the car.

Mike watched as Jody Douglas turned the patrol car

around and drove back down the driveway. He stood there, wondering if the man had really changed since his teenage years. Surely the cruelty he seemed to enjoy in his younger days was nothing more than the stupidity of youth, or the raging hormones of a teenager. In a rural county like Hudson there probably weren't too many ways for young people to vent off steam. Tormenting Mike's grandmother, as mean-spirited as it had been, was probably nothing more than a way for a handful of boys to break the boredom.

At least Mike hoped Jody Douglas had buried his mean streak in the past, for a sheriff who still acted that way would be a terrible thing indeed.

Chapter 5

Long, long ago, when the world was still new, the ancient people and the ancient creatures did not live on the top of the earth. They lived beneath it. There were four worlds: this one on top of the earth, and below it three cave worlds, one below the other. The Hopi people lived in the underworld, which was the original place of all human life. In the beginning life was good, and the people were happy.

But evil came to the underworld of the first Hopi, entering the hearts of the high priests. Instead of keeping the sacred rites and leading their people, as they were supposed to do, the high priests began to cheat the people. The underground world soon became a terrible place to live, and the people longed to live elsewhere.

Knowing they had to find a way out of the underground world, the people of good hearts gathered together to talk over their problems and to pray for a solution. They had heard stories that a world existed above theirs, and wanted to know if those stories were really true.

The people called upon the birds for help, asking if they would fly up into the sky to see if there was an opening to the other world. They called upon the canary, the swallow, the hawk, and even the mighty eagle for help. While each bird flew as high as he could—and several of them saw that there was indeed an opening to another world—none were strong enough to fly through that opening to see the world that awaited beyond.

The situation was beginning to seem hopeless, when the good-hearted people called upon the catbird for help. The catbird, who is the cousin of the mockingbird, flew so high that he passed right through the narrow opening separating the underworld from the world above it. Nearly faint from exertion, the catbird returned to tell about the wonders that awaited the people in the world beyond darkness.

Knowing they could not fly up to the opening, the people called upon chipmunk for help. The chipmunk planted the seed of a spruce tree, singing magical songs to make the tree grow quickly into the sky. But the spruce was much too short for the people to climb up through the opening.

Determined to help the people reach the next world, the tiny chipmunk planted the seed of a pine tree, but it was also too short to reach the opening. Next he planted the shoot of a bamboo plant, covering it with sacred cornmeal and praying that the bamboo would grow higher than the evergreen trees he had planted. The little chipmunk continued to sing his magical songs until the bamboo plant grew high enough to pass through the opening into the world above.

Gathering together their meager possessions, and carrying prayer offerings, the people cut an opening in the bottom of the bamboo plant and climbed up through its inside to the new world. They left behind an elderly wise man who waited for the people to make their climb into the new world, then cut down the bamboo plant so none of the evil people or *creatures that lived in the darkness would follow them to their new home.*

Sam Tochi had learned the creation stories of his people, in all their variations, when he was just a small boy living on the Hopi reservation in Arizona—years before the white man had taken him from his parents, forcing him to go to the Indian boarding school in Phoenix—but it wasn't until he was a young man that he understood the truth in those stories. He had seen the truth with his own eyes, but few people believed him. To most he was nothing more than a crazy old Indian.

"Crazy old Indian. Maybe it is the white people who are crazy. They do not listen to the old legends, and have even forgotten the history of their town. The old people were believers, but they are all gone now. Vivian believed, but she too has crossed over to the spirit world."

Dressed in blue jeans, moccasins, and an old green work shirt, Sam sat cross-legged in his backyard and watched as the fading sun painted the western sky in shades of red and orange. Before him a small altar of sand had been spread upon the ground, the sand held in place by a frame of four boards each measuring two feet in length. In the center of the altar was a wooden bowl containing water, and for each direction an ear of corn had been placed. Each ear of corn was a different color: white for the east, red for the south, blue for the west, and yellow for the north. In addition to the corn, two prayer sticks and an eagle feather had also been placed upon the altar.

On the ground beside him was his medicine bundle: a beaded leather bag containing his sacred pipe, assorted herbs, feathers, prayer sticks, and other items of medicine. Opening the bag, he removed the pipe and a small leather pouch containing tobacco. The Hopi used three varieties of native tobacco in their smoke; the tobacco in Sam's pouch was the same type used by his people in the kivas for important ceremonies. Sam did not have an underground kiva in his backyard, but he knew the spirits would still help him as long as he prayed with a pure heart.

Opening the bag, he removed his medicine pipe and placed it on his lap. The clay bowl of the pipe was about an inch in diameter and a little over twice that in depth, decorated with zigzag lines that represented both snakes and lightning. Snakes were sacred to the Hopi people, for they were considered to be the bringers of rain which guaranteed a good harvest.

Sam had once been a member of the Snake religious society, and had taken part in many Snake ceremonies while living on the Hopi reservation. The Snake ceremony was conducted by the Snake and Antelope societies and lasted for nine days. For the first few days of the ceremony, the members of the societies, all men, would prepare themselves by praying, making prayer offerings, and setting up altars inside the kivas. Then for four days they would go out into the desert to capture snakes, both poisonous and nonpoisonous, which were kept in special pens inside the kivas.

On the morning of the ninth day, Sam and the other members of his society would remove the snakes from their pens. They would wash the snakes in water, and then dry them in sand. As a test to see if their hearts were pure and fearless, the men would then drape the snakes over their bodies. The snakes would sleep on those who passed the test, and they would sometimes bite those who failed.

At sunset on the ninth day, the Snake society members would dance in a circle around the village plaza carrying the reptiles in their mouths. Accompanying each dancer was a second man who carried a snake whip made of eagle feathers. The snakes were terrified of eagles and the touch of the feathers was often enough to keep one from striking the dancer who held it. After the dance the snakes were returned to the desert, carrying the prayers of the people to the spirits so rain would come again to the land of the Hopi.

Sam smiled. It had been a long time since he was a member of the Snake society, longer still since he last danced with a live rattlesnake in his mouth. He no longer danced the Snake dance, but he still had his society kilt and feathered headdress. They were his most precious possessions, and he would not trade them for all the money in the world.

He opened the small leather pouch and removed a pinch of tobacco, placing it in the bowl of his pipe. A second pinch soon followed, and then a third. Closing the pouch, he removed a butane lighter from his shirt pocket and lit the pipe.

Sam inhaled deeply, bringing the flame to the bowl and drawing the sacred smoke into his body. He exhaled, raising the pipe above him in offering to the Great Spirit. He inhaled again, and offered the pipe to the earth and the spirits of the four directions. He prayed to the winds, and to the sacred spirits, asking them to watch over his people. Last he raised his pipe and asked the spirits to please tell him what had happened to him on Tuesday, because, while he could clearly remember the Snake dances and creation stories of the Hopi, he could not remember what he had done the day before.

"Great spirit, please hear my prayer. I offer this pipe to you in a sacred manner. Please open my ears so I may hear your voice. Open my eyes so I may see the things you put before me to see. Let the cloud that covers my mind be lifted so I may know of the things I have said and done. Please, if it be your will, let me remember."

It was not the first time Sam had had a blank spot in his memory, and it would not be the last. He remembered yesterday morning, but then a spell brought on by his sickness had occurred and everything else was a blur. He must have gone to the pharmacy to have his prescription of pain medicine refilled, for the bottle once empty was now full, but he could not remember going or coming back. Nor could he remember if he had talked to anyone along the way. He had been out of his head yesterday, pure and simple, a babbling old Indian driven to the point of insanity by the pain of an ever growing brain tumor.

His memory of the previous day was gone, and in its place was the feeling that something bad was about to happen. It was a feeling he could not shake, no matter how hard he tried. Even taking twice his normal dosage of pain medicine had not helped. The pain had gone away, but the bad feeling had remained to haunt him.

Finished with his prayers, he dug a small hole in the ground and buried the ashes from his pipe. To the west the colors of the sunset were being quickly swallowed by the darkness of the coming night. A shudder of fear passed through the old man as he watched the approaching darkness, remembering the terrors that nighttime had once brought to the area years earlier. Again the feeling came over Sam that something bad was about to happen.

Chapter 6

Thursday.

Tommy was excited, but Megan was less than thrilled about going to a new school, especially one in a town as small as Braddock. She had tried to stall for a few more days off, claiming exhaustion from the move, but her parents wouldn't hear of it. They said she had already missed a week of school, and could not afford to miss any more days.

Nor did Megan like the idea of having to ride a school bus, crowded in with a bunch of kids she didn't know. Country kids. They probably wore bib overalls, smelled of livestock, and chewed tobacco. Gross.

Of course, Megan had never met any real country kids before, so she couldn't swear they all wore overalls and chewed tobacco, but that's what they always looked like on television. Shows like those shown on Nickelodeon always portrayed country kids as social misfits spawned from cousins marrying cousins, and even brothers marrying sisters.

Boys weighing three hundred pounds, in raggedy jeans, with a pack of Redman in their back pocket, or a tin of Skoal, carrying a six pack of Pabst Blue Ribbon beer, on their way to the junkyard to steal hubcaps, or the fishing hole to feed frogs firecrackers to watch them explode. Girls wearing gunnysack dresses, with long stringy hair never touched by either conditioner or shampoo, missing front teeth because their daddies got drunk one night and decided to beat someone besides the wife, putting out for any boy in the trailer park who would even look their way, smelling of cheap wine, sweat, and odors best not thought about.

Standing where the driveway connected to Sawmill Road, Megan wished she was back in New York City among the sights, sounds, and friends she loved. Why did her father have to move to the country in the first place? There was nothing but trees, fields, and old farmhouses, absolutely nothing to do.

It wasn't like they were poor and had to move to the country. Her parents were wealthy enough to afford living in a nicer part of the city, sending her and Tommy to private schools. Crack dealers didn't hang out on the street corners where they had lived; gangs didn't run rampant, spray painting their graffiti on the walls, like they did in other neighborhoods. Upper Manhattan wasn't like the bad places they always showed on *20/20* and *Dateline*.

Just because a friend of her father's had been killed they had to move. It wasn't fair. It wasn't her friend who had died, nor did the murder happen anywhere near their neighborhood.

For all she knew the guy might have deserved to die. Maybe he was a gangster with ties to organized crime. Perhaps he was a crooked drug dealer, or he had fooled around with someone's wife or girlfriend. She wasn't sure why her father's friend had died, but she knew it had nothing to do with her or where they lived. And she wasn't scared because of it.

But the murder had scared her father. He had come home that night as white as a ghost, trembling and crying. He had told the story to Holly, his fingers clutching a full glass of scotch, shaking so hard the ice cubes rattled like bones. He had kept his voice low so the children wouldn't hear, but Megan had heard every word he said.

Her father had changed that night. He had lost his nerve, growing afraid of the city he once loved. The very next day he had called a company to install an alarm system in their apartment, and an extra deadbolt lock. They had started staying home more, having "family nights" instead of going out like they used to do.

New York was fun in the daytime, but the city was at its best at night. Lit up in fiery brilliance, all shiny and glimmering, like some fabled city out of a fantasy. Before her father had lost his nerve, she used to go out with her friends at night to do a little shopping, take in a movie, or grab a sandwich at one of the many little coffee shops. Sometimes they would even venture down to Times Square to look at the lights and watch the tourists. Forty-second Street was always exciting and vibrant, a circus performance of humanity acted out on a stage of concrete.

Megan sighed. The town of Braddock didn't even have a shopping mall, no place for kids her age to hang out and be seen. Nor was there a skating rink, public swimming pool, or teen club. The only hot spot seemed to be the local Dairy Queen, and that was only because it was at the end of the official car cruising strip. She had gone there with her family the previous evening, watching as carload after carload of kids had pulled into the parking lot. With horns honking and lights flashing, they circled the building once or twice before driving back off in the direction from which they had come.

At first she thought it was different cars she was seeing, but then, after a half hour or so, she noticed it was the same vehicles over and over again: beat-up pickups, late-sixties muscle cars in need of mufflers and body work, Japanese imports with low-profile tires and dark tinting, a 1957 Chevy with red flames painted on the hood. Apparently this was the local wild bunch: bored teenagers with nothing but time on their hands, no place else to go, and absolutely nothing to do.

Looking upon the local youth of Braddock, she wondered if she too would end up like them in an attempt to escape what would probably turn out to be a boring life in an equally boring town.

Megan's thoughts of her future life in Hudson County were shattered by the appearance of a big yellow school bus barreling down the narrow gravel road. The bus looked prehistoric, like a creature spawned in the dim darkness of the Jurassic Period. A man-eater. She took a deep breath and tried to calm her fears, but her heart started to jackhammer.

"Damnit Dad, how could you do this to us?" she muttered under her breath. "How could you do this to me?"

"What did you say?" Tommy asked, turning to look at his big sister.

She shook her head. "Nothing. I was just talking to myself."

Tommy looked at her a moment longer, then smiled. Megan was glad he accepted her answer, because she would catch hell from her parents for upsetting him on his first day at a new school. Though they were in different levels, and went to different schools, the grade school and high school were located next to each other on the same street. Both schools started and ended at the exact same time so students could share the same buses. That made her Tommy's official baby-sitter during the bus ride.

The bus slowed to a stop in front of them, the door opening with a squeak as sinister as that of a coffin lid. Grabbing the handrail, Tommy climbed the three steps to get into the bus. Megan swallowed hard and did the same.

The bus driver was a heavyset woman with flaming red hair. She greeted them with a smile. Tommy said hello back to the lady; Megan only nodded as she turned to look upon a sea of faces she did not know. She stood there, searching for a seat, feeling every eye upon her. There was no talking, laughter, or other sounds normally associated with children on their way to school; silence had descended over the passengers as she and Tommy climbed aboard.

Megan wanted to turn and flee the silence, but she put on her bravest face and ushered her brother forward, choosing an empty seat a few rows behind the bus driver. Despite the bus being almost filled to capacity, the one seat remained strangely vacant, as though it had been deliberately left for them. Did the others know there would be new kids riding this morning? If so, did the empty seat mean no one wanted to sit with them?

Megan felt her face warm with embarrassment as she sat down. The bus started moving, yet the silence remained. Only a few whispers from the very back of the bus broke the quiet.

Feeling as if every eye were still upon her, she faced forward, not daring to turn her head and look at anyone.

She managed to steal a few glances from the corner of her eye, and was greatly relieved to discover no one was wearing bib overalls or straw hats. Nor, from what she could see, was anyone going to school barefoot. So much for how television portrayed country kids.

Judging by the boys and girls sitting in the seats across the aisle from her, kids in Hudson County seemed to dress in much the same way as those back in New York City. Though none of them appeared to be wearing expensive brand names, they were dressed in modern apparel: baggy jeans, pullover shirts, and basketball shoes for the boys; knit tops, casual shoes, and shorts or dresses for the girls.

She should have known from the giggling around her that something was amiss, but Megan had never been the victim of the viciousness of other children. At the private school in New York she had been popular with her fellow classmates, never threatened by anyone. She didn't know a trap had been set until something struck the back of her neck.

Ouch.

Grabbing her neck, Megan discovered she had been hit by a tiny wet ball of paper. A spit wad. Horror seeped through her as she realized she had just touched someone else's saliva. Throwing the spit wad to the floor, she quickly wiped her fingers off on the leg of her jeans.

A second spit wad buried itself in her hair. Megan felt it hit, combing her fingers through her hair until she found it. She had just flung the second spit wad to the floor when a third struck Tommy hard on the right cheek, nearly bringing tears to his eyes.

"Ow, Megan, what was that? Something hit me."

Angry, Megan turned around in her seat. She looked

past a sea of smiling, giggling faces searching for her attackers. It only took a moment to find the culprits, for they made no effort to conceal their identities.

The spit wads had been fired by a group of older boys sitting in the last row of seats. Tall, hard-muscled boys who looked much too old to still be in high school. Dressed alike in blue jeans, T-shirts, and ball caps, they sported tans that spoke of long summer days working in the fields of their family farms. One of the boys held the casing of a cheap Bic pen in his left hand, a makeshift blowgun from which to fire the nasty projectiles. The boy looked at Megan defiantly as he popped another small piece of paper into his mouth and began chewing, openly daring her to say or do anything.

Megan could not physically challenge the boys, nor could she report them to the bus driver. Being labeled a snitch would destroy any chance of her making new friends. It would also put her and Tommy in danger of retributions from the boys if she got any of them into trouble. She couldn't fight back, nor could she ask for help from anyone. Her only option was to retreat.

Turning back around, she slouched down in the seat until her head was no longer a target. A quick tug on his wrist caused Tommy to do the same.

As a barrage of spit wads sailed over their heads, the other children openly laughed at them. Several kids even yelled out taunts, and a rhyming little ditty about the insanity of Megan's great-grandmother, Vivian Martin.

> Old lady Martin has gray hair
> Claims to see them everywhere
> Boogers in the attic, boogers in the walls
> Boogers under the bed nine feet tall

Come, let's get them before she's dead
Let's get the boogers out of Martin's head

Megan was stunned by what was being said. Did everyone in town know about her great-grandmother's apparent insanity, and were she and Tommy now being labeled social outcasts because of it? If so, then they were doomed to a life of torment and unhappiness in their new school and community. The bus rides alone would be unbearable. Better to die now than face this kind of humiliation every morning.

Damnit, Dad. Why did we have to leave New York? Why did you have to inherit that stupid house?

A tear formed in the corner of her left eye. She wiped it away quickly, not wanting Tommy or the other kids to see it. She dared not let anyone know they had made her cry; it would only make matters worse, ensuring such torments were carried out on a regular basis.

Nor could she let Tommy see her cry. If he saw her tears, he would know that what was going on around him was more than just a harmless game. He would feel badly for her, feel bad for himself, and his tears would come. Not just a drop of two, but in great sobbing buckets. She couldn't allow that to happen, because it would label him as a crybaby. The other kids would take great delight in picking on him then in the hope of making him cry again.

Wiping away the tear, Megan clenched her jaws and sat staring at the seat in front of her. The taunts and laughter eventually faded out, and so did the spit wads, as the children grew bored with the game. Her anger, on the other hand, burned all the way to school.

Chapter 7

The house was slowly shaping up. Very slowly. There seemed to be no end to the cleaning still needing to be done. Practically everything was dirty with years of accumulated grime. That which had not already been replaced or painted needed to be scrubbed and disinfected. Moldings, drawers, woodwork, bathroom fixtures—all were in need of a loving touch and plenty of serious elbow grease.

Holly stood in the middle of the library trying to decide what to clean next. The room looked a thousand percent better than when she first laid eyes on it—the new carpeting helped—but there was quite a bit of cleaning left to do. The walls were paneled so they had not been painted, and the books adorning the walnut shelves all needed a thorough dusting, as did the shelves themselves. Cobwebs hung down from the ceiling like finely spun cotton candy, covering the upper rows of books and the shelf containing the kachina dolls.

Deciding the cobwebs were just too much to tackle right then and there, she focused her attention on the hideous masks hanging on the one wall. They were hand-carved and obviously quite old, the wood almost black with age. Like something from a late-night horror movie, the twisted features of the masks sported crooked mouths, bulging eyes, and devilishly long tongues. Some were painted with bright paints, mostly reds and blues. Others had been left unpainted, their eyes formed with hammered sheets of copper inserted into the wood.

Notches had been carved in the outer edges of the masks, a place to fasten leather cords, so Holly knew the masks were made to be worn. She wondered if any of them had ever been used in ancient ceremonies to ward off evil demons, conjure up spirits, or cure the dead.

Maybe the masks had been used by old men to frighten naughty children on cold winter nights, when the wind howled and a full moon caused leafless trees to stretch shadowy fingers across new fallen snow. Such masks would surely have frightened her when she was a little girl, causing her to pull the covers tightly over her head for protection.

Perhaps the masks were not American in origin, coming instead from the mysterious black forests of Northern Europe. Maybe they had been carved by a lonely woodcarver in a country where legends of vampires and werewolves still filled the land, and where portly housewives hung garlic over the windows to keep out unwanted night visitors. They could also have come from Africa, or South America, born in the jungles where ancient medicine men held control over tribal people through terror, intimidation, and ritual magic.

Holly shook her head. For some strange reason she didn't think the wretched masks had been imported from another country. There was something about them that made her feel the masks were definitely Native American in origin. It was almost as if she could visualize the men who had once worn them: half-naked savages with bronzed skin, dancing around shimmering fires in forests of towering oaks and pine trees, carrying out ceremonies of ancient magic and medicine. Tied to a wooden post next to the fire was a beautiful white woman, her body trembling with . . .

She smiled at the image suddenly filling her head, chiding herself for letting her imagination run away on her. "Enough of that. Leave the make-believe to your husband. You don't have time to stand here and daydream."

No matter what the origin of the masks—be it Africa, Europe, or a toy shop in Cleveland—they had to go. Period. Mike had promised to remove them, but they still remained on the wall. Being a horror writer, and having a deep fondness for the strange and bizarre, he was probably hoping she would change her mind about getting rid of them.

"Not this time, mister." She crossed the room and lifted one of the masks from its supporting pegs. The wood was lightweight and smoothly polished. She could almost admire the craftsmanship that had gone into it had the mask itself not been so hideous to look at.

As Holly lifted the mask from the nail holding it on the wall, a strange tingling surged through her hands, as though a small electrical current had passed from the mask to her. She was about to dismiss it as nothing more than a static discharge when the room seemed to groan. It was more of a vibration than an actual sound, coming from deep within the bowels of the house and passing upward through the ceiling. The vibration lasted for no more than a second or two, passing as quickly as it came.

"What the hell?" Startled, she stepped back and looked around. Nothing had changed. She stood there for a few moments waiting to see if the strange vibration would be repeated, wondering if Mike or one of the contractors had briefly switched on an engine somewhere. When the sound wasn't repeated she looked down at the wooden mask she held.

"So you don't like being taken off the wall. Do you?" she joked, dismissing the events that had just transpired as nothing more than static discharge, the settling of an old building, and a bad case of overactive imagination. "Too bad. You're going into a box and that's final."

She placed the wooden mask in an empty cardboard box and then turned back to the wall to remove another one. She almost expected the room to groan again as she removed the second mask from the nail holding it, but nothing happened. No groaning. No shaking. Nor did she experience another tingling in her fingers.

Taking her time to carefully pack the masks, not wanting to damage any of them in case they turned out to be valuable, she was about to reach for the last mask on the wall when movement caught her attention. Something small and dark had darted past the open doorway, gliding quickly down the hall.

"Pinky?"

She crossed the room and stepped out into the hallway, knowing it wasn't the family cat she had seen. Pinky never moved that fast, not even in his younger days. And the cat never, ever passed a member of the family without first stopping for a quick rub. Nor was it a mouse she had seen, or even a rat. It was bigger than that, whatever it was.

Holly looked both ways down the hall. There was no

sign of a cat, or any other furred creature. It must have darted into one of the other rooms. Curious, she crossed the hall and entered her studio.

Most of her art supplies had already been put away in their proper places upon the shelves, leaving few boxes left on the floor that a cat or small animal could hide behind. Entering the room, she stepped forward and checked behind the remaining boxes, praying she wouldn't uncover a rodent in the process. Not that she was scared of rodents, but if one suddenly darted out from behind one the boxes she might scream. Such a cry of terror would result in endless laughter and ridicule from her husband.

Nothing was lurking behind the boxes. No rats, cats, or grinning green goblins. Turning around, she crossed the room and quickly searched through the closet, leaning the paintings forward one by one until she had checked behind all of them. Nothing was hiding in the closet either.

Leaving the art room, she walked across the hall and entered Mike's office, which was a cluttered mess compared to her studio. Numerous boxes, books, and stacks of manuscripts were piled upon the floor, creating places where any number of small furred creatures could easily hide. Switching on the work lamp that sat on top of the desk, she eased forward between the boxes and stacks of books and paperwork, carefully checking behind each stack as she went. She reached the end of the room without finding anything and then checked the closet. Again nothing. The door connecting the office to the library was closed, so nothing could have gone that way.

Okay. Where did you go?

Leaving the office, she followed the hallway to the

stairs. At the top of the stairs the contractors were installing new carpeting, so she knew nothing could have gone that way either. Not even Pinky. Had the big tomcat tried to get in the way, the men would have shooed him back down the stairs.

She was about to dismiss the whole thing as a trick of the lighting, when a loud noise echoed from the library. It sounded like a pistol shot, or the crack of a wooden baseball bat. The contractors heard it too, for they paused in their work and looked up.

"Now what?"

Hurrying back into the library, she was surprised to find the last wooden mask, which had still been hanging on the wall, lying in the middle of the floor broken into two pieces. The mask had been snapped in half, broken lengthwise between its slanting eyes.

She stepped forward and picked up the pieces of the mask, wondering what had caused it to fall. The mask was lying a good six feet from the wall, which meant it hadn't just fallen. Instead it had been knocked off the wall, sent sailing with enough force to snap it into two pieces. Holly tested the mask in her hands, attempting to bend the wood. But the wood was solid, and of such strength it would have taken a considerable force to break it.

Perhaps there was a flaw in the wood, maybe a hairline crack, and the normal atmospheric pressures of heating and cooling had finally taken their toll on the mask. Houses and driveways were subject to such conditions, why not a wooden ornament? Maybe the mask had been broken before, though Holly could see no evidence of it ever having been glued.

But even if the wood was flawed, or if the mask had

been broken and glued back together, that still did not explain how it had been knocked off the wall.

Turning to look at the place where the mask had hung, she was astonished to discover a large crack running vertically down the wall from floor to ceiling. The crack was over eight feet long, and at least a quarter inch wide. Closer inspection showed that not only was the crack in the wood paneling, but it was also in the wall behind the paneling.

Holly stared at the mask, and then at the wall, wondering what could have caused the damage. "Damn. This place really is falling down around our ears."

Chapter 8

Mike and Holly were sitting at the kitchen table, discussing the recently formed crack in the library wall and what to do about it, when the kids came home from school. Tommy came bursting through the front door, anxious to tell his parents all about his new school. Grabbing a cookie from the jar sitting on the counter, he described his school, teacher, and some of the other kids.

"Mrs. Wilson. That's my teacher. She's nice. But she has these funny glasses that make her eyes look real big." He set down his cookie and made circles with his fingers to show how his teacher's eyes looked. "Like this. Big eyes. Kind of like a frog. They look funny when she's looking at you."

"Just don't call her frog eyes," Holly warned. "I don't think she would like that."

"I wouldn't do that," Tommy said, shaking his head. "She might get mad at me and send me to the principal's office. I heard she can be mean if she wants to. That's what Jimmy Foss said. That's a boy in my class. He sits next to me. Jimmy said Mrs. Wilson can turn into a witch when she wants to. Today she sent two boys to the principal's office just for talking."

"You didn't go to the principal's office today, did you?" Mike asked, teasing.

"Oh no. But I saw it."

He described the principal's office as a circular glass enclosure in the middle of the school. While the office was a highly unusual structure, what really impressed him was the cases of stuffed birds lining the walls directly across from it. Dozens of cases. Hundreds of birds. Everything from a tiny blue-green hummingbird to a bald eagle. They were dead, of course, and their eyes were glass, and some of the feathery bodies were aged to the point they were starting to fall apart. But they were still pretty neat, at least according to Tommy.

"Are you sure they were real birds?" Holly asked.

"Oh yes. They were real. I even asked my teacher about them. She said they've been there since the school was built."

Despite keeping a smile firmly in place, Holly did not share in her son's enthusiasm about a collection of murdered and mounted birds. She thought wildlife should be just that, wild, and not part of someone's morbid collection. She worried what kind of message such a collection could be giving to young children, especially those brought up in the rural country where guns and hunting were a way of life.

Megan entered the house a minute or two later, her demeanor the complete opposite of her brother's. Her first impression of her new school had obviously not been a good one. She didn't like her classes, teachers, or fellow classmates.

"You have to give it a chance," Mike said. "It's only

your first day. Things will get better once you make friends. You'll see."

"Give this a chance," Megan said, obviously upset. She reached into her jeans pocket and pulled out a carefully folded paper napkin. Unfolding the napkin, she deposited several tiny balls of paper on the kitchen table.

"What are those?" Holly asked, leaning forward to get a better look.

"They're spit wads," Megan replied, her voice angry. "I pulled six of them out of my hair this morning on the bus."

"Yeah, I got hit in the face." Tommy said, his mouth filled with cookie. "It hurt, but I didn't cry. Did I, Sis?"

"No, you didn't cry," Megan said, trying to ignore her brother. "All the kids on the bus were saying things. Mean things."

"What sort of things?" Holly asked.

"They were saying things about Dad's grandmother, how she was crazy in the head. Some of them even had a little poem about it. I can't remember the words, but it wasn't very nice." Megan's eyes started to glisten and Mike knew she was fighting to hold back tears of anger. "I think the kids on the bus hate us because of Vivian Martin. I think they think we're crazy like her because we live in the same house."

"Old lady Martin has gray hair. Claims to see them everywhere. Boogers in the attic. Boogers in the walls. Boogers under the bed nine feet tall," Tommy said, remembering some of the words to the poem the children on the bus had been singing. He giggled suddenly, perhaps thinking what it would be like for an old woman to have boogers under her bed.

Holly arched an eyebrow, giving Mike a look that

said she wanted an explanation. Mike looked at his wife and daughter, trying to come up with something soothing to say to make things better. He knew kids could be cruel, but still he suspected the spit wads had been fired in jest rather than maliciousness. When he didn't say anything, Holly spoke up.

"I'm going to call the school and put a stop to this right now."

She got up and started toward the phone, but Mike stopped her. "You don't want to call the school about this. Not yet."

"Why not?"

He held up his hands, trying to calm her. "Look. I'm sure this was nothing more than a harmless prank being played on the new kids. Things will be different tomorrow. You'll see. Besides, if you call the school the bus driver will yell at the kids and things will only get worse."

Holly turned and stared at him. "I will not have my children terrorized on the bus."

"Neither will I," he said. "But let's give it a day. Okay?"

Holly thought about it for a moment, then nodded. "All right, I'll wait. But if this happens again, I'm calling the principal."

"Fair enough." Mike nodded. He turned to the kids. "What about you guys?"

Megan knew how bad things could get if she snitched on the other kids. "Okay," she said. "But tomorrow I'm going to wear a helmet."

"Me too," Tommy said. He pulled another cookie out of the jar, but the cookie slipped out of his finger and rolled under the table. Not wanting his afternoon snack to get away, he chased after the cookie.

"Hey, Dad. What's this?" Tommy asked, retrieving the chocolate chip cookie from beneath the table.

"What's what?" Mike asked, scooting his chair back to see what his son had found. Tommy was pointing at a dark stain on the floor directly beneath the table, an irregular oval about six inches long and four inches across.

"That wasn't there earlier when I swept," Holly said, looking under the table.

Mike looked at the stain for a moment, wondering what possibly could have caused it. The pale yellow tiles had just been installed the day before; maybe the workers had spilled something on the floor and it had taken this long to soak up through the tiles. Leaning forward, he ran his fingertips over the stain. The tiles weren't wet, or sticky.

"I'm not sure what it is," Mike said, straightening back up. "Something must have soaked through from the other side. It doesn't feel like mildew. Maybe it's just a piece of bad tile. I'll give the workers a call in the morning and have them come out and replace it."

"You'll never get someone out on such short notice," Holly said, staring at the stain.

"Sure I will," Mike argued. "You forget we're living in the country now. There can't be that much work for contractors going on around here. I imagine most people do their own repairs, especially when it comes to something as simple as laying floor tiles."

"It looks like a face," Tommy said, interrupting them.

"What was that, son?" Mike asked.

"It looks like a face."

Mike looked back down at the stain. He hadn't noticed it before, because he was looking at it from a different angle, but the stain did look sort of like a person's face, minus the ears. There were two darker patches within the stain that formed the eyes, with another dark smear making up the mouth. And it was lighter where the cheekbones and the bridge of the nose would be.

"It's just the way the light is hitting it," Holly said, studying the stain.

"No, it isn't, Mom. See." Tommy stepped closer to the stain, blocking the glow from the overhead lights. The image didn't change. As a matter of fact it now looked more like a face than it had moments before. Exactly like a face.

Though Mike knew what he was looking at was nothing more than a discoloration on the tile, he couldn't stop the chill that suddenly marched down his spine. The stain did look eerily like a face, as if someone or something was peering up at him from the floor, looking through the tiles as one would look through a window.

"It's just a funny-shaped stain. That's all," he said, reassuring Tommy before the boy's imagination ran away with him. Still, from deep inside Mike's head a little voice whispered that what he was seeing was much more than just a stain. Much, much more.

Chapter 9

Awakening early the first Saturday in their new house, Mike found Tommy sitting in front of the television watching cartoons. They still only had about six channels, but it was obviously more than enough to keep the boy happy. At least he wasn't screaming about missing his favorite shows, which Mike knew from experience would happen if his son missed an episode of whatever was currently at the top of his list.

No matter what his current favorite show was, Tommy was at the moment watching an old Bugs Bunny cartoon. Bugs and Daffy were arguing in front of Elmer Fudd about whether it was actually "Rabbit Season" or "Duck Season." Mike paused in the doorway to watch for a moment, smiling when Bugs Bunny pulled the old word switch-a-roo, making Daffy say that it was duck season. Quick as a flash Elmer Fudd pointed the business end of his trusty shotgun at Daffy's head and squeezed the trigger, blasting the duck's bill around to the back of his head.

Mike was especially pleased to see the cartoon had not been edited by television censors. There was a time when it seemed just about every kid's show had come under attack by parents' groups for being too violent for young viewers. The Three Stooges were usually at the top of the hit list, but cartoons also suffered, including the classic Looney Toons from Warner Bros.

The groups put pressure on the various networks, forcing them to either remove the shows from their lineups or edit them until none of the violence remained. It didn't matter if the supposed violence was slapstick comedy, or a parody. All of it had to go.

It also didn't matter if no one could prove that watching a Three Stooges episode had resulted in a child becoming a violent maniac. Mike had never read about a child watching Curly, Larry, and Moe and then whacking his or her mommy in the face with a frying pan, or putting Daddy's head in a vice.

And did the parental censor groups really believe a child would try to drop a safe on someone as Wily Coyote had often tried to do to the Road Runner? Maybe they were afraid a misguided teenager would paint a tunnel on the side of a mountain, or a building, and hapless motorists would smash their vehicles into it. Perhaps they were terrified that children all across America would save their lunch money to purchase rocket-powered roller skates, or other high-tech gizmos, from the Acme Company.

It was truly a sad world when such groups focused their attention on old slapstick comedy routines, and cartoons, as the cause for all the bad things in the world, rather than face up to the reality that they were just lousy parents. If the same people would take time to teach their children right from wrong, and if those children would be held responsible for their own actions, then the world would be a much better place.

Maybe people were already starting to see things for

what they truly were, because many of the cartoons that had come under attack in the 1980s were no longer censored. At least the one Tommy was watching had not been censored. Mike was glad about that, because a Bugs Bunny cartoon wasn't the least bit funny when it had been chopped and shredded to pieces. And he wanted Tommy to receive the same enjoyment he had from watching the classics.

Sitting on the floor directly in front of the television, far enough back so as not to be fussed at by his mother, Tommy cradled a box of Corn Pops in his lap, eating the crunchy sweet cereal right out of the box. He giggled as the antics of Bugs and Daffy continued, totally oblivious that his father watched him from the doorway. Mike considered joining his son in front of the television, but knew if he did he would probably waste the better part of the morning watching cartoons.

Instead he smiled and continued down the hallway to the kitchen. He thought about preparing breakfast, something other than Corn Pops right out of the box, but Holly and Megan were still sleeping and he hated to go through all the trouble of fixing a meal just for himself. Deciding Tommy had the right idea—the quick way was the best way on a Saturday morning—he grabbed a couple of strawberry Pop Tarts out of the cabinet and prepared a pot of fresh coffee.

As he pulled a chair away from the kitchen table, Mike noticed there were now two stains on the tile floor. Like the first, the second stain was a dark gray oval about six inches long and four inches wide.

"What the hell?" He moved the chair out of the way so he could see the stains, annoyed such things should be appearing in a brand-new floor. There had to be an explanation for it. Perhaps moisture was getting under the tiles. Maybe one of the water lines had sprung a leak.

"Great. Just what we need. More repairs."

Setting the Pop Tarts on the table, he crossed the room to the door opening onto the basement. Since moving in, he hadn't had time to take more than a quick look at the basement. If a water line had sprung a leak, that's where he would find it, because the pipes connected to the kitchen fixtures ran along the wooden beams beneath the floor.

Opening the door, he flipped the light switch at the top of the wooden stairs. Two light bulbs came on in the basement below, their pale glow doing little to push back the darkness. Holding onto the handrail, Mike descended the narrow steps. A barrage of odors rose up from the shadows to greet him: the smell of mold, dampness, dust, and perhaps cockroaches. There was also a noticeable difference in the temperature as he descended the steps. The basement was as cool as a cave.

Reaching the basement floor he turned to his right, navigating between an old oil furnace and a small stack of empty paint cans. He walked into a spiderweb, the sticky strands clinging to his face and hair, causing him to jump back in alarm.

"Damn. Damn. Damn," he cursed, tearing off the strands of web and swatting at the imaginary spiders he was certain now crawled all over him. He should have brought a flashlight, but he hadn't known the basement would be so dark. Turning around, he looked for the row of tiny windows set high along one wall that should have allowed light in. The windows were there, but all the glass panes had been painted black.

Mike stood and stared at the windows, realizing he was looking at yet another visible indication of his grandmother's eccentric behavior. The old woman must have painted over the glass to keep anyone from seeing into the basement. Not that there was anything worth looking at.

Making a mental note to purchase a razor blade scraper to use on the windows, he turned back around and counted off his footsteps. Reaching the spot he estimated to be directly beneath the kitchen table, he stopped and studied the ceiling above him. Where he stood there were no water pipes, nothing to cause a leak or produce enough moisture to stain the kitchen floor.

Knowing leaks had a peculiar way of traveling, he slowly crossed the basement until he found the water lines. Again he found nothing to indicate a leak. No puddles. No drips. Not even any excess moisture.

Determined there had to be a leak somewhere, he followed the lines from one end of the basement to the other. Nothing. He had just started to retrace his steps, double-checking the lines, when he caught a glimpse of movement, a shadow darker than the blackness around it. Something small scurried along the wall beneath the windows. The movement caused him to stop, his heart pounding.

What the hell was that? It must have been a rat. No way. Too bloody big to be a rat. Maybe it's a possum. Or a skunk. Mike sniffed, but didn't smell anything. *God, please don't let it be a skunk.*

The thought of having wild animals in his basement upset him, especially with the children in the house. He knew there wasn't much chance of them getting bitten, but he was not going to put up with unwanted critters.

His gaze focused on the wall beneath the windows, Mike slowly walked across the room. He moved as quietly as possible, his head cocked slightly, listening for the pitter-patter of tiny feet. The only sounds he heard, however, were those made by him.

It must have left, probably escaped through a hole in the wall or floor. Maybe down a tunnel. I probably scared it off.

He turned his attention to the area directly beneath the windows, and almost walked into one of the other walls. He stopped, momentarily disoriented by the sudden appearance of the wall before him. Looking around, he realized the basement was not a perfect rectangle. Instead it was shaped like the letter L, and he was now standing in an alcove jutting off from the main room.

Standing there getting his bearings, he spotted something dark and furry directly above his head. Startled, he jumped back, a scream nearly escaping his lips.

Jesus!

He expected the animal to lunge at him, its pointed teeth going for his unprotected throat, but nothing happened. The creature and Mike remained frozen in place, each staring at the other. At least he suspected it was staring at him. He couldn't see its eyes.

All right, big fellow, make your move. Let me see just how bad you really are. If I had a baseball bat right now, I would show you just how bad I am.

A few moments passed. The animal still didn't move.

What are you doing? Sleeping? Or are you already dead? Maybe the cat's got your tongue.

Realizing something wasn't right, he slowly relaxed his stance. He took a step forward, discovering that what he thought to be an animal was actually a carved wooden statue, about twelve inches high, covered with fur. The statue stood on a wooden shelf lining the wall. Other statues stood with it.

Mike let out his breath. "A fucking kachina."

Unlike the other kachinas he had seen so far, this particular doll was completely covered with brown fur. It also wore moccasins, armbands, and a brightly colored apron about its waist. Judging by the menacing clawed hands, and the shape of its head, he assumed the statue represented a bear spirit.

"You gave me quite a start." He turned the statue around to see its face. Like those in the rooms upstairs, all of the kachinas in the basement had been placed on the shelf facing the wall. The bear kachina's face was rather furious looking, with an open snout lined with pointy white teeth. Above the furry snout angry red eyes stared at Mike, challenging him.

"Jeez, you're enough to give a guy nightmares." He turned the statue to see it better in the dim light. "Yeah. Pretty scary, all right. Let's say we give you a new home upstairs."

He dusted off the statue and walked back across the basement. He hadn't found a leak, which meant the stains in the floor above were probably the result of defective tiles. He would give the contractors a call. They wouldn't be happy about coming out to repair the floor, but that was tough shit. He had paid for a new kitchen floor, without defects, and that's exactly what he was going to have.

Transferring the bear kachina to his left hand, Mike grabbed the handrail and started up the steps. Had he turned around just then and looked behind him, he would have seen a small shadow gliding along the bottom of the wall nearest the stairs. Not the shadow of a possum, skunk, or of any living creature. Just a shadow and nothing more.

Chapter 10

Mike carried the bear kachina into the kitchen and set it on the table. He wanted to call the contractors about the stains on the floor, but knew he would not be able to get hold of anyone on Saturday. Instead he went into the library and begin sorting through all the old books on the shelves.

The volumes on folklore, magic, and the paranormal his grandmother had collected were a welcome addition to his collection of reference books. Unfortunately he now had so many books only a fraction of them would fit on the shelves. Keeping the most desirable volumes on the shelves, he packed away the rest of the books into boxes until he could build more bookcases.

As he sorted and packed, he came across a rather nice book on kachina dolls. Curious, he opened the book and flipped through the pages, delighted at the numerous full-color photos the book contained. He paused when he found a picture of a bear kachina similar to the statue he had just retrieved from the basement. Reading what was written under the photo, he learned that the Hopi believed bears were the advisors, doctors, and assistants of their people. Through their assistance the Hopi had overcome monsters and witches, and cured strange diseases. It was believed the greatest doctor of the animals was the badger, but the bear also shared in this ability, knowing about the curing property of all the roots and how to administer them. The bear was also a warrior and knew the ways of danger, and could aid men in becoming more bearlike.

According to the book, all animals could remove their skin at will and hang it up like an article of clothing. With their skin removed, they appeared exactly as men, sitting around in their kivas, smoking and discussing serious matters. If they needed to become animals again, it was just a simple matter of slipping back into their skins.

"I'll be damned," Mike said, smiling. "You learn something new every day." Fascinated by the bit of Hopi tribal lore he had just read, and wanting to learn more about his grandmother's collection of kachina dolls, he placed the book back on the shelf, in a spot where he would be able to find it again easily. He wanted to read more, but resisted the temptation, knowing that if he started seriously reading the book he would never finish the cleaning.

Finished with sorting the books, he grabbed a chair from the kitchen and climbed up to dust off the collection of kachina dolls adorning the solitary shelf that ran along the walls near the ceiling. Oddly enough, in addition to the dust and cobwebs covering the statues, each and every one of the statues had been sprinkled with tiny reddish wood shavings and sawdust. Curious as to what kind of wood the shavings were, he lifted a pinch from one of the statues and sniffed it. The odor was very faint, but he could still detect the sweet scent of cedar.

He wondered why his grandmother had sprinkled cedar over the kachina statues, but then he remembered reading that many Native American tribes considered cedar to be sacred. It was often used in ceremonies, either burned in a fire to give off a purifying smoke or sprinkled over a person or object to be blessed. Eagle feathers and medicine pipes were often stored in boxes made from cedar to ward off negative energies. The aromatic wood was also great at keeping away moths, which is why long ago many people stored their most beloved clothing in cedar chests.

Apparently his grandmother felt the kachina dolls contained special properties and was trying to protect them from any negative energies that might exist in the house. Perhaps the dolls had once been used in Indian ceremonies to heal the sick or injured. Or maybe she was using the cedar to keep away moths and other unwanted bugs. Maybe she ran out of bug spray and cedar was all she had left.

Whatever the reason for the sprinkling of cedar shavings and sawdust, Mike did not share the same beliefs as his grandmother and felt there was no reason not to clean off the statues. It would be impossible to retain the cedar and remove the dust and cobwebs; therefore, it all had to go. Blowing and wiping, he carefully cleaned each and every one of the kachinas.

As he wiped off the statues, he turned them around so they no longer faced the wall. He wondered why his grandmother had chosen to display her collection backward, but only for a moment. She was an odd woman, her mind functioning quite differently from those of rational people. To her there had probably been a logical reason for displaying the wooden statues backward. To her and her only. Mike's grandmother was a cuckoo. It was as simple as that.

Later that afternoon Holly and Mike decided it would be a good idea for them to attend the dance being held at the VFW Hall in Braddock. Actually it was Holly who decided. He was a little reluctant, but she convinced him it might be just the thing to make new friends. And since the paper had done an article about him, it was almost expected that he be there.

The kids were less than thrilled to learn they would be staying home on a Saturday night while their parents went out. When Holly mentioned she had made arrangements to have a baby-sitter come over, they were downright upset.

"A baby-sitter? For us?" Megan asked, disbelief in her voice. "I'm fifteen, much too old for a baby-sitter. What are you trying to do, ruin my reputation in this town before I have a chance to even get one?"

"Now, now," Holly said. "Don't think of Tammy as your baby-sitter; instead think of her as a house-keeper."

"It's the same thing," Megan retorted. "And whatever you want to call it, I won't see her because I will be in my room all evening." With that she went upstairs to her room and slammed the door.

The baby-sitter arrived promptly at seven o'clock. She was a tall, skinny girl with a pleasant smile, probably in her late teens or early twenties. Giving her a list of instructions, Holly left her in charge of Tommy. Megan still had not come down from her room and wasn't likely to do so before the night was through.

The parking lot at the VFW Hall was full, forcing Mike to park the van in an empty lot across the street.

From the looks of things half the town of Braddock had showed up for the dance. He wondered if the dance always drew such a crowd, or if some of them were actually there just to see their newest celebrity resident. The thought that he and Holly were about to be put on public display for the locals made him more than just a little uncomfortable.

The inside of the VFW was just as crowded as the outside. Small wooden tables encircled a rectangular dance floor where couples danced to a four-piece band. The music was mostly country, but a few jazz tunes were also thrown in now and then for variety. Aware of the eyes upon them as they entered, they slowly made their way across the room to the bar.

Getting the bartender's attention, Mike ordered a Budweiser for himself and a rum and Coke for Holly. Having paid for the drinks, he turned in search of an empty table. Unfortunately all of the tables were full.

"Looks like we're going to have to sit at the bar," he said, handing Holly her drink.

"Looks that way," she said and nodded, speaking loud enough to be heard over the music.

"I guess we should have gotten here earlier."

She smiled. "What? And miss the chance of making an entrance?"

Mike laughed and took a sip of his beer. He noticed a tall, dark-haired man crossing the dance floor toward the bar and had a feeling the man was coming over to talk to him. He was.

"Mr. Anthony. I'm Jim Cowen. I'm the editor of the *Braddock Tribune.*" He stuck out his hand. "I just wanted to welcome you to the neighborhood."

Mike set his beer down and shook hands. "This is my wife, Holly."

"It's a pleasure," Jim said, shaking hands with her. "Listen, these stools are awful uncomfortable. My wife and I have a table in the corner. We'd love to have you join us. It's also a lot quieter over there than it is here. Not quite so close to the speakers."

"Intelligent company and the preservation of our eardrums?" Mike smiled. "You have yourself a deal."

Grabbing their drinks, they followed Jim Cowen across the room. Again it seemed as if all eyes were upon them. Mike received so many looks he wondered if his fly was open, but resisted the urge to reach down to check it.

Jim led them to a small round table in the back corner of the room, far enough away from the band to make conversation possible, and far enough from the dance floor to keep from being elbowed or bumped by those in the throes of country music delight. A strikingly beautiful woman sat at the table. She was thin and athletic looking, with blue eyes and thick blond hair that cascaded over her shoulders like a waterfall. Her dress was bright red and loose fitting; a maternity dress. Mrs. Cowen was obviously pregnant, but she was probably only in her first few months.

"Mike, Holly, this is my wife, Karen," Jim said, making the introductions.

Karen flashed them a warm smile and shook hands. "It's a pleasure to meet you. I was afraid you wouldn't want anything to do with us after that article Jim wrote about you. I told him to wait until later to publish it, but you know how newspaper men are."

Jim hung his head sheepishly. "A writer moving into town is big news around here. I hope you weren't offended by what I wrote."

Holly laughed. "No. No. Not at all. Although I did wonder why everyone was staring at us."

Setting their drinks down, Mike and Holly joined the Cowens at their table. The women paired off in conversation, their talk soon turning to children and childbirth. It was Karen's first pregnancy and she was very excited about the prospect of becoming a mother. Soon both women were swapping stories and laughing in delight.

Mike and Jim's conversation centered more around community events and local politics. Jim also discussed his job as an editor of the town's only newspaper, a position he had been in for less than two years.

It was about an hour later, and Mike had gone off to use the rest room, when Holly suddenly remembered the crazy old Indian who had confronted her in the supermarket parking lot. "Jim, you're the editor of the newspaper, so you must know most of the people in town."

"Most of them," Jim smiled. "It's not hard in a town this small."

"Do you know an old man named Sam Tochi?"

Jim's smile faded, and he exchanged a quick glance with his wife. "Yeah, I know Sam. I wish I didn't, but I do. He's the official town oddball. An old Hopi Indian that should have gone back to the reservation a long time ago. He's a real pain in the butt, but harmless. I guess every town has such a character; Braddock is no exception. I take it you've already met him?"

Holly nodded. "He approached me outside the Kroger store, and started ranting about 'boogers.' He said I have their house, whatever that means. It's pretty funny now, but at the time it was rather upsetting. Any idea what he could have been talking about?"

Again Jim and his wife exchanged a quick glance. "You have to understand that Sam Tochi has been around this area for a long time. He knows a lot of the old stories and legends, and was once considered to be a local authority on them, but that was back when he still had all of his mental faculties. Now he just goes around muttering bits and pieces of local folklore, mixing it up with Indian legends, and scaring the hell out of the kids. The town has tried to have him locked up for his own good, but the old cuss somehow keeps convincing the doctors that he's sane enough to take care of himself."

"But what are boogers?" Holly asked. "And what does he mean that I have their house?"

"The people who originally settled this area came from northern Europe. They were a very superstitious lot, bringing with them a lot of their fears and phobias. When anything went wrong—a cow dying, a horse taking sick—they used to blame it on the bogeyman, boogers, or hobgoblins. It became such a common practice in the old days that some people thought the woods were filled with mischievous little creatures."

"What woods?" Holly asked, suspecting she already knew the answer.

Jim smiled. "The woods that are now part of the property you own. But it's only legend and superstitions, tall tales told by backwoods hillbillies and crazy old Indians."

Mike returned from the rest room, taking a seat beside Holly. "Did I miss anything?"

"Not really," Jim said. "I was just telling your wife about Sam Tochi."

"Who?" Mike asked.

"The town's official nutcase."

"The old Indian I told you about," Holly added. "The one who approached me the other day."

"Oh, that one," Mike nodded. "Is he dangerous?"

"No. He's perfectly harmless," Jim said. "The only danger is having your ear talked off."

"Not much danger in that," Mike laughed, "because I'm not going to give him the chance to get that close."

The Cowens proved to be charming company, but they had to depart early in the evening, leaving Mike and Holly alone at the back table. They weren't alone for long, however, for during the night several people approached their table to introduce themselves and say hello.

Most of the people they met that night were warm and friendly, but some were rather offputting. A few even made a point of saying something negative about Mike's books, which was shrugged off by the author as nothing more than a bad case of jealousy.

A little after midnight Mike got into a heated argument with one of the local drunks. The man had staggered up to their table, looked Mike in the eyes, and begun criticizing his grandmother.

"You must get all of your stories from her. She was a real mental case, all the time seeing things that weren't there. What a loon; it must run in the family."

Mike wanted to punch the drunken bastard, but Holly held his arm. Deciding it was time to leave, they slipped on their jackets and headed for the door. They were still angry when they arrived home, but that anger quickly faded as they crossed the front yard to the porch.

Having paid the baby-sitter, they waited for her to drive off before locking up for the evening. Mike had

just gone into the living room to turn off the television
when Holly called him from the kitchen.

"Mike!" she yelled. "Come in here!"

Hurrying into the kitchen, he saw what his wife was
so upset about. There were now six oval stains on the
floor. Three under the table, two by the counter and another one near the door. They were all similar in size
and shape, although the first two that had appeared
were much darker than the rest.

Mike felt the hairs on the back of his neck start to rise
as he stepped forward to take a closer look at the two
original stains. Because they were darker, there was no
mistaking what they were. They were tiny faces, magically drawn on the tiles. Faces with open eyes that
stared at him unblinking from the kitchen floor. They
were faces all right, no doubt about it, but they were not
human.

Chapter 11

Mike would have slept longer, but a dull ache in the hollow of his back caused him to wake a little after 7:00 A.M. Try as he might he could not get back to sleep. Worse yet, his tossing and turning woke Holly. Since sleeping late on Sunday was now out of the question, they decided to get up and prepare a breakfast of pancakes and sausages.

Entering the kitchen, he flipped on the light and took a close look at the six oval stains on the floor. They looked no different in the daylight than they had last night. The stains looked like faces, as if someone had drawn them on the tile floor with charcoal or some other dark pigment. Of course they couldn't be faces; that was absurd. There had to be a logical explanation for it, but damned if he could think of what that would be.

Holly was just as puzzled about the stains as he was. The floor didn't feel wet, or sticky, and there was no noticeable smell of mildew to the room. She even got down on her hands and knees and sniffed, hoping for a clue as to what was causing the stains. But there was no odor. Nothing. Nada. Zero. Zip. The stains remained a mystery.

Trying to keep his mind off of why his perfectly good floor was getting ruined, Mike helped Holly prepare breakfast. But as he beat the pancake batter in a mixing bowl, his gaze kept returning to the stains on the floor. He would call the contractors first thing in the morning. There was probably a simple explanation to the problem.

After mixing the pancake batter, he set the table and then went upstairs to wake the kids. He thought Megan might still be upset about having a baby-sitter in the house last night, and refuse to come downstairs and eat, but when he knocked on the door his daughter yelled that she would be down in a minute. He guessed the fragrance of sausages cooking, which could clearly be smelled upstairs, was enough to coax anyone out of his or her room.

Megan and Tommy were both downstairs by the time the pancakes and sausages were served. Sunday breakfasts were sort of sacred at the Anthony house, with whatever problems and arguments currently taking place set aside until later. Rather than risk hard feelings, Holly steered clear of any discussion about the baby-sitter or last night's dance.

"Mom, can I eat my breakfast in the living room?" Tommy asked, stopping in the kitchen doorway.

Holly set the last of the plates on the table and turned to her son. "Tommy, you know we always have Sunday breakfast together. It's a family tradition. And if I let you eat your pancakes in the living room, you might get syrup on the carpet."

"Please, Mom. I'll be careful."

"I don't think so," she said. "Why? Is something special on television?"

Tommy shook his head and pointed at the kitchen

floor. "I just don't like the faces looking at me. They're spooky."

"No spookier than your face," Megan said, stepping past her brother to enter the kitchen.

"They're not faces," Mike said, sliding his chair back and taking a seat at the table. "They're stains. That's all."

"They look like faces to me," Tommy argued.

"They may look like faces, but they're not," Holly said, trying to reassure her son. "Honest. Now, come eat before your food gets cold."

Tommy remained standing in the doorway. "But I don't want to step on them. They might bite me."

Mike made a point of looking at his son's feet. "You're wearing shoes. If they try to bite you, just give them a good stomp."

Holly shot Mike a quick look of warning, but what he had just said to Tommy obviously worked. The boy entered the kitchen and took a seat at the table, being careful not to step on any of the stains in the process.

Wanting to change the subject from spooky-looking stains, Holly hinted that Mike might go into town and see about getting a satellite dish antenna for the television. Such a suggestion delighted the kids and turned the talk to all of the television shows they would soon be enjoying.

After breakfast Mike helped to clear away the dishes and then went into the library. He was about to select a book from the shelf when he noticed that all of the kachina dolls had been turned back around to face the wall.

"What the hell?" He stepped closer to the shelf. Each and every one of the statues had been turned. None had been left untouched. "Who the hell did this?"

Angry, he crossed the room and stepped into the hallway. He started to go back into the kitchen, but entered the living room instead. A quick glance around the room showed him that all of the kachina statues in the living room had also been turned to face the wall.

"Holly! Kids!" he yelled, never taking his eyes off of the statues. "Come in here a minute."

"What is it, dear?" Holly entered the room, wiping her hands off on a dish rag. The children followed her.

"Is this someone's idea of a bad joke?" He pointed at the collection of kachina dolls lining the shelf. Turning to the children, he asked, "Did you guys turn the statues around last night while we were at the dance?"

Tommy shook his head. "I didn't do it. Honest. I can't reach up that high."

"How about you, Megan?"

A look of hurt flowed into the girl's eyes, followed by a flash of anger. "I didn't do it. I was upstairs all night. Ask Tommy. Maybe the baby-sitter did it."

"Why would the baby-sitter turn the kachinas around?" Mike asked, not entirely convinced his daughter was telling the truth. He suspected she had turned the statues around to get back at him and Holly for hiring a baby-sitter. Perhaps she and Tommy were both in on the prank. Such a thing would not surprise him, although he had never known Tommy to tell a lie.

Megan shrugged. "Maybe she didn't like them looking at her."

Megan's answer surprised Mike, and made him consider a possibility he had not thought of before. Perhaps his daughter was right. The baby-sitter might have been a little unnerved at having several hundred frightful statues staring at her, especially in an old farmhouse late at night. Even so, it seemed an unusual course of action, for it would have been far easier just to ignore the kachinas than climb up on a chair to turn each and every one of them around.

Holly was also suspicious that her children were playing a prank, but she could not scold them without adequate proof. Wanting to take the pressure off of the kids, she said, "Well, it looks like someone went to an awful lot of trouble just to play a joke. Megan might be right. Maybe the baby-sitter didn't want the statues staring at her. Can't say that I blame her. I wouldn't want them staring at me either.

"We can turn the statues around later," she said. "After we get back from church."

Still wanting to be accepted into the new community, Holly had decided to take the children to the Methodist church for Sunday service. She wasn't a regular church-goer, but she did like to attend services once in a while.

Mike declined to go with them, wanting instead to stay home and work on his new novel. He hadn't touched the story in almost two weeks and was afraid of it growing cold on him. Besides it would be good to be alone for a while to get the old creative juices flowing.

The Braddock United Methodist Church was an impressive red brick building on the corner of Main Street and Ashmore Drive. It was one of only two churches in town: the other being the First Baptist over on Mission Street. Catholics had to drive all the way to Warrenton to attend service.

Sunday service was just beginning when Holly pulled the van into the side parking lot. She cast a quick glance into the rearview mirror to make sure her hair and makeup looked presentable, then climbed out of

the vehicle and waited for the children to join her.
Having locked the van, they crossed the parking lot to
the church.

Truthfully, Holly was not all that strong on religion
and did not regularly go to church. In the last year she
had only attended services twice, and then only because she had gone with someone else. She considered
herself a Christian, because she believed in God, but
she didn't think it was necessary to attend church to be
saved from the eternal damnations of Hell.

Not that she really believed in Hell. Or the Devil. She
suspected both were made up by religious leaders in an
attempt to scare the masses and fill the collection
plates. The Devil was probably nothing more than the
religious equivalent of the bogeyman, something to tell
to naughty children and half-senile old women.

She climbed the stone steps leading up to the church
and opened one of the massive wooden doors for
Tommy and Megan. Her children didn't enjoy church
services, another reason why Holly never attended
them on a regular basis. She wanted them to have a
working understanding of religion, all religions, but
she didn't want to shove it down their throats as most
parents did.

Holly's mother had once been a stout Baptist, forcing
her to attend church on a regular basis in an attempt to
brainwash her into believing everything the preacher
said. Those beliefs had been shattered when their minister was caught being serviced by a local hooker in a
two-bit motel. It was hard to believe in the righteous-
ness of a congregation leader who had been caught
with his pants down around his ankles and his penis in
someone's mouth.

No. The children would make their own decisions

when it came to religion. Intelligent decisions based on their own reasoning, not based on the influence of family members. And if they chose no religion at all, then Holly would stand behind them one hundred percent.

Entering the church, she led the kids down the side aisle until she found space in one of the pews. Once seated, she picked up a program book from the holder in front of her, gave it a quick glance, and then turned to admire the architecture.

Above her a lofty vaulted ceiling of polished redwood had been carefully constructed to draw one's gaze upward in spiritual contemplation. The roof and beams supporting it acted as a sounding board for the organ, sending vibrations bouncing throughout the building like the ominous voice of the Almighty. Four large stained glass windows were set in the walls that ran parallel to the pews, each depicting a famous biblical scene.

Wood was put to good use at the front of the church in the form of beams, paneling, and the altar's decorative rail. It all seemed to glow under the light cast by the fixtures suspended from the ceiling. As the choir finished their opening hymn, the minister stepped forward to start the day's sermon, offering first messages of condolences to congregation members who were sick and injured.

Holly settled back to enjoy the service, only having to remind Tommy twice not to talk while the minister was speaking. The two times he said something he had kept his voice to a whisper, but she knew even whispering could be very annoying to those around them.

As the service progressed, she noticed several congregation members cast glances and stares her way. At first she suspected they were just curious about the new arrivals, especially those who were obviously strangers to the religious community. But some of the looks she received were outright hostile, making her feel that her presence was less than welcomed. Remembering how she and Megan had been similarly treated in the supermarket, she wondered if the looks and stares had anything to do with the newspaper article about her husband.

I'll sure be glad when some other celebrity moves to town so they'll quit looking at us.

Service ended without any embarrassing mishaps. Megan didn't fuss too much about having to endure the ceremony, and Tommy fidgeted no more than was normal for a boy his age. Nor did he try to sneak a quarter from the collection plate as he had once done during midnight mass at St. Patrick's Cathedral. All that remained was the customary shaking of hands with the minister and other church dignitaries as they filed out of the building. Since she was new, Holly made a point of introducing herself and the children as she shook the minister's hand.

"Oh, I'm quite aware of who you are, Mrs. Anthony," Reverend Mitchell replied, a frown touching the corners of his mouth. "I'm also familiar with your husband, and the things he writes."

Holly knew by the tone of his voice that Reverend Mitchell was going to say something negative about Mike's books. It would not be the first time a religious leader had said such things; after all, Mike wrote horror and dark fantasy novels. Even in this day and age, many people considered him in league with the Devil. She wanted to walk away from the reverend, get in her van, and just leave. Instead, she asked, "You've read some of my husband's books?"

The minister shook his head. "No, I haven't, and for good reason I might add. Neither I nor my congregation approve of such books. Nor do we like it that your husband has chosen to use this fine community as the setting of several of his witchcraft stories."

Holly was taken back. "There must be some mistake. Mike has never used this town in any of his books."

The minister smiled a patronizing smile, which infuriated Holly. "He uses different names, makes some minor changes to enhance the story, but anyone familiar with Braddock will easily recognize it as the same town described in several of his novels."

"He may have borrowed a few things from this town—a street or two, the name of a road, even the description of a cemetery or cave—but all writers do that," Holly argued. "They write about what they know, and for Mike this town was an important part of his childhood. His roots are here. If he puts a little bit of Braddock into his stories, I assure you he does so as a way to honor the town, not to embarrass the people living in it."

"Mrs. Anthony, the novels your husband writes have made many of the people in this town quite angry. They don't want to be associated with works of literature about witchcraft and Satanism. My congregation feels very strongly about this matter, as do I; therefore, I feel it would be in the best interest of all if you and your family found another church to attend."

Holly felt a flush of anger creep across her face. It was all she could do to keep from swearing. "Reverend Mitchell, you said you have never read any of my husband's books. Is that correct?"

He nodded. "That's correct, but—"

"Then how can you possibly judge him or what he writes fairly? Mike's books aren't evil. If anything they're a warning against the dangers of evil. His last novel, *Pentagram Dreams,* was the story of a father fighting to save his child from a Satanic cult. It was a story of good versus evil, with good winning in the end. Surely you can't think badly of a book that warns others about evil. Can you?"

"It doesn't matter what I think of your husband's books, Mrs. Anthony," Reverend Mitchell replied, speaking to her as if she were a child who didn't understand. "What matters is what my congregation, and the town of Braddock, thinks of your husband and his books. And I have already told you what they feel about the situation."

Holly wanted to argue the matter, but the minister dismissed her with a slight wave of his hand.

"Good day, Mrs. Anthony. We will pray for you and your family."

Holly took a deep breath and smiled, suppressing the anger about to overtake her tongue. "And I will pray that you, and the rest of your congregation, be saved from total and complete ignorance. But I'm afraid it's much too late for that."

With that parting remark Holly turned away from Reverend Mitchell, leaving him red faced and sputtering. Steering the children through the crowd, she didn't look back until she had reached the van. The reverend still stood on the sidewalk, staring after her. She thought about flipping him the bird just for the hell of it, but decided against it. No sense dropping to the level of others when she didn't have to.

"Mom, we won't be coming back to this church, will we?" Tommy asked, looking up at her.

Suddenly realizing she had been holding her breath, Holly breathed out, releasing some of the tension seizing her. She looked down at Tommy and smiled, patting him on top of the head. "No. We won't be coming back here."

Tommy thought about it for a moment, then smiled. "Good. I didn't like this place."

"I didn't like it much either." Unlocking the van, she climbed in and started the motor. She waited for the children to climb in and slip their seat belts on, then backed out of the parking space and started down the street. Reverend Mitchell continued to watch her as she drove away.

Chapter 12

The empty computer screen stared at Mike, challenging him to fill its gray brightness with words. The cursor flashed mockingly. He stared back at the screen, typed a few words, then changed his mind and deleted what he had just written. He turned to look at the clock sitting atop his desk and frowned.

An hour had already gone by, yet he had nothing to show for it. No visions of a literary masterpiece had floated up from the deep dark recesses of his mind. Not one page. Not a paragraph. Not even a single line of dialogue worth keeping. Leaning back in his chair, he rubbed the bridge of his nose and wondered where his talent had gone.

Oh, sure, he could blame his lack of creative flow on the unfamiliarity of his new office. He could even ascribe it to the newness of the house, or a mental drain brought on by the move. That wouldn't be the truth, however, because his flow had stopped weeks before he even thought about moving from New York.

Writer's block.

Mike shook his head. No. No. No. He dared not even think such thoughts. Writer's block was the dreaded curse of the literary world. It came without warning or reason, robbing an author of the inner voice that guided him through lonely nights and countless blank pages. Writer's block could last for months, even years, ending the career of even the most talented author.

I do not have writer's block!

If he did have writer's block, there had to be a reason for it. Maybe the pressure of writing had finally taken its toll on him, planting the seed of doubt deep in his mind that his talent was all used up.

He knew the critics were just waiting for him to make a mistake, hoping his next novel would not be nearly as good as the one before it. Like lions at a watering hole they were waiting to pounce, dragging him down into the world of bad reviews and warehouses full of unsold books. No matter how much he chose to deny it, the pressure was on and Mike knew it. The next novel had to be as good as those before it or he was finished as an author.

He had hoped moving to the country, away from the domain of publishers, agents, and critics, would take some of the pressure off of him and loosen up the old creative juices. But from the look of things, his mind was just as stopped up in the country as it had been in the city. He only had three months to complete the first draft on the novel he was currently writing, and he was less than halfway through.

Think happy thoughts. Or gory thoughts since this is a horror novel. But write. Damnit. Write.

Maybe a walk would help loosen up the old creative juices. He really hadn't had much of a chance to get out and walk around the property, so maybe now would be a good time to do so. Besides, the house was kind of spooky when it was empty; he kept getting the strange feeling he was being watched. He also kept catching movements out of the corner of his eye—small shadows that seemed to flit and dart across the room—but whenever he turned his head to look, nothing was there.

Deciding a walk was exactly what he needed, he exited out of the word processor he was currently using and switched off his Gateway 2000. He stood up and pushed his chair back under the desk, then covered his computer and turned off the lamp.

He went upstairs to grab his house keys and a pair of sunglasses. Pinky, who had been napping at the top of the stairs, followed him when he came back down.

"Want to go for a walk, boy?" The big cat rubbed against his legs as he unlocked the front door, and then quickly shot past him when the door was opened. Slipping on his sunglasses, Mike stepped outside and locked the door behind him.

As he circled around the house to the apple orchard, Pinky ran ahead of him, stopping to sniff a strange scent or chase a bug through the tall grass. Grasshoppers proved to be an obvious delight to the feline, and he took great pleasure in stalking them in his best jungle cat fashion.

Only about half of the trees had apples on them; the rest were leafless and looked to be the victims of some form of disease. Mike wondered if the disease could spread to the other trees, and made a mental note to find out from someone who knew about such things. If there was a chance of the disease spreading to the healthy trees, then it would be best to hire someone to cut down the diseased trees before the entire orchard was wiped out. No reason to lose a supply of fresh fruit if he didn't have to.

Beyond the orchard the forest grew thick and wild. For the most part the trees were elms and oaks, but there were several places where strands of tall pines reached for the sky. Noticing the straightness of the rows, Mike realized the pine trees had been carefully planted by someone.

Apparently the oaks and elms were part of the old grove, while the pines had been planted in recent times to replace trees once removed. He knew a sawmill had once been located in the area, so maybe the woods he now owned had been part of their logging operation. The pines must have been planted as replacement trees because of their rapid growth. He wasn't an expert on trees, but he estimated the pines he saw to be about sixty or seventy years old.

Following a winding animal trail, it wasn't long before he stumbled upon Bloodrock Creek. The creek was about ten to fifteen feet across at its widest point, and no more than a foot or so deep, although there were places where the swirling water had scooped out earth and rock to form pools that were probably deep enough for swimming.

Soothed by the creek's gentle gurgling, he took a seat on a large rock and watched the dark water swirl past him. He dipped his hand in and took a drink, invigorated by both the clarity and coldness of the water. No way would he ever think of drinking from a stream in New York, but here it seemed perfectly natural to do so. He just hoped the stream didn't pass through a cow pasture farther upstream. Still, drinking water laced with a little cow shit was probably a whole lot healthier than the chemical-tainted poison that flowed from the tap back in the city.

Sitting on the rock, he allowed his mind to relax as he

enjoyed the wildlife around him. He spotted several species of birds, as well as an abundance of squirrels in the area. There were also quite a few insects making their homes along the creek, including a rather pesky yellow fly who insisted on making his presence known. A few well-aimed swats finally persuaded the insect to seek attention elsewhere.

The serene calm of the forest made it hard to imagine that a battle had ever been fought in the area. But according to local history, Bloodrock Creek had earned its name because of a minor skirmish waged along its banks during the early days of the Civil War. The Battle of Bloodrock Creek wasn't a planned campaign. Two opposing generals had not led their troops in grand charges, as often portrayed in books and movies.

On the contrary, the skirmish had been the result of a Union patrol becoming lost and accidentally stumbling upon an encampment of Southern sympathizers. The sympathizers in the encampment, as well as the soldiers in the patrol, had been drinking heavily that day, so many of the shots fired in the exchange missed their target. Only three soldiers were killed: two of the sympathizers, and the Union officer responsible for getting his troops lost. Several other soldiers were wounded, but none seriously enough to be considered life threatening.

Since blood had been spilled in the battle, the local residents felt inclined to change the name of the creek from Johnson's Creek (much to the displeasure of Nathan Johnson, for whom the creek had been originally named) to its more ominous nomenclature of today.

His creative juices inspired by thoughts of ancient forests and forgotten battles, Mike decided to head back to the house and take another crack at his writing.

Calling Pinky to make sure the big cat followed him, he left the forest and made his way slowly back through the orchard.

Arriving back at the house, he stopped suddenly when he spotted movement in an upstairs window. The window was one of the two belonging to Tommy's room.

Alarm bells sounded in his head. Holly and the kids weren't back yet, and Pinky the cat was with him, so there should not be anyone in the house. Yet he had definitely seen something slip past the window. As he stood there, he saw it again, a patch of darkness gliding past on the other side of the glass. It wasn't a trick of the lighting. Nor had the shadow been caused by a curtain blowing, because the window was closed.

Positive someone was inside Tommy's room, Mike hurried to the rear of the house. He tried the back door, but found it locked. Whoever was inside probably had not come this way.

Stepping away from the back door, he circled the house, keeping close to the wall so as not to be seen from above. He checked the windows as he went, but they all appeared to be securely locked. Arriving at the front of the house, he stepped up on the porch and slowly approached the front door. The door was still closed, but that didn't mean it had not been recently opened.

As he reached for the doorknob, Mike suddenly realized that he was unarmed. If there was someone inside the house, a burglar perhaps, then it could be very dangerous coming face to face with him. Hesitating for a moment, he thought about retreating to search for something to use to defend himself. He might find a tool of some kind in the barn, or even a sturdy board that would suffice for protection. But if he went to the barn to look for such an item, the person inside the house might get away.

He stood there, not knowing what to do, feeling a little afraid at the possibility of coming face to face with an intruder while unarmed. He was also angry that someone had violated the sanctuary of their home. In New York City he had protected his apartment with alarms and triple locks, but had never thought to do such things here. The country was supposed to be safe, or at least it used to be.

Not wanting to retreat off the porch for fear the intruder might slip away, Mike finally decided to enter the house. Taking a deep breath, he tried the doorknob, and was surprised to find it locked.

Of course it's locked. The burglar probably relocked the door to make it appear exactly as he found it.

Fishing his keys out of his pocket, he slipped the house key into the lock and slowly opened the door. Entering quickly, he closed the door quietly behind him. He stood just inside the door, carefully listening to the sounds around him. The house was dark and quiet, slumbering peacefully under a midday sun.

Moving as quietly as possible, he slowly proceeded down the hall to the living room. He paused just before the doorway, again listening for sounds, before peeking into the room. The living room was empty and apparently undisturbed. A quick glance to the hutch showed that his Bram Stoker Award still sat safely on the shelf.

Withdrawing from the living room, he continued down the hallway. The kitchen was on the left, but it also proved to be empty. He quickly circled the kitchen table and removed a butcher knife from the drawer beside the sink. Feeling much better now that he was armed, he quietly slid the drawer closed and left the kitchen.

Holly's studio and his office were also empty and apparently undisturbed. As he entered the office, he thought about snatching up the phone and dialing 911, but refrained from doing so. He had no proof yet that someone had broken into the house, and was reluctant to make a call to the police without it. Better to wait until he was sure than look like a complete idiot later.

The bathroom on the first floor was also vacant. That left only the bedrooms and bathroom on the upper floor to be checked.

Truthfully Mike didn't expect to find anyone lurking on the lower level, because he had seen the movement in the window upstairs. Still he wanted to check each of the rooms as he passed them to prevent anyone from sneaking up behind him. Approaching the stairs, he paused, again listening for noises from upstairs: drawers being slid open, furniture being moved, footsteps, voices, something to indicate an intruder was present. The house remained quiet; the only sound was his nervous breathing.

He took the stairs slowly, cautiously, one step at a time. His heart nearly skipped a beat when the fifth step squeaked as he placed his weight fully upon it. He had forgotten the step squeaked, and now he was certain the noise would warn of his presence.

Knowing he no longer had the element of surprise on his side, Mike charged up the rest of the stairs and raced down the hallway. With the butcher knife gripped tightly in his right hand, he threw open the door to Megan's bedroom and stepped inside. The bedroom was empty and looked exactly as he had last seen it that morning.

Quickly entering the room, he checked under the bed and inside the closet, making sure no one was hiding. Satisfied the room was empty, he stepped back out into the hallway.

The bathroom was next, followed by the master bedroom. Both proved to be empty. That left only Tommy's room, the same room in which he had spotted movement from outside the house. The door to his son's room stood open a few inches, but as he started down the hallway that door slowly closed.

Mike froze, his bowels turning to ice. No doubt about it, someone was inside Tommy's room. They must have heard him coming and closed the door. Were they waiting for him just inside the door, a weapon in hand? Or were they seeking a place to hide, maybe an avenue of escape? Was it a kid who waited, a local teenager, or was it a full-sized adult?

These questions bombarded him as he stood there in the hallway, wondering what action to take. Mental images flashed through his mind, pictures of being attacked and beaten, perhaps even killed, by the man— or thing—waiting for him beyond the door.

Yes, thing. For now, at the worst appropriate moment, his writing muse decided to go on line, conjuring up images of werewolves, vampires, and slobbering creatures waiting for him inside the tiny bedroom. Facing danger was never easy, but it was especially difficult when you were a horror writer gifted with an imagination that always portrayed the worst case scenarios.

What are you, a man or a mouse?

He continued to think of all the things that could be lurking on the other side of the door and knew the answer.

A mouse.

But this was his house, damnit, and he was not about to back down from a possible threat to the sanctuary of it. He owed it to Holly, Megan, and Tommy to be the protector, the brave knight in shining armor.

Determined to do or die, he took a deep breath and stepped forward. The door wasn't closed all of the way; he could see a tiny crack between the door and the frame. Knowing he didn't need to turn the knob, he stepped forward and kicked the door as hard as he could.

The door slammed open with a bang, hitting the wall behind it hard enough to render unconscious anyone foolish enough to be hiding there. He had started through the doorway when something lunged at him with an unholy screech. A howling demon of yellow fur and claws shot past him and raced down the hall.

"Pinky!"

Mike thought he had left the cat outside, but Pinky must have slipped past him when he entered the house. He was so intent on searching the lower rooms he hadn't even noticed the big cat following him. Tommy must have left his room door open enough for the feline to slip in. Pinky probably bumped the door once he was inside, trapping himself. Kicking the door had scared the hell out of the cat.

Pinky scared the hell out of me too.

A troubling thought crossed his mind. What if something else had frightened the feline?

Turning his attention back to the task at hand, Mike hurried through the open doorway into Tommy's room. He looked quickly right and then left as he entered the room, but no one was hiding on either side of the door.

Nor was anyone in the closet or under the bed. The room was empty.

"There's no one here. I must have been imagining things."

He was just about to step back out of the room when he heard a strange banging coming from downstairs. Three bangs and then silence. Very loud. Very sharp. Like someone striking wood with a hammer. It sounded like it was coming from the kitchen.

"I'm not imagining that!"

Rushing out of Tommy's room, he hurried downstairs to the kitchen. He again found the kitchen empty, but someone must have been there only moments before. Entering the kitchen, Mike discovered that the bear kachina had been knocked off the table and was now lying broken in several pieces on the floor.

Certain an intruder was in the house with him, he left the kitchen and rechecked all of the rooms on the first floor, again finding them empty. He also checked the basement and hallway closet, and went outside to look around, but found no one. After checking the barn, he returned to the house and went back into the kitchen.

Setting the butcher knife on the table, he picked up the broken pieces of the bear kachina. Someone had to be playing a prank on him; there could be no other logical explanation. Someone must have gotten into the house, hiding when he searched the rooms on the lower floor. They must have then broken the kachina and run away before he could get downstairs. But why? And who?

Setting the broken kachina on the counter, he started to leave the room. As he turned to leave, Mike noticed a large crack in the floor directly beneath the kitchen table. The crack was about thirty inches long and a quarter inch wide, running zigzag between the oval stains.

"Son of a bitch," he said, kneeling down to examine the crack.

It was the second crack to appear since their moving into the house. Like the one in the library wall, the crack beneath the kitchen table must have been formed by severe stress or pressure of some kind. Perhaps the house was settling, but surely a house so old would have settled long ago.

A panicked thought entered his mind. What if they were living on an unknown fault line, and the cracks were the result of two land masses moving? The infamous New Madrid fault was only about two hundred miles south, so maybe there were other, smaller, faults running through the area.

Mike shook his head. He had seen the geological reports for the region, and there was no indication of any faults in the area. Nor, as far as he knew, had the house been built over an underground cavern.

If the sudden appearance of the cracks could not be attributed to nature, then there had to be something wrong with the house itself. A flaw in the foundation, or even in the building design. Maybe there had been other cracks before, and his grandmother had covered over them.

Running his fingers over the crack, he felt a cool dampness seeping up from the floor. For some strange reason the dampness reminded him of ancient tunnels and deep, dark wells. Again he wondered if there was a water leak somewhere.

One thing for sure, he would call the contractors the first thing in the morning. He already had to call them about the oval stains, so he might as well kill two birds with one stone.

He was just about to stand back up when he noticed that the oval splotches on the tile floor looked considerably darker than they had earlier in the day. Oddly enough, they also looked more defined, as though someone had shaded them in with a colored marker. Like the first two stains, the other splotches also looked like faces . . . faces with eyes that watched his every movement.

A chill danced down his spine. He had been trying to pass off the stains as a flaw in the tiles, or a leaky pipe. But he could no longer deny that the splotches were anything other than faces. Angry faces.

Chapter 13

Holly and the kids arrived home from church shortly after 1 P.M. Hearing the van pull up in the driveway, Mike went out on the porch to greet them. He could tell from Holly's expression that things had not gone as planned, but he waited for her to tell him about it rather than ask. Taking a seat on the steps, she waited for the kids to go inside before telling her husband about what had happened.

"I still can't believe the nerve of that man," she said, finishing her story. She dug a pack of cigarettes out of her purse, lit one and took a puff, then added, "And to think he calls himself a minister of God. A minister of bigotry and stupidity is more like it. He really pissed me off. I'm still furious."

"That's what you get for marrying the spawn of Satan," Mike teased, knowing he too would have been upset had he been there to hear the reverend's words against him.

"This isn't funny," she said and frowned. "How are we ever going to be part of this community if the locals think we are bad people?"

Mike shrugged. "Country people are kind of funny.

Most of them are real slow about taking to outsiders." He sat down beside her and took a puff off of her cigarette. "I'm sure they'll come around, eventually, once they see that we don't ride around on broomsticks or sacrifice small children during the full moon. It just might take a little time to win them over."

"It's going to take a lot of time with that minister telling everyone we're evil and no good."

"Actually, I'm the one he said was no good," Mike corrected. "And it's not like I haven't been called such things before, and by much more influential people. I'm quite sure the good reverend will quit ranting once he sees we're not all the things he thinks we are. The best thing for us to do in the meantime is to go about our business and just ignore him."

She let out her breath, releasing some of the anger inside of her. "Maybe you're right. I'm just worried about the kids. They have a hard enough time trying to fit in and make new friends the way it is."

He smiled. "Our kids are New Yorkers. They can make friends anywhere. And if they can't, then they can kick ass with the best of them."

Holly laughed, the anger she had felt earlier all but gone. "And how was your day?"

Mike told her about finding the bear kachina lying on the floor broken, and about the crack in the middle of the kitchen floor.

"Do you think there's a connection between the two?"

"I don't think so," he said. "Truthfully, I don't think there could be a connection. Not unless we got hit by an earthquake tremor strong enough to knock the statue off the table and put a crack in the floor. And if that's what happened I would have felt it, because I was in the house at the time."

"Do you think Pinky could have knocked the statue off the table?" she asked.

"That's possible, but not likely," he turned to face her. "That kachina is made of cottonwood. It wouldn't have broken into so many pieces just from falling off the table."

"I don't understand. I thought you said you found it on the floor?"

"I did, but I don't think it just fell off the table. I think it was slammed on the floor, and maybe even stomped on."

A look of surprise crossed her face. "Stomped on? You think someone broke the kachina on purpose?"

Mike nodded.

"But that would mean someone was in the house. Who? And how did they get in?"

He shook his head. "I don't know. I was having trouble getting started on the new chapter, so I decided to take a walk with Pinky. I wasn't gone long, maybe an hour at the most. I locked the front door when I left; the back door was locked from the inside. Both doors were still locked when I got back, and there was no sign of a forced entry. Even so, I could have sworn I saw someone in one of the upstairs windows."

Holly glanced up, even though she couldn't see any of the upstairs windows from where she sat. "Which window?"

"One of the ones in Tommy's bedroom."

"Did you see who it was?"

"No. Not really. I just saw a shadow move. I came in and looked around, but I didn't find anything that had been disturbed . . . other than the broken kachina. I'm going to call the contractors tomorrow about the cracks, and the stains on the kitchen floor. I'll have them change all of the locks while they're out here, just in case someone is playing a joke on us."

"A joke?" Holly asked. "Do you think someone's playing a joke on us?"

He shrugged. "Maybe. I'm not sure. A teenager might have gotten into the house, not knowing it was occupied. But if this is their idea of a joke then I'm not laughing."

That night at the supper table Holly and Mike avoided talking about the day's events in order not to upset the children. When Tommy brought up the subject of his visit to church, the conversation was quickly changed to something else. The boy didn't mind. He knew there was cherry pie for dessert and he was happy to talk about anything his parents wanted to talk about, or nothing at all.

Finished with dessert, the children went into the living room to watch television. The subject of not having HBO or MTV had come up during dinner, and Mike promised to check into purchasing a satellite dish antenna. Holly was just starting to stack the dirty dishes in the sink when Tommy reentered the kitchen, a frown on his face.

"Mom, have you seen Pinky?"

"No, dear," she said, wiping her hands off on a dish towel. "Did you look upstairs? He's probably taking a nap on one of the beds."

"I looked upstairs, but he's not there. I haven't seen him since this morning. Do you think he's hiding?"

Mike had been wiping off the table. He stopped and looked toward Pinky's bowl in the corner of the room. The can of cat food he had opened earlier was still untouched. "That's odd. Pinky hasn't touched his food. Come to think of it, he didn't come around to beg for a handout at dinner."

As a matter of fact, none of them had seen the big tomcat all afternoon. It wasn't normal for him to miss an opportunity to hang around the dinner table begging for a handout.

Holly set the dish towel on the counter and turned off the water in the sink. "Pinky never misses a meal, not if he can avoid it."

"Maybe he got himself locked in somewhere." Mike pushed the chairs in at the table. "You said you already looked upstairs?"

Tommy nodded. "I called his name, but he didn't answer."

"Well, let's say we go have ourselves another look. If I know that silly cat he's probably napping in a closet somewhere. Or under a bed. Go get your sister and tell her we have a missing cat to find."

Mike, Holly, and the kids searched through every room in the house for the missing tomcat, but he was nowhere to be found. They looked under beds, and in closets, even opened up dresser drawers to see if he was mixed in with the clothes.

Thinking Pinky might have slipped out when they weren't looking, Mike grabbed a flashlight and looked around the outside of the house. He checked behind all of the bushes and shrubbery, and beneath the front porch, but the only thing he found was an old rubber ball and a couple of spiders the size of silver dollars.

"All right, cat. This isn't funny. You're cutting into my coffee drinking time." Mike stood up and brushed himself off. He swept the beam of the flashlight across the front yard toward the road, hoping to see the reflection of green eyes in the darkness. Nothing.

Deciding the barn would be the next best place to look, he circled the house to the old wooden structure. The barn was probably a haven for field mice. Maybe Pinky had decided to test out his hunting skills. After all, a cat couldn't be a country cat unless he could prove himself as a hunter. What would the neighbor cats think if Pinky couldn't catch at least one lousy mouse?

Mike approached the barn slowly, suddenly aware the old wooden structure looked a heck of a lot spookier at night than it did in the daytime. In the daytime it was just an old wooden building, its red paint blistered and peeled away by the sun and numerous Midwestern thunderstorms. A place of quiet memories which spoke of long, lazy summers, fields of ripening hay, and maybe even the hint of forbidden teenage love.

By night, however, the barn took on an altogether different image. Gray as a crypt in the silvery moonlight, it was now a place of shadows and darkness—a place where ghosts might pause to rest as they strode across the haunted countryside, doing whatever it was that ghosts did on their nightly outings. Mike remembered some of the supposedly true ghost stories he had read over the years, realizing that many of them took place in just such a building as that which he now faced.

"I do not believe in ghosts," he said aloud, reminding himself that, while he often wrote ghostly tales, he never really believed in the existence of spirits, haints, and other such supernatural visitors. He did, however, believe in rabid rodents, poisonous spiders, snakes, and dastardly evil insects, all of which he was certain inhabited the old barn at night. Still, he had a cat to find and nothing was going to stop him from taking at least one quick peek inside the barn.

Pushing his way through the high weeds, he circled around to the big double doors in the side of the barn. Only one of the doors was still standing; the other had fallen off years ago and was now nothing more than a slab of wooden boards rotting on the ground. Stepping up to the opening where the door had once stood, he aimed the beam of his flashlight inside the barn.

The interior of the barn was divided into sections. The area closest to the double doors had once been used for storing farm equipment. An old hay rake sat upon iron wheels just inside the doorway, looking like something once used as a weapon of war. Beyond the rake low walls partitioned off a place to keep cattle or horses during times of bad weather. Overhead a small hayloft extended half the length of the barn, its hay long since removed.

"Pinky?" Mike called, shining the flashlight back and forth. Most of the dividing walls had gaps in them, places where the boards had fallen out or been removed to be used for other things, allowing him to see much of the interior without venturing too far beyond the opening. He caught movement to his left, but when he pointed the flashlight in that direction he only saw a small scurrying beneath a pile of dead leaves. It was probably only a cockroach escaping the beam of the bright light. One thing for sure, Pinky was not inside the barn.

Stepping back outside, he thought about searching the orchard, and maybe part of the forest, but decided against it. If Pinky had decided to stake out his territorial claim, he could be halfway to town by now. Not that he really believed the big cat was out laying claim to anything. Pinky, bless his heart, had been fixed years ago at Holly's insistence. He was no longer a lover and a fighter, and had no reason to set out in search of adventures and cat kingdoms to conquer. He was a cat of leisure. A fat, happy, lazy cat.

Mike thought about the untouched food dish back inside the kitchen. He didn't want to admit it to Holly and the kids, but the last time he had seen Pinky was when he kicked open Tommy's bedroom door. He had frightened the big cat, and he wondered if that was the reason he was now missing. One thing for sure, it wasn't normal for Pinky to miss an evening meal. Not normal at all.

Part II

There are things we don't know about. Strange things that lurk in the darkness. Just because we don't know about them doesn't mean they're not there.

—Jay Little Hawk

Part II

Chapter 14

Some Mondays are bad. Some are worse than others. This particular Monday soon proved to be the mother of all bad days.

The contractors arrived shortly after the kids left for school. Examining the kitchen floor, they claimed there was nothing wrong with the tiles they had installed. Nor could they find any indication of a water leak. Rather than argue with them, Mike decided to go ahead and pay to have new tiles put down in the kitchen.

He also had the contractors patch the crack in the floor, and the one in the library wall. As with the stains, they could not determine what had caused the cracks. The house's foundation appeared to be in good condition, and there was no evidence of settling.

While the contractors were busy ripping up the kitchen floor, Mike decided to clean out some of the mess in the basement. He had been at it for less than an hour when he discovered Pinky's lifeless body beneath a pile of old boxes.

"Oh, dear Jesus," he said, jumping back. He turned to make sure Holly hadn't entered the basement when he wasn't looking—she was still upstairs supervising the work in the kitchen—and then stepped back toward the dead housecat.

Pinky lay on his left side, legs outstretched, tongue protruding between his front fangs. The big cat had been killed and mutilated, his eyes gouged out and his throat ripped open. There were several other minor cuts on his body, and his fur was torn and matted, indicating he had been in one hell of a fight. Oddly enough there was no blood beneath the body. He hadn't been injured and crawled beneath the boxes to die. On the contrary, something had dragged him beneath the boxes after the cat was already dead.

Mike turned and looked around the basement, searching for blood droplets, bits of fur, something to indicate where the battle had taken place and what Pinky had tangled with. When he could find none of these things, he became suspicious that maybe it wasn't an animal that had caused the beloved cat's death. Maybe a person had murdered Pinky and then hidden his body beneath the boxes.

The last time he had seen the big tomcat was yesterday when he was searching through the house looking for a possible intruder. Pinky had scared the hell out of him when he bolted out of Tommy's bedroom after Mike slammed open the door. The feline had also been startled, fleeing down the stairs to the first floor. The cat had been downstairs when the bear kachina was broken. Maybe the person who broke the statue had decided to carry out a wanton act of cruelty on the Anthony family cat. It would be an easy task to accomplish. Pinky was quite friendly toward people, often approaching complete strangers for a rub. Had the cat approached the wrong person?

"But how did he get down here in the basement?"

Mike thought maybe he knew the answer. Yesterday, after seeing someone upstairs in Tommy's room, he had quickly searched the rooms on the first floor and then hurried upstairs, never thinking to look in the basement for the intruder. Whoever it was must have hidden there after seeing him approach the house, waiting for an opportunity to escape. Before leaving the house, the intruder, for whatever reason, had decided to break the bear kachina. While he was destroying the wooden statue, Pinky had entered the kitchen, and the intruder had taken the opportunity to enact further crimes against the family.

Tears welled up in his eyes as he looked upon Pinky's body. Slicing the cat's throat had been a violent act of murder, but cutting out his eyes went far beyond that. It was an unspeakable act that could only be performed by a sick and dangerous individual.

But why? Why had someone done such a terrible thing? He and his family had no enemies, no reason for someone to seek revenge on them by torturing the family housecat. He thought about his wife's confrontation with Reverend Mitchell, wondering if one of the minister's congregation had killed the cat in an effort to get them to leave the community. If so, what kind of poison was the good reverend spouting at the pulpit?

Mike shook his head. He didn't think the minister or any of his congregation was behind the killing. They might boycott his books, ban his family from church, even call upon the saints to boil his soul in oil, but he doubted if any of them had the stomach it took to murder and mutilate an innocent cat, especially one as lovable as Pinky.

"Oh, no."

The voice startled him. He turned and found Holly standing a few feet behind him. Mike hadn't heard her come down the steps, because he was so upset over finding Pinky's body. He didn't want her to see the cat like this, wanted to break the news of his death gently to her after he had buried him, but now it was too late. She stood just behind him, staring in wide-eyed horror at a pet that was more hers and the kids' than it was his.

"Oh, no," she repeated, her lips forming the words so carefully it appeared she was incapable of any other speech.

Mike stepped in front of her, blocking Holly's view of the lifeless cat. "I'm sorry, honey. I just found him a few minutes ago."

Holly looked up at him, perhaps seeing her husband for the first time. She stepped slightly to the side, her gaze returning to the floor behind him. "His eyes," she said, her voice almost a whisper. She looked at Pinky a moment longer, then looked at him. Her face grew dark with anger. "Who did this?"

"I don't know," he said, stepping forward to comfort her. He could tell Holly was fighting back tears, using anger to keep control of her emotions. She didn't like to cry, not if she could help it.

"Call the sheriff," she said, clenching her fists at her sides. She looked at Pinky, and then back at him. A tear slowly formed in her left eye, then trickled down her cheek. "What will I tell the children? What will I tell Tommy? He'll be heartbroken."

"We'll think of something to say." He placed his arm around his wife's shoulders and steered her toward the stairs. "Come on, let's go upstairs and call the sheriff's office."

Mike looked up the phone number of the Hudson County Sheriff's Office in the directory. He told the dispatcher what had happened, and then waited a few moments while he was put on hold. When the dispatcher came back on line, she told him they would have someone out to his house as soon as possible. Mike thanked her and hung up.

A patrol car pulled into the driveway about an hour later. Mike was surprised to see it was Sheriff Jody Douglas driving the car rather than one of the county deputies. He wondered for a moment if the county even had deputies, because he had never seen any, and then decided the sheriff probably answered the call himself because he knew the person who had called. Maybe he wanted to check up on the local celebrity writer. Then again, maybe it was just a slow day in law enforcement and any excuse to get out of the office was a good one.

Greeting the sheriff, Mike led him down into the basement and showed him Pinky's body. Holly did not accompany them. She had already seen the mutilated cat once and that was enough. Instead she stayed in the kitchen, scrubbing pots in an effort to occupy her mind and not think about the death of the family pet.

Pulling a flashlight from his gun belt, Sheriff Douglas squatted down and carefully examined Pinky's body for a minute or two. Standing back up, he switched off the light and turned to Mike. "Your cat's throat was not cut by a knife, if that's what you're thinking. The cut is much too jagged and rough. Same way with the minor cuts on his body, and around his eyes. Offhand, I would say that he probably died of old age and something got to him after he was dead."

"There must be some mistake," Mike argued. "Pinky

was not that old. And he was in perfect health; we had him checked out by a vet before we left New York. It couldn't have been sickness, or old age."

"Then what do you think killed him, Mr. Anthony?" the sheriff asked. "There's nothing bigger than raccoons and possums in this county, and I doubt if you would find too many of those down here in this basement."

"I don't know what killed my cat. Or who. All I know is that Pinky was not that old, and there isn't a possum big enough to take him on."

"Mr. Anthony, I don't know how it is in the big city, but here in the country cats die from all kinds of reasons: some get run over by cars, some get killed by dogs, others just up and die for no apparent reason at all." The sheriff slipped his flashlight back into his belt.

"You're not going to do anything?" Mike asked, frustrated.

"Look, I can't even write a report about your cat, because there's no evidence of foul play. Now, if someone would have shot him, that would be different. But they didn't. And I seriously doubt if anyone tiptoed down here to—"

"I think I saw someone here in the house yesterday," Mike interrupted.

The sheriff cocked an eyebrow. "Oh? When was this?"

"Around noon. I was just coming back from a walk, and I thought I saw someone in the upstairs window."

"What did they look like?"

Mike shook his head. "I didn't get a good look at them, just caught a glimpse of movement. I came in and looked around, searched all of the rooms, but I didn't see anyone. But when I was upstairs I heard a loud banging in the kitchen, like someone was hitting the floor with a hammer. By the time I got back downstairs the noise had stopped, and the kitchen was empty, but the bear kachina was broken."

"The what?" Sheriff Douglas asked.

"The bear kachina," Mike explained. "It's one of the Indian statues. I had it sitting in the center of the kitchen table. It was there when I came into the house, because I saw it. I went into the kitchen and grabbed a butcher knife out of the cabinet drawer before I searched the house. The kachina was sitting on the table, not a scratch on it. But when I came back downstairs to investigate the banging noise, I found the statue on the floor in pieces."

Sheriff Douglas glanced past Mike, obviously looking at the statues that lined the shelf on the wall. "Was anything else broken besides the statue, or anything taken that you know of?"

"No. Nothing's missing. And the only thing I found broken was the kachina."

"Did you see anyone when you came in the house?"

"No. They must have gotten away."

"How about the doors and window, were they all locked?"

Mike nodded. "Everything was locked."

"From the inside?"

"Yeah, from the inside. Why?"

The sheriff shook his head. "Nothing. Just seems kind of odd that someone could get past you without being seen, especially if they were upstairs and all of the windows and doors were locked from the inside."

Mike suddenly realized that Sheriff Douglas was patronizing him, treating him like a child who was telling a whopper of a story. His face warmed with anger, but he held his tongue. The sheriff must have seen the anger in Mike's eyes, or in his facial expression, because he smiled.

"I just don't see how I can help you, Mr. Anthony. A break-in isn't a break-in unless someone actually breaks in. Nor is it a robbery unless something is taken." He stepped past Mike and started up the stairs.

"What about the broken kachina doll?"

The sheriff stopped and looked at him. "What about it? I'm sure you have plenty of replacements. If not, I suggest you get yourself a bottle of Elmer's glue. You might also want to get yourself a shovel and bury your cat before your kids get home from school."

With that parting shot, Sheriff Douglas climbed the stairs and left, leaving Mike alone in the basement. Alone and very angry.

Chapter 15

Mike buried Pinky out behind the barn, taking time to cover the grave with dried leaves and grass. He and Holly didn't want the children to know what had happened to their pet. Not yet anyway. Moving into a new neighborhood, adjusting to a new school, was upsetting enough without adding to the situation. They would tell them later, at a more appropriate time.

Patting down the grave with his shovel, Mike wondered if a few words of remembrance would be appropriate. He had never buried a family pet, and wasn't sure what were the proper procedures. Did one say a prayer, and if so, why? He wasn't sure if animals had souls, so he didn't know if a few words directed toward the big kahuna in the sky was the right thing to do. Was there a kitty heaven, a place where felines romped and played to their hearts' content? He didn't really think so, but it was still nice to imagine that such a place existed.

As he stood there, leaning on the shovel used to dig the grave, he could almost picture Pinky in a place where cats spent the days lounging around on feathery clouds, sipping from silver chalices filled with cream, and snacking on bits of fresh liver and tuna. There would be no dogs in kitty heaven, only fat, tasty mice to swat about and chase. They wouldn't need wings either. Nope, no angel wings in kitty heaven, because they would get in the way of daily grooming. No need for wings when you could run, jump, roll, and tussle with all the other cats in the kingdom.

If there was a kitty heaven, then he was quite certain that's where Pinky had gone. The big cat was probably already up there, stuffing himself on bowls of his favorite treats. It didn't matter if there wasn't really a kitty heaven, because that's what he would describe to Tommy when it came time to tell the boy that his beloved cat was dead.

A wave of anger surged through Mike, turning the corners of his mouth down in a frown. Someone or something had killed his cat. Pinky had not died of old age, as the sheriff had suggested.

The more he thought about what Sheriff Douglas had said, the madder he got. The sheriff didn't believe Pinky had been killed by a person. Fair enough. Every man was entitled to his opinion. But he hadn't believed anything Mike had said, going so far as to openly insult him. His looks, his gestures, everything about the man told Mike that he was being looked down upon, silently laughed at like he was some sort of nutcase.

Just like he used to laugh at my grandmother.

A chill danced up his spine as another long forgotten piece of childhood memory clicked into place, playing on the magic movie screen behind his eyes. The bit of data had been all but forgotten, eradicated from his memory bank as efficiently as if someone had pressed the delete key. But now it was back, in living color, complete with sound.

It had only been a few months after he had come to live with his grandmother, a few months after his parents had been killed in that god-awful car wreck. Mike was in the upstairs bedroom, the same bedroom Tommy now claimed as his own. Funny, but up until that moment, he had also forgotten that the room his son stayed in had once been his.

My memory has so many holes in it.

He had been in the upstairs bedroom, lying on the bed and reading a children's book his grandmother had gotten for him at the library. He couldn't read all of the words, but that was okay because the book was lavishly illustrated with paintings of distant worlds and magical kingdoms. What he couldn't read he could figure out from the pictures. He had become enthralled with the story when he heard shouts coming from the front of the house, and the roaring of a car engine.

Curious, he had laid the book on the bed, carefully marking the page he was reading. The sound grew even louder as he walked down the hallway and descended the stairs. He had to go down the stairs slowly so as not to trip over the boxes and bags lying in the way. Even then his grandmother had not been right in the head, but she wasn't nearly as bad as she later became.

The downstairs was flooded with bright light, every bit as sinister as the light portrayed in movies about alien abductions. But the light he saw did not originate from a spacecraft; it came instead from a more down-to-earth vessel.

Mike had moved slowly forward, nearly blinded by the brilliant white light, seeking the source of it and the noise he heard. He was halfway down the hallway before he realized the front door stood open.

This concerned him because his grandmother never left the front door open, especially at night.

"Gramma," he called, his tiny voice swallowed up by the roaring engine sound. He didn't call her name again, because he was afraid. He wanted only to run back up the stairs and seek the safety of his bedroom, seek the safety of the book he was reading. But he couldn't run away. He had to look.

The lights scared him most of all, because they made him remember bad things. There had been lights the night his parents were killed: the lights of the car driven by the drunk driver who had crossed the center line and hit their vehicle. The blinding white light of pain as Mike had been thrown forward from the collision, striking the back of his mother's seat. The lights of other cars stopping on the road, and the flashlights of policemen and firefighters as they sawed through twisted metal to free the victims of the accident.

The lights had turned everything bright white that night, bleaching the color from all that he saw. But the lights hadn't bleached all the colors away. The color red appeared twice as bright as any red he had ever seen before. And the color red was everywhere. It was poured across the front of his favorite Batman T-shirt, splattered in big, gooey droplets across the shattered windshield and crumpled dashboard of his father's Chevrolet.

There was also red on the woman's hand that protruded from the white sheet in the middle of the road. That's all he saw, one hand. It lay palm-up in the middle of the highway, attached to the mangled body hidden beneath the bloody white sheet. Another bloody sheet lay a few feet beyond the first, carefully pulled over a somewhat larger body.

Mike had seen the sheets when they pulled him out of the car, and somehow he knew that the bodies of his parents lay beneath them. He didn't cry, or scream, because he could not find his voice. Instead he just stared at the once perfect hand of his mother, white as fine porcelain under the bright lights. Stared at the redness of her fingernail polish, and the crimson blood that ran down her hand to encircle her wrist like a bracelet of death. Red. Red. Red. The color was everywhere, bright as a lover's lips in the harsh white lights.

The lights had come again to his grandmother's house, and the roaring of a car engine. They had come to take her away, as they had taken his parents.

Mike continued down the hallway until he reached the front door, where he stopped to stare through the open doorway at the bright lights. They were the lights of a sports car pulled dangerously close the house, the front bumper just inches away from the porch. Behind those lights faces leered out at him from inside the car. The twisted, grinning faces of demons trapped behind a sheet of glass. They were the faces of drunk teenage boys, out for a night of troublemaking. Mike recognized the faces, because he had seen them before. The face behind the steering wheel belonged to Jody Douglas.

Blinking from the glare of the bright light, he heard his grandmother shout at the boys in the car. She stood on the porch, standing behind one of the wooden pillars. A little woman, terribly thin, armed only with the broken handle of a rake. She stood behind the wooden post and shouted at the boys to go away and leave her alone, pleaded with them for her safety and that of her grandson.

The shouts had no effect on the teenagers. They

laughed at the old woman. The driver gunned the car engine and inched even closer to the porch, threatening to drive the vehicle right through the front of the house. The car suddenly lunged a foot and Mike cried out, screaming because he knew the car had come to take him away, as one had taken his parents from him. He saw the lights of the teenagers' car, and he saw the lights of the drunk driver's car, superimposed one over the other.

His scream of terror startled his grandmother, caused her to turn in his direction. She had been standing behind the safety of the post, but nothing lay between Mike and the threatening car. Alarmed she crossed the porch at a run, she grabbed him roughly by the wrist and dragged him back inside the house. She slammed the door and locked it, hurrying him into the living room. There they knelt and hugged each other, waiting until the teenagers outside grew tired of their game and drove away.

Four teenagers had been in the car that night. Jody Douglas was one of them. It wasn't the first time he had tormented Mike's grandmother, nor would it be the last time.

The image of that night faded, leaving Mike shaking and short of breath. So many of his childhood memories had been forgotten, pushed deep down inside of him, to the place where he kept the memories of the night his parents had died. When one of those memories broke lose and floated to the surface, it left him physically drained.

The memory was all but gone now, leaving only anger in its place. Anger over the death of a family's housecat, and anger at the county sheriff.

* * *

Tommy and Megan arrived home at 3:30 P.M. Both asked almost immediately if Pinky had come home yet, and if they could go looking for him in the van. Mike reassured them that Pinky was probably just out exploring the area and would no doubt be back soon. He hated lying to the kids, and wasn't sure how long he could keep at it, but for now his explanation seemed to satisfy them.

To change the subject, Holly asked them how things were going at school. It would seem that things were gradually getting better, at least Megan and Tommy hadn't been the target of any spit wad attacks on the bus since their first day. And while they weren't exactly Mr. and Ms. Popular, they had both made a couple of friends from fellow classmates.

A couple of the students in Megan's gym class had suggested she try out for the volleyball team with them. They were quite impressed by the fifteen-year-old's athletic ability, and felt she would be a shoo-in for the team. Megan had never played on a volleyball team, other than an occasional game at school back in New York, but she could do just about anything once she put her mind to it.

"So why don't you try out for the team?" Holly asked, encouraging her daughter.

"I don't know. I might," Megan said, considering the possibility. "The uniforms are pretty lame, and I don't have a ride to practice or the games."

"I'm quite sure that even a geeky uniform will look good on you." Mike smiled. "I tell you what, you make the team and I'll make sure you get to all of the practices and games on time."

Megan said she would think about it, and then left to watch a little television before doing her homework.

Tommy raced after her in an attempt to get to the television first.

After dinner, Mike grabbed his glasses and a Clive Cussler novel and went out on the front porch to do a little reading. He rarely read horror novels, despite writing them, preferring instead to read something outside of the genre he worked in. He loved thrillers and mysteries, and sometimes even indulged in a western or two. He had only read a few pages in the novel when Holly called him from the library.

"Now what?" he said, setting the book down and standing up. Things were supposed to be quieter in the country, but there seemed to have been more peace and quiet back in New York City. Allowing the screen door to bang closed to protest his displeasure over being interrupted, he walked down the hallway and entered the library. Holly was standing at the other end of the room, staring at the wall.

"You screamed?" he joked, but the smile quickly slipped off his face. His wife was looking at the place where the contractors had repaired the crack in the wall earlier in the day. They had removed the damaged paneling and plastered the wall, replacing the split paneling with a new piece. The repairs had obviously done little good, however, because the crack was back. Not just back, but far worse than it had been before. Now two ragged cracks ran the length of the wall, from floor to ceiling, forming the shape of a giant V.

"This is getting ridiculous," Mike said, walking up to where Holly stood. He ran his fingertips along one length of the crack and was surprised to feel an icy coldness seeping from the wall. The coldness was unexplainable, for the house was anything but cold. Nor was it cold outside. In fact, the temperature was in the seventies.

"It feels cold," he said, speaking more to himself than to Holly.

"But why?" Holly stepped forward to touch the other crack.

He shook his head. "I don't know. It shouldn't feel cold. No reason for it, not unless there's dampness seeping up from the basement."

"But the basement isn't damp," she pointed out.

"I know," he quickly agreed, "but there has to be a logical explanation for it. Moisture has to be getting into the wall somehow. Maybe there's a broken water pipe upstairs somewhere, that would explain the—"

A sudden movement caught his eye. Mike turned in time to see a shadow glide along the hallway opposite the door. At first he thought it was one of the kids going into the kitchen, but the shadow was the wrong size and shape. It was smaller than a kid, about the size of a dog.

"What was that?"

"What was what?" Holly asked.

"I saw something," he replied.

"Where?"

"Something ran down the hallway."

Hurrying out of the library, he caught a glimpse of something scurrying into the kitchen. He didn't see what it was, spotting only its shadow moving along the opposite wall.

"There," he said, following the shadow. "It went into the kitchen."

"What is it?" Holly asked, leaving the library behind him.

"I don't know."

Mike raced into the kitchen, but when he got there the room was empty. Whatever he had seen had somehow managed to get away. Quickly crossing the room, he checked the back door but found it locked. He also opened the lower cabinets, and looked behind the trash can, but found nothing. The door to the basement was also locked.

"What is it?" Holly asked, appearing in the doorway. Mike stopped his search and turned to face her.

"I thought I saw something, but it must have been a trick of the lighting."

Holly looked at him unconvinced. "What do you think you saw?"

He shrugged. "I thought I saw a shadow move past the doorway. Something small. An animal perhaps." He looked around one last time for good measure. "Must have been just my imagination."

Mike had started to leave the room when a funny look came over his wife's face. She was looking past him, at the floor. He turned, dreading what he might see there, but somehow knowing what he would find.

The crack beneath the kitchen table was also back, bigger than ever.

"Son of a bitch," he said, turning around. "They just fixed this. The floor can't be cracked again."

He crossed the room and knelt down beside the table. Leaning forward, he ran his fingertips over the crack. As with the crack in the library wall, there was a feeling of cold ebbing from the crack in the kitchen floor, as though an icy wind flowed up from the basement. But the basement was not that cold, which made him wonder exactly where the chill came from.

As he knelt there, fingertips pressed against the crack, Mike was overcome with the impression that what he felt came from someplace far deeper than the basement. It was as if the cold was a breath of wind issuing from a fissure deep within the earth, a subterranean cavern formed by ancient ice floes. A place of dark secrets where blind things whispered in the blackness. Though he knew this to be nothing more than a writer's imagination, he couldn't suppress the shiver of fear that walked down his back on a spider's legs. Nor could he stop himself from snatching his fingertips away from the crack.

Chapter 16

It was a little after 10 P.M. when Sam Tochi entered Jim's Bar & Grill, a quiet little drinking establishment that catered to the Braddock working class. Since it was a weeknight, there were only a handful of customers in the place. Selecting an empty stool at the bar, Sam sat down and ordered a bottle of Budweiser. He wasn't much of a drinking man, but he did enjoy an occasional beer if his mind was troubled. And at that particular moment his mind was very troubled. Very troubled indeed.

Despite the prayer ceremony he had held in his backyard, he still could not remember what had happened to him last Tuesday. The events of that particular day remained lost in a fog, the result of a spell brought on by his ever growing brain tumor. Nor could he shake the feeling that something bad was about to happen, and that really bothered him.

Being raised in the traditional ways of the Hopi, he was not about to dismiss such a feeling as nothing more than an overactive imagination. No way. He was a believer in visions and premonitions, and knew that a bad feeling might be a message sent to him from the spirit world. Perhaps one of his spirit guides was trying to warn him that danger was present, though—except for the tumor—there was little in his life that could be considered truly dangerous. He had no enemies, and knew of no one who would wish him harm. A few of the town's residents might like to see him locked up in a crazy home, but he doubted if they would like to see him physically hurt. At least he hoped this was the case.

Paying for his beer with a pair of crumpled dollar bills, he put the bottle to his lips and tilted his head back. The beer was cold enough to have a bite, and he didn't stop drinking until half the bottle's contents was gone. Setting the bottle down on the bar, Sam wiped his mouth with the back of his hand.

Maybe a good sweat would help him see things more clearly. He had not been in a sweat lodge for several years, so maybe that's what he needed. A good sweat always helped to open up the pores and cleanse the body. It also helped to put one's spirit back in the proper balance, making it easier to see things for what they truly were. He had built a sweat lodge in his backyard several years ago, but an August thunderstorm had blown it down. Maybe it was time he built another one.

Too much work.

Sam smiled to himself. That was the problem with growing old: everything seemed to be too much work. It was much easier to think about building a sweat lodge than to actually do it. The pain medicine he took also didn't help, because it made him sleepy. Tired old Indians did not build sweat lodges in their backyards; they built castles in their dreams.

He was about to take another sip of beer, when three

young men entered the bar. Sam recognized them as local contractors, but he did not know their names. The three men took seats at the bar, a few stools over from where he sat. No sooner had the three men sat down, then one of them spotted Sam.

"Hey, old man. What are you doing in here? I thought you would be on the side of the road somewhere telling your stories."

Sam took a sip of beer and shook his head. "No one listens to the old stories anymore. They would rather play Nintendo."

The three men laughed. Having placed their order with the bartender, one of the men turned back to Sam. "Maybe you could tell some of your stories to that writer fellow who moved into town. I bet he would listen. Hell, he might even pay you. Or buy you a beer."

Sam set his bottle down. "Why would he listen to an old man like me?"

The contractor grinned. "Because that guy is as crazy as his fucking grandmother. That's why. We just had to tear up a perfectly good kitchen floor because he decided to paint a few faces on it."

"Faces?" asked Sam.

The contractor nodded. "That's right. Faces. Real scary ones. The boss says they're the same kind the old woman used to draw. I guess her grandson plans to carry on the family tradition. Not that I care one way or the other, because I'm getting paid by the hour. He can paint faces all over that house for all I care."

"How many faces were on the floor?" Sam asked.

The contractor took a sip of his beer and scratched his head. "Six, I think. Maybe seven."

Sam felt a feeling of dread settle in the pit of his stomach. It was starting again. That explained the bad feeling he was having. The feeling was a warning of things to come. "What about the Indian statues? Are they still in the house?"

The contractor nodded. "They threw everything else away, but they kept the statues. I heard that writer likes them. I can't see why; those damn things give me the creeps."

Sam smiled, feeling somewhat relieved. The statues were still in place at Vivian's old house, so maybe things were not so bad after all. Maybe he was just an old man, worrying over nothing. The kachinas were guardians. They would warn their owners if danger was present.

The old Indian's smile faded. The kachinas were guardians, but what if their new owners did not know this? Maybe Vivian had not told her grandson about the magic of the statues. Maybe he and his family did not know about the house they now lived in, or about the property upon which that house stood. Not knowing such things would be bad. Very bad indeed.

Megan had gone to bed at eleven, but she was unable to sleep. She kept thinking about her friends and all of the wonderful things she had left behind in New York City. She missed the city terribly. Why on earth did her parents want to move to Missouri of all places, to a house in the country? Her father had money, plenty of money. It wasn't like they had to move. They could have stayed where they were. Instead she had been forced to move into a house she didn't want to live in and attend a school she didn't like.

"It's just not fair," she whispered, a feeling of desperation coming over her. At the very least her parents could have allowed her to stay behind in New York

City. She could have attended boarding school, or maybe even moved in with one of her friends. But they wouldn't hear of it, refused to even talk about such options. They said she was far too young to live on her own and that family should stay together, even if it meant giving up all the things she loved just so her father would be happy.

I wish Vivian Martin wasn't my dad's grandmother. I wish she had never died and left this stupid house to him. If it wasn't for her we would still be living in New York. I hate her; I hate this house.

Frustrated at being unable to sleep, angry that she had been taken away from everything she loved, Megan tossed her covers off and climbed out of bed. The floor squeaked softly beneath her bare feet as she crossed the room. Flipping on the light, she slipped on her robe and opened the door.

The house was quiet; her parents had gone to bed hours ago. She stood outside her bedroom, listening to the soft sound of her father's snoring that came from the next room. Normally the sound didn't bother her, but tonight even the sound of his nocturnal breathing irritated her. How could he sleep so peacefully? Didn't he know that he had ruined her life? Didn't he understand the crime he had committed against her?

Turning, she saw a soft amber glow coming from beneath the door across the hall. The glow came from the small bulb of Tommy's Daffy Duck nightlight. Megan smiled, despite her angry mood. Tommy was still young enough not to trust the dark entirely. He wasn't scared of it like a lot of kids his age, didn't scream his head off if you turned out all the lights. He hadn't even used the nightlight much the last year in New York. Tommy used one now, however, because the house they lived in was different, strange, and that strangeness could be frightening to an eight-year-old late at night in the dark. He would probably give up the nightlight in another month or so, but for now its pale illumination was comforting.

Megan followed the hallway to the stairs, and slowly climbed down to the lower floor. She stepped over the squeaky fifth stair to avoid waking her parents. A little squeaking probably wouldn't disrupt their slumber in the least bit, but she didn't want to wake them and then have to explain why she was still up.

Starting down the hallway to the kitchen, she began to realize just how creepy the old house was at night. The darkness seemed to close in around her, shadows stretching forth to grab at her with hungry claws. In that darkness something moved.

"Pinky?" She stopped, her heart beating faster. "Is that you, boy?"

Had the big tomcat finally returned from exploring the surrounding countryside? If so, how had he gotten into the house? Her father always locked the doors at night, and made sure all of the windows were fastened tight. There was no way for a cat to get inside once everything was locked up—at least she didn't think there was.

"Pinky?" she called again, her voice no more than a whisper. She didn't know why, but suddenly she was very afraid to make any noise that would call attention to herself. The darkness surrounding her seemed menacing, as if it hid some terrible secret.

No answer came from the darkness. Had it been the cat, he would have answered with a meow, especially when it was one of the children who called. If it wasn't Pinky, then what was it she had seen move?

Megan had started to take a step backward when she saw it again. A dark shape, blacker than the darkness around it, moving rapidly along the baseboard of the wall. Definitely not Pinky.

Alarmed that there might be some kind of animal inside the house, she turned and hurried along the hallway. She entered the library and switched on the lamp, only to find that the light didn't work. Confused, she took a step forward and felt something crunch beneath her feet. Pain flashed through her right foot and up her leg, tearing a cry from her lips.

Megan stumbled backward and stopped. The pain shot fiery ribbons up her leg. Reaching down, she felt something hard and sharp sticking in the bottom of her foot. Glass. She tried to pull it out, but the piece of glass was slippery with blood. Her blood.

"Ow," she said, trying to balance on her other foot. "Ow. Ow. Ow."

Limping forward, she grabbed the table to steady herself. Once steadied, she gripped the piece of glass with a thumb and index finger and carefully worked it out of her foot. She pulled on the piece slowly, fearful the glass would break if she snatched at it too fast. A few careful tugs later the embedded object was removed.

She had just pulled the piece of glass from her foot when something entered the library. Megan paused, motionless, holding her breath.

Even though the room was cloaked in darkness, she saw a patch of blackness move from the hallway into the library. It was small, no bigger than a medium-sized dog, but there was something about it that filled her with dread.

The dark shape seemed to change as it entered the library. One second it was long and thin, while the next it was short and stocky. It moved as if it were liquid mercury, flowing into the room, pooling from one patch of darkness to the next. If it was an animal, then it was like none she had ever seen before.

Whatever the mysterious creature might be it had followed her down the hall, and that was reason enough for Megan to be scared. It stopped just inside the door of the library.

It's looking for me. It knows I'm here. Maybe it can't see me in the darkness. Maybe if I stand real still it won't find me.

But she knew that most animals could see better in the dark than people. And even if it couldn't see her, it could probably smell her. Either way, standing still was not going to do her any good.

Keeping the unknown creature in sight, she slowly backed across the room. She had almost reached the opposite wall when she bumped against her father's chess table, causing pieces to topple over with a clatter.

Alerted by the noise, the shadow moved in her direction. Megan retreated until her back was flush against the wall. As she bumped against the wall, a strange coldness seemed to envelope her. Startled, she turned to find the source of the chill, and was shocked by what she saw.

She stood in front of the crack that ran the length of the wall, from floor to ceiling. Though it was very dark in the library, she could clearly see the crack, for it appeared much darker than everything else. An eerie cold spilled out of it. With the cold came whispering sounds, as though someone—or something—spoke deep within the wall.

She spun around, searching for the unknown creature she had momentarily forgotten. She couldn't see it, but knew the thing following her was close. Very close. Things in the wall, something in the room with her. She was trapped between the two.

Trapped. The thought terrorized her. If only she could turn on the light and see what was in the room with her. But she couldn't, because the light didn't work.

Why? Why didn't the light work? It had worked earlier in the evening, but now it didn't. Why?

Megan felt the pain shoot up her right leg and knew why the light didn't work. It didn't work because the bulb was broken. Someone had taken it out of the lamp and shattered it on the floor. That's what she had stepped on. Someone had broken the bulb; that's why the light didn't work.

But why?

To keep me from turning on the light.

Someone, or something, had removed the light bulb to keep her in the dark. And now that shadowy something was between her and the only exit from the room, hiding somewhere in the darkness.

She might have stood there all night, her back against the wall, too afraid to move. Instead, she pushed herself away from the wall and ran toward the doorway. Something lunged at her from beneath a coffee table, tried to stop her, but missed.

Reaching the doorway, she turned right and raced down the hall. She took the stairs two at a time, too frightened to slow down or look behind her. As she reached the top of the stairs, a scream escaped her lips.

"Daddy!"

Megan screamed again, even louder. The door to her

parents' bedroom opened. The hallway light came on. In that instant as the darkness was pushed away, she glanced down and saw something just behind her left ankle. A shadow as black as old motor oil raced to catch her. Only there was no creature from which this shadow sprang. The shadow *was* the creature, visible but see-through at the same time. Dark as the night, with eyes the color of smoke.

She saw the shadowy creature for only an instant, for the light caused it to vanish as though it had never been there at all. But Megan was positive that what she had seen was real, and she continued her flight until she was safely in her father's arms.

Chapter 17

The screams shattered the stillness of the night, waking Mike from a sound sleep. He sat up in bed, disoriented, thinking what he had heard might be the nocturnal cry of an animal. An owl perhaps. The bedroom windows were open, so the sound could have come from the forest. But then he heard it again: a sharp piercing cry, the scream of a young woman. Definitely human, and definitely belonging to his daughter.

Throwing back the covers, he jumped up and hurried across the room. It took a few panicked moments of fumbling in the dark before he could locate the light switch. Turning on the light, he opened the door just as Megan came racing into his arms.

"Daddy . . ."

The girl crashed into him and nearly knocked him over. He staggered back, feeling a twinge of pain shoot up the muscles in his back.

"Megan, what is it? What's wrong?"

Holly appeared at his side, slipping a robe on over her nightgown. She looked down and saw her daughter's injured foot. "Oh, my God. What happened? You're bleeding."

Mike looked down and saw the blood on his daughter's foot. Bloody footprints lined the hallway behind her. "Oh, Jesus." He turned to Holly. "Quick, get the first aid kit out of the bathroom."

"I'm okay, Daddy," Megan said, trying to calm her voice. "It's just a cut. A small one."

"How did this happen?" Mike asked, trying to control the anger in his voice. He was still half-asleep, so what he saw upset him. His daughter shouldn't be bleeding, there was no reason for it, especially when she was supposed to be safely asleep in her bed. What on earth had she been doing to earn such an injury?

He squatted down to take a look at the wound, hoping it wasn't serious. He also hoped the blood would come out of the newly installed carpeting. A frown tugged at the corners of his mouth. He shouldn't be worrying about the carpeting. It wasn't important. What mattered was whether or not his daughter was seriously hurt.

"I stepped on a broken light bulb in the library," Megan explained as Mike turned her around to get a better look at her injured foot. "Someone must have broken the lamp."

It took a moment for what Megan was saying to sink in. "The lamp in the library is broken? How did that happen?"

Megan shook her head. "I don't know. I tried to turn on the lamp, but it wouldn't work. That's when I cut my foot. Someone must have taken the bulb out and dropped it on the floor."

Alarm bells sounded in the back of Mike's head. "Someone took the bulb out of the lamp?" he asked, repeating what his daughter had just said.

She nodded. "Someone must have broken it. I went

in there to get away from the thing in the hallway, but the light wouldn't come on."

Again the bells sounded. "Megan, darling, what thing? What are you talking about?"

Holly returned with the first aid kit. Mike helped his daughter hobble across the room, and sat her on the edge of the bed so Holly could take a look at the injured foot. Hurrying into the bathroom, he wet a clean washcloth to wipe away the blood from around the cut. There didn't appear to be any more glass in the wound, but it was hard to tell because the cut was still bleeding.

Folding the washcloth over, he applied pressure against the cut for a minute or two to slow the flow of blood. Once the bleeding stopped, he reexamined Megan's injury. Luckily, the cut was only about an inch long, and not deep enough to require stitches.

"That's not so bad," he said, putting on his best happy face. The cut looked far worse than it actually was, and he was quite sure the sight of so much blood had badly frightened his daughter. "No need to even go to a doctor. We'll patch it up and you should be good as new in the morning."

Relieved the cut was not a serious one, he turned over the rest of the doctoring to Holly. Opening the first aid kit, she removed several gauze squares, a roll of white medical tape, and a bottle of antibiotic spray.

"Now this may sting a bit," Holly said, turning Megan's foot so she could get a better look at the cut.

"Ow," Megan yelped as her mother sprayed the cut several times with the antibiotic spray. She tried not to move, but flinched each time the cut was sprayed.

As Holly bandaged the cut, Mike pulled his jeans on over his pajama pants. He then slipped on his shoes and turned back to his daughter. "Megan, what exactly did you see downstairs?"

Megan looked up and shook her head. "I don't know. I couldn't sleep so I went downstairs to get a drink. Something followed me down the hallway. At first I thought it was Pinky, but it wasn't him."

"What was it?" Holly asked.

"A shadow," Megan answered, her eyes watering at the memory of what she had seen downstairs.

"You saw a shadow?" Mike asked, suddenly wondering if his daughter had been spooked by her own imagination. "What was it a shadow of?"

"I don't know. I couldn't see what it was, because it was too dark. All I saw was its shadow."

"But, honey, how could you see a shadow in the dark?" Holly asked, putting the final touches on the bandage.

"Because it was darker than the darkness. Real black. Like a night without stars. That's it. What I saw was darker than night. But it was only a shadow." Megan looked from one parent to the other, looking for reassurance that what she said was being believed. "I swear, I'm not making this up. That's what I saw."

"Was it a big shadow, or a little one?" Mike asked.

"Small, like a dog."

Mike let out a sigh of relief. He had been worried someone had broken into the house while they were sleeping. Before going to bed, he made sure all of the downstairs windows were locked and the deadbolts engaged on both the front and back doors. Still, with everything that had been happening lately, he was beginning to believe the house was unsafe. From what Megan had just told him, however, it was probably just a raccoon that had gotten into the house. Or maybe a possum.

Leaving Megan with Holly, he left the room and slipped down the hallway. Flipping on the lights at the top of the stairs, he could see a trail of blood drops leading down to the lower level.

Christ, it looks like I'll be renting a carpet cleaning machine in the morning. I doubt if there's anyone in town who does carpets.

Knowing there was probably broken glass on the floor, Mike entered the library slowly, being careful of where he stepped. He tried the lamp, even though he already knew it wouldn't work.

It didn't.

Turning the switch until it clicked twice, he traced his fingertips up the side of the lamp, under the shade, to where the bulb should have been. Careful not to let his fingers slip into an empty socket, and give himself a rather shocking surprise, he discovered that the bulb was in fact missing from the lamp.

Megan's right about the lamp. Someone has removed the bulb. But why? And who?

He wondered if Tommy was behind the missing bulb, but it wasn't like the eight-year-old to carry out that kind of mischief. And he certainly wouldn't remove the light bulb and then break it on the floor, especially when such actions would land him in a world of trouble.

Mike doubted if raccoons were capable of such feats, nor would a raccoon have a reason for doing such a thing. Open cabinet drawers in search of food, yes. Knock over a trash can to get at the goodies inside, certainly. But not enter a darkened room and carefully remove a light bulb from a table lamp, especially without knocking over the lamp in the process.

But maybe it *was* a raccoon. He knew very little about the masked marauders other than what he had read in books and magazines, and seen in comical Disney movies. Leaving the library, he retrieved a flashlight from the hallway closet. He returned a few minutes later, shining the light beam across the library's floor.

Pieces of the broken light bulb shone like milky jewels in the light. Mike looked at the broken pieces for a moment, then turned to survey the rest of the room. There was no other evidence that a raccoon might have been in the library. None of the books had been knocked off the shelves. A few of his chess pieces were toppled, but his daughter might have done that. He crossed the room and checked the windows, but they were still locked.

He had started to turn away from the windows, when something out of the corner of his eye caught his attention. Turning back around, he aimed the beam at the shelf running above the window, shining the light on his grandmother's collection of kachina dolls.

Sunday night, after looking for Pinky, he and Holly had climbed up on chairs and turned all the statues back around to face the room. Their work had been in vain, however, for the statues no longer faced him. Each and every one of them had been turned around backward to face the wall.

"What the hell? This is a joke, right? Someone's attempt at bad humor?"

He turned, sweeping the light across the shelves on the other walls. The kachinas on those walls had also been turned around backward. Leaving the library, he hurried down the hallway to the living room. A quick

check showed that all of the kachina dolls on the shelf
in the living room had also been turned around.

"I am not amused!" Mike said, feeling anger well up
in his chest. There could only be one explanation for
what he saw: while he and Holly slept, Megan had
sneaked downstairs and turned all of the kachina dolls
around backward. Maybe this was her way of protest-
ing the move from New York to Missouri. He knew she
wasn't happy living in the country, being taken away
from all of her friends back in the city. Her actions were
probably just a way to get back at him for disrupting
her life.

"She's getting back at me by trying to drive me
crazy," he said, returning to the library.

His daughter was probably also responsible for the
kachinas being turned around the night they went to
the dance, though he couldn't imagine how she had
done it without being caught by the baby-sitter. Unless
the baby-sitter had been in on it. That was possible. The
baby-sitter was also a teenager; maybe she enjoyed the
opportunity to team up with Megan to play a prank on
the older generation.

Was Tommy also in on the practical joke? Mike didn't
think so, because the boy was not very good about
keeping secrets. He would have given the whole thing
away. If not by outright blabbing, then by giggling
every time he or Holly came near the kachina dolls. No,
Tommy was definitely not a part of the fun and games.

Mike still wondered why the light bulb had been
taken out of the lamp. Maybe the bulb had burned out
and Megan had been in the process of replacing it. Perhaps she had dropped the bulb, stepped on it, and cut
her foot. Knowing she would be in trouble for her practical joke with the kachinas, she had concocted the

whole story about coming downstairs for a glass of
water and seeing the mysterious shadow chasing her.

*Clever. Very clever. My daughter has the imagination of a
future writer. But that still doesn't get her off the hook for
what she's done.*

Since he had already been awakened from a sound
sleep, and since he was already downstairs, Mike decided to go ahead and check all of the windows and
doors on the lower level just to make sure they were
still locked.

From the library he proceeded into his office, and
then into Holly's studio. Nothing in either of the rooms
had been disturbed, and the windows in both rooms
were locked tight. He entered the living room next,
looking behind the furniture to make sure a furry intruder wasn't hiding there. He also checked the bathroom and then made his way to the front door.

The front door was still locked, the deadbolt and
chain in place. The deadbolt was the type that could
only be opened from the inside. Even if it could be
opened from the outside, the chain was still in place,
which meant no one had opened the front door since he
had gone to bed.

Retracing his steps, he followed the hallway to the
kitchen. The back door was still closed and locked, as
was the door leading to the basement. The window
over the sink was also locked.

Satisfied that everything was on the up-and-up,
Mike turned to leave the kitchen. As he turned, the
beam of his flashlight danced across the newly installed tile floor. What he saw in the yellow glow of that
beam stopped him dead in his tracks.

"What the hell?"

The oval splotches on the floor had returned, staining the new tiles as they had before. Six of them, bigger and darker than ever.

"There's no way. This is a brand-new floor. Brand-new tiles. This just can't be happening. First the crack returns, and now this."

Mike's stomach knotted as he stepped closer to the stains. There was no mistaking what they were this time. Six faces had been drawn on the tiles of his kitchen floor in shades of grays and black. Six eerie, unholy faces, peering up at him from the floor like the souls of tormented spirits.

The eyes of the faces were unnerving, for they were all open, staring, watching him with pupils as dark as burnt wood. He almost expected them to blink, or perhaps wink at him, but they didn't. They only stared, quietly questioning his presence in a kitchen that was fast becoming their unearthly domain.

Of the six, four were obviously the faces of men. Or rather, they had characteristics that were male, because none of the faces really appeared to be human. They had certain human qualities, but there was something about their shape—and the way they were drawn— that made them less than human. They reminded Mike of gargoyles and other hideous creatures carved in stone upon medieval cathedrals.

The other two faces looked to be female, but they were not the faces of women. No stunning beauties looked up at him from his kitchen floor. No images of supermodels or silver-screen goddesses. Like the other four, the two faces that appeared female also possessed a grotesque quality. Had Dante been an artist and not a writer, he might have drawn such images to express

what he had witnessed during his fabled trip to the
land of eternal damnation.

"This has got to be a joke," Mike said, stepping
closer. "That's it, a fucking joke. Someone has to be
drawing these things." He rubbed the toe of his right
shoe across the face closest to him, but the damn thing
didn't smear. If it had been drawn, or painted, the artist
had done a very good job about it. He or she had also
been quite fast, for none of the faces had been on the
floor when he and Holly went to bed.

Had Megan drawn the faces?

No way. His daughter was not that good of an artist,
and it would have been nearly impossible to draw the
faces, and turn the kachina dolls around, in the time
since he and Holly had retired for the evening.

Perhaps a stencil had been used. A cardboard cutout
from which several layers of gray and black paint had
been applied to the tile floor. Mike knew certain types
of spray paint dried fairly fast. With a stencil, and spray
paint, it would have been possible to create the six faces
he saw in the time between going to bed and coming
back down to the kitchen again.

If a stencil and spray paint had been used, then that
let his daughter off the hook as the possible culprit.
There wasn't a can of spray paint in the house, and
Megan had not had an opportunity to go to the store by
herself to purchase any. Nope. Rule out his teenage
daughter as the artist behind the eerie faces on the floor.

So who had painted the faces, and why? A much
better question was how could they have gotten into
the house? The windows and doors were all locked
tight.

What if someone didn't draw them?

He paused to consider the question. If the six faces

hadn't been drawn by someone as part of an elaborate joke, then there could be no logical explanation for them. That left only the supernatural.

"Nonsense."

Even though he made a living writing horror novels, Mike did not believe in the supernatural. Not really. The belief in ghosts, spirits, witches, goblins, werewolves, vampires, and other things that went bump in the night was for backwoods country people and those who read the tabloids at the checkouts in the local supermarkets. He had no use for such beliefs, other than to make money off of them with the books he wrote.

Still here was something that could not be logically explained, at least not by him. There had to be a rational answer, but damned if he could think of one.

Turning away from the faces, he left the kitchen and went back upstairs. Megan was still in his bedroom, sitting on the edge of the bed. Holly sat beside her, quietly talking with the girl. They ended their conversation and looked his way when he entered the room.

"Did you see anything?" Holly asked.

Mike closed the door behind him and approached the bed. "I saw plenty, but not a raccoon or any other furry animal."

Megan's eyes widened a bit and Mike wondered if she was afraid of what he was about to say. "You didn't see the shadow?"

"No. No shadows other than the ones I made myself." He looked down at his daughter for a moment, then said, "Megan, I want the truth. What were you doing downstairs tonight?"

"I told you. I couldn't sleep, so I went downstairs to get a drink. I saw something following me in the hallway, and I got scared. I ran into the library and cut my foot on a piece of broken glass."

Mike listened to his daughter's explanation and said, "You sure you didn't go into the library to play a trick on us? Maybe you're mad because we moved from New York? Maybe you don't like this house, or the town, and want to get back at us somehow?"

Megan shook her head. "No. That's not it. I didn't like moving away from my friends, but I didn't go downstairs to play a trick. I was thirsty, and I went downstairs to get a drink."

"Mike, what's this all about?" Holly asked, obviously upset.

He turned from Megan to his wife. "Someone took the bulb out of the lamp in the library and broke it, just like Megan said. But the kachina dolls have also been turned around backward, each and every one of them."

"I didn't do it!" Megan protested.

Mike turned back to his daughter, fixing her with an icy stare. "Are you sure this isn't your idea of a joke? You didn't sneak downstairs to turn the statues around, accidentally cut your foot, and then make up the story about the shadow to keep from getting in trouble?"

"No!"

Holly intervened. "Megan, this isn't very funny. If that's what you did, you'd better tell us. You'll get in less trouble for doing something wrong and then telling the truth, than you will for trying to lie about it."

"I'm not lying," Megan responded, tears forming at the corners of her eyes.

"You didn't turn the statues around tonight?" Mike asked again.

"No."

"And you didn't turn them around the night the baby-sitter was here?"

Megan looked hurt. "I didn't even go downstairs that night. Ask Tommy."

"And you didn't draw the faces?"

"What faces?" Holly asked.

"The faces on the kitchen floor. They're back, all six of them."

"The faces are back?" Holly asked, concerned.

Mike nodded. "Every last one of them, even darker than before."

"I didn't draw them, Dad," Megan said, feeling she was still on the hot seat. "You know I suck at art."

Holly turned to her daughter, putting a comforting arm around her shoulder. "Megan, honey, if you say you didn't turn the statues around, or draw the faces on the kitchen floor, then we believe you. No one's mad at you, your father and I are just trying to figure out who's doing it. That's all." She looked at Mike. "Isn't that right, dear?"

Mike realized that he had raised his voice to his daughter, had almost been yelling. He took a deep breath and let it out. "That's right, sweetheart. I'm sorry if I sounded mad at you. I'm not. I just wanted to know if you had anything to do with what's been happening. That's all. If you say you only went downstairs to get a drink, then I believe you."

"I was only downstairs for a few minutes," Megan said, looking up at her father.

"Okay. I believe you." Mike nodded. "You'd better get back to bed and give that foot a rest. Might be a good idea to prop it up on a pillow while you sleep. You wouldn't want it to start bleeding on you again and ruin your sheets."

Megan got up and slowly left the room. Mike waited until she had closed the door before turning back to Holly.

"Show me," she said, standing up.

Mike led Holly downstairs, stopping at the library first. He swept the beam of his flashlight over the shelf that ran along the walls, displaying the collection of kachina dolls. "There. See. Each and every one of them is turned around backwards. It's the same way in the living room."

From the library they went into the kitchen. The lights were still on, so there was no need for the flashlight. Mike could see a look of shock in his wife's eyes as she spotted the faces adorning the floor.

"Oh, my god," she said, pausing in the doorway. Entering the room, she circled around the kitchen table, carefully studying the faces at her feet. She agreed with Mike, there was no way the faces could be just stains. They were not the result of mildew, bad tiles, chemicals, or a busted water pipe. They could only have been drawn by someone.

Kneeling on the floor beside one of the ovals, she ran her fingers over the faces, attempting to smear it.

"I tried that," Mike said. "It doesn't smear."

"It doesn't feel like paint," Holly observed. She leaned over, putting her nose only an inch or so above the floor, and sniffed. "It doesn't smell like paint either. If it was paint, there would still be an odor, even if it was just a faint one."

"Maybe it's ink," he suggested.

She wet the tips of her fingers and rubbed them over the face. "I don't think it's ink either. It hasn't been here very long, so it would have smeared if it were ink. Besides, it doesn't look like an ink drawing. Offhand I would say charcoal was used, but then that also would have smeared easily and it doesn't."

She looked up at Mike. "One thing for sure, Megan didn't draw these. They're too lifelike, and the technique used is too sophisticated for her to have done it."

"If not Megan, then who?" Mike asked.

Holly stood back up and looked around nervously. "Someone else. Someone who was in this house, here in this kitchen, while we were upstairs sleeping."

"But I checked all of the doors and windows. They're still locked. There's no way someone could have gotten in here tonight."

"Someone must have," she argued. "Maybe there was a window you missed."

He shook his head. "All checked. All locked."

She turned. "What about the basement? Maybe someone got in through one of the windows downstairs."

"I don't see how," he said. "The only door is here in the kitchen and it was also locked when I checked."

"Maybe it was unlocked earlier," Holly suggested. "Maybe someone came in, drew the faces, and then locked the basement door on the way out."

"It's not that kind of lock. You can't set it and then close the door. You have to close the door first and then flip the lock. It can't be locked from the other side."

Holly turned back to him, her eyes suddenly widening in fear. "Maybe they didn't leave. Maybe they're still in the house with us. Megan might have come downstairs and frightened them. Maybe they're still here, hiding somewhere."

"I didn't see anyone . . ." he started to say.

"But you didn't really check. Did you?" Holly asked. "You came downstairs looking for something small: a raccoon, or a possum. Not a person. Did you check all of the closets, or the bathrooms? Did you look upstairs in the bedrooms, under the beds? Maybe there's a hiding place we don't even know about in this old house."

"You're right," he said, feeling the fear his wife did. "I'll go upstairs and start searching again. You stay here. Call the sheriff's office, tell them we've had an intruder tonight. If someone was here tonight, they might still be around, either in the house or somewhere on the property."

Holly crossed the room and snatched the telephone off the cradle to dial the sheriff's office. Mike turned and grabbed a steak knife from the kitchen drawer, then hurried up the stairs to search the children's rooms. He didn't think someone was still hiding in the house, but it would be wise to be cautious just in case.

"We'll see about this," he said, starting up the stairs. "We'll just see."

Chapter 18

It was nearly 4 A.M. when the headlights of a vehicle illuminated the big trees at the end of the driveway. Mike and Holly had been sitting in the living room, watching out the windows. Seeing the lights, Mike got up and went to the front door. He had just opened the door when a patrol car pulled in front of the house and parked. He expected it to be one of the county deputies, and was quite surprised when Sheriff Douglas climbed out of the vehicle.

"Good evening, Sheriff," Mike said and stepped out onto the porch. "I didn't know you worked the graveyard shift."

Sheriff Douglas grabbed his hat and a clipboard off the front seat and then closed the door. "I usually don't work this late," he said, walking around the front of the car, "but the wife of one of my deputies is having a baby so that leaves us kind of shorthanded. I agreed to come in a few hours early to take his place so he could be at the hospital with her."

The sheriff saw Holly standing in the doorway and nodded toward her. "Morning, ma'am."

Holly smiled. "Would you like some coffee, Sheriff? I

can make a fresh pot." She stepped back out of the way as Mike and Sheriff Douglas entered the house.

"Thank you anyway, but I just had a cup at the diner in town. If I drink anymore, I'll get the jitters." Stepping through the doorway, he turned toward Mike. "The dispatcher said you called in a report about a possible prowler."

"Yes, sir," Mike nodded. "At least I think we had a prowler. I didn't see anyone, but I have reason to believe someone was here in the house tonight who wasn't supposed to be."

Mike and Holly led the sheriff on a tour of the lower rooms, explaining what had happened earlier in the evening. They started in the library, pointing out the broken light bulb and the kachina dolls that had been turned around backward. They also pointed out the statues in the living room that were now facing the wrong way.

As they moved from room to room, Jody checked the windows and doors, looking for evidence that someone might have broken in. Mike explained that he had already checked all of the windows and doors, and found them locked, but the sheriff went ahead and double-checked anyway. He also paused at several of the windows to shine his flashlight outside, looking for footprints or other evidence that an intruder had been present.

The tour concluded in the kitchen, with Holly and Mike pointing out the drawings of the faces that now adorned the tile floor. Sliding a kitchen chair back out of the way, Jody squatted down to better examine one of the faces. As Holly had done earlier, he ran the tips of his fingers over the drawing then sniffed them to see if there was any odor of paint. Straightening back up, he walked over to the door leading to the basement.

"This door was locked when you came downstairs?" He asked Mike.

"Yes, sir," Mike answered.

"And you're sure it was locked before you went to bed?"

"I checked it before I turned the lights off," Mike replied.

The sheriff opened the door and worked the lock a couple of times, then tried to turn the knob. Shutting the door he tried the knob again. "There's no lock release on the other side, but this door might have been opened with a credit card. Did you have the chain on?"

"I always use both the lock and the chain," Mike answered.

Jody slipped the chain in place then unlocked the door, opening it until the chain stopped the door. "It would be a tight squeeze, but someone might have jimmied the door open then slipped their hand through to remove the chain." He closed the door again and removed the chain. "Did you check downstairs to make sure all of the basement windows were locked?"

Mike admitted he hadn't. "The door was locked, and the chain was still on, so I didn't see any reason to check the basement."

Jody opened the door then removed the flashlight from his utility belt, switching it on. "I'd better go have a look."

"Here's the switch for the basement lights," Holly said, pointing out the switches at the top of the stairs. The sheriff thanked her and then started down the stairs. He was only gone for a minute or two before returning to the kitchen.

"All of the windows down there are still locked from the inside, so there's no way someone could have gotten into the house through the basement—not unless you have some sort of secret tunnel down there." He closed the door to the basement and locked it.

"No tunnel that we know of," Mike said.

Jody turned toward him. "Those Indian statues down there, which way were they facing last you looked?"

"They were facing out, their backs to the walls," Mike answered. "I turned them around myself when I was cleaning down there the other day."

Jody Douglas smiled. "Well, they're not facing out now; they're all facing the wall."

Mike felt the tiny hairs on the back of his neck stand straight up. "You're kidding."

"I'm serious as a heart attack," Jody replied. "Whoever turned the other statues around must have also turned the ones in the basement."

Slipping the chain back on the basement door, the sheriff asked, "Do you mind if I have a look at the library again?"

"Sure, by all means," Holly answered.

Entering the library, the sheriff walked around the room for a moment, obviously thinking about something, then walked back over to the lamp with the missing bulb.

"Did you check the windows upstairs?"

Mike nodded. "The windows in the kids' bedrooms and bathroom are locked. The one in our bedroom is open, but the screen has a locking latch on it."

"And you say nothing was taken?" Jody asked. He bent over and picked up a piece of the broken light bulb to examine it.

"Nothing is missing that we know of. But you know

how it is with these things: you never realize something has been taken until you go to look for it." Mike frowned. "Uh . . . shouldn't you be wearing gloves? I mean, you might be able to get fingerprints off of that."

The sheriff dropped the piece of glass and straightened back up. "You watch too much television, Mr. Anthony. It would be rather hard to get fingerprints off of a fragment that small. Not that there is a reason to take fingerprints."

"What do you mean?" Holly asked.

"I mean, as far as I can determine, there was no crime committed here."

"You don't call breaking and entering a crime?"

He rubbed his chin and nodded. "Of course, breaking and entering is a crime. But so far I've seen no evidence that anyone has broken in here. You said yourself the doors and windows were all locked before you went to bed, and they were still locked when you came back downstairs."

"Yes, but someone must have broken in," Mike argued. "How else could you explain the light bulb being broken? And my daughter saw something moving in the hallway."

"Something? You said your daughter saw a shadow." He looked around. "A big old house like this, late at night, probably has lots of shadows. I bet it creaks and groans a bit when the wind gets to blowing. I imagine it can be downright spooky to a child, especially to a child not familiar with her surroundings. I suggest you leave the hallway light on at night; that should get rid of any scary shadows."

Mike was reluctant to accept the sheriff's explanation. "What about the kachina dolls? It wasn't a shadow that climbed up and turned those statues around backward."

The sheriff looked at the shelf for a moment, then turned his attention back to Mike. "You sure those statues were facing this way when you went to bed?"

Mike nodded. "I'm positive. I remember looking at them before I went upstairs."

"Hmmm . . . but when your daughter woke you they were turned around the other way?"

Holly didn't like the tone of Jody's voice. "What are you suggesting, Sheriff?"

"Oh, nothing, ma'am. It just seems kind of funny to me that the dolls were turned around after she was in the library."

"You're not saying you think Megan had anything to do with this?"

"The thought had crossed my mind. Maybe she was playing a practical joke on you. You know how kids are nowadays. Maybe she thought she would have a good laugh at your expense, but cut her foot and got scared. She might have made up the part about something in the hall following her just to stay out of trouble."

"Megan wouldn't do something like that," Holly said, taking her daughter's defense.

Again the sheriff shrugged. "Maybe. But you can never be too sure with teenagers."

"What about the faces on the kitchen floor?" Holly asked. "You're not suggesting she made those too."

"No, ma'am. I'm not. Not unless the art supplies I saw in the room across the hall belong to her."

"The art supplies are mine, but . . ." Holly's face suddenly went red with anger. "Are you suggesting I drew the faces?"

"That's the most ridiculous thing I've ever heard," Mike added, also becoming angry.

"Is it?" the sheriff asked innocently. "Perhaps it is, but you have to look at things the way I see them."

"And just how is that?" Mike asked, crossing his arms across his chest.

Jody smiled, apparently amused by Mike's display of anger. "Well, I wasn't going to say this, you being a big-shot writer and all, but how do I know you're not making all of this up?"

"Making it up?" Mike was shocked.

The sheriff nodded. "You grandmother claimed to see things all the time in this house that weren't there. She used to call the sheriff's office on a regular basis, at least three or four times a week. How do I know you're not doing the same thing? Maybe it runs in the family."

"I'm not making this stuff up."

"So you say." Jody nodded thoughtfully. "I've also heard that the last book you wrote didn't do as well as expected."

Mike was confused. "Just what are you saying?"

"Maybe all of this is a way to drum up some free advertisement for your next novel. A newspaper article or two about a horror writer being besieged by an unknown prowler would be great press."

Mike couldn't believe what he was hearing. "And you believe this?"

Jody Douglas shrugged indifferently. "I'm just repeating what some of your contractors are saying."

"Contractors? What contractors?" Holly asked, jumping back into the argument. "Which ones?"

The sheriff turned to her. "The contractors who had to tear up a perfectly good floor because someone decided to draw a few spooky faces on it."

"We did not draw those faces on it!" Holly exploded, her anger getting the best of her. "How dare they say such a thing."

Jody just shrugged again. "They think you did, especially since they're the same kind of faces the old woman used to draw."

Mike's heart skipped a beat. "Wait a minute. Hold on. You're saying my grandmother used to paint faces on the floor?"

"Floors, walls, and on the ceiling too. Painted them everywhere, then claimed they were the faces of demon spirits trying to get through from the other side. She drove the previous sheriff nuts; that's why he hired a painter to paint the downstairs a dark green. The old woman couldn't bug him about the faces if she couldn't see them." He stared hard at Mike. "Painting the walls and floor put a stop to the nonsense. At least it did up until now."

Holly started to say something else, but Mike stopped her. "Sheriff, I assure you we aren't the ones who painted those faces—if they were painted. I can also assure you we won't be calling you again; Holly and I will get to the bottom of this ourselves. And we *will* get to the bottom of it."

"See that you do, because I don't want to keep coming out here for nothing." With that, Jody Douglas bid them a good night and left, leaving Holly and Mike standing in the hallway.

Chapter 19

Even though Mike went back to bed after the sheriff's visit, he didn't get much sleep. What the sheriff had said upset him. It also got him to thinking. He lay in the bed, looking up at the ceiling, wondering who had drawn the faces on the floors and walls that had so badly frightened his grandmother, and why?

He lay there, his mind filled with all kinds of possible answers, some as wild as the Hardy Boys mysteries he had read as a teenager. Were criminals behind the faces? Was an international ring of diamond thieves trying to frighten his grandmother, and now his family, away from the house so they could recover a stash of precious jewels hidden beneath the flagstones in the basement? Had gold been discovered on the property? Did the house sit overtop of a lost mine? Maybe oil had been struck when the deep well was drilled, the discovery a secret known only to the men who dug the well.

Mike smiled. Diamonds. Gold. Oil. Now all he needed was a ragtag band of pirates and he'd have the perfect plot for a young adult adventure novel. With these thoughts dancing through his mind, he finally drifted off to sleep, awaking an hour later when the alarm clock rang.

Megan's foot was still sore that morning, so they decided to let her stay home from school. Tommy, on the other hand, had no excuse to stay home. Despite his protests of unfair treatment, Holly and Mike made sure he got dressed on time, finished his breakfast, and was standing at the end of the driveway before the appearance of the big yellow school bus.

Once Tommy was safely on his way to school, Mike and Holly sat down to a breakfast of French toast, low-fat turkey bacon, and several cups of coffee. Both of them found it rather difficult to enjoy breakfast in the kitchen, however, because of the faces that looked up at them from the tile floor.

Although it was silly, Mike couldn't shake the feeling that he was being watched, and their conversation listened to. It was all he could do to resist the urge to stomp on the face closest to him. For a brief moment he imagined stomping on the face and feeling flesh not tile, and the sensation of bone and cartilage breaking beneath the heel of his shoe, blood oozing bright red across the floor. That mental image did little to improve the taste of his food. In fact it made the syrup-laden French toast difficult to swallow.

Nor would they have been more comfortable in the living room, for in that room the row of kachina statues lining all four walls were now turned around backwards. That was another mystery to be pondered, another sign that someone had been in their home last night while they slept. Whoever it was had been careful about turning the statues, for each and every one of them was turned around perfectly. None of the kachinas were half-turned, or only turned a quarter of the way. Nor had any been toppled over or knocked askew. They were exactly as they had been earlier in the day yesterday, only now they were facing the opposite direction.

Trying not to look at the kitchen floor, they finished their breakfast and then cleaned the dishes. Anxious to research some of the things Sheriff Douglas had said about Vivian Martin, Mike decided to make a trip to the Braddock Public Library. He invited Holly to go along with him, but she wanted to remain at home in case Megan needed anything.

The drive into town was rather pleasant. It was a beautiful day out, the sky so blue it almost hurt his eyes to look at it. As he drove along State Road #315, Mike tried to imagine what the area had looked like before being settled by the white man.

Here was the place the Osage Indians had once called home, living close to the land, taking only what they needed and no more. From what he had read, the Osages were supposed to be rather statuesque in height, with most of the men well over six feet tall. They had hunted the land long before the white man, their moccasin trails now the highways and service roads that cut across the state of Missouri. Where their villages had once stood were now cities and towns, communities filled with people.

The Osage people were long gone, forced from their land by the encroaching white settlers. Only the names they had used for the land remained to mark their passing; only an occasional arrowhead or spear point found along the creeks and rivers spoke of their once proud nation.

Cut down all of the trees and then name a street after them. Slaughter all of the Indians and then give their names to the towns, cities, and states. Put their images on currency, tobacco products, and automobiles to make a dollar off the things that are lost forever. It was the American way.

As Mike drove along State Road #315, he wondered about the neighbors living closest to him. Could one of them be responsible for what was happening at his house? Had the same thing happened to any of them?

Passing a farm on his right, he spotted an old man on a tractor plowing a field near the road. On impulse Mike slowed the van and turned into a graveled lane running parallel to the field. Parking the van, he climbed out and watched as the tractor slowly approached him.

He thought the old farmer was going to pass right by him, but then the tractor slowed to a stop not ten feet from where he stood. The farmer switched off the engine and then turned to look at Mike.

"Good morning," Mike called. "My name is Mike Anthony. I'm your new neighbor. I live in the old Martin house, on Sawmill Road."

The farmer nodded. "You that writer fellow they wrote about in the newspaper?"

Mike smiled. "That would be me, only don't believe everything they said about me. Newspapers have a tendency to exaggerate."

The farmer climbed down off of the tractor and walked over to the barbed wire fence that enclosed the field. "I usually take what they print in newspapers with a grain of salt, especially if they're talking about politicians, celebrities, or cutting our taxes." He reached across the fence, offering his hand. "I'm Otto Strumberg."

Mike shook the man's hand. "Strumberg? Sounds like a German name."

"It is," Otto said. "My great-grandfather was from

Germany. He was one of the first farmers to settle this area. One of many it seems. All of this area was originally settled by Germans. Some of the old people still speak the language. Don't speak a word of it myself, but my father could talk it like a native. He could also drink most men under the table when it came to good German beer. There used to be a brewery not too far from here, but it closed down a long time ago. My father used to work at the brewery, after he lost his job at the sawmill."

"Wasn't there a sawmill around here once?" Mike asked.

Otto nodded. "That's the one. Used to be located on that property you now own, pretty much near where your house is now standing."

"What happened to it? Why did it shut down?"

"It didn't shut down," Otto corrected. "It burned down."

"Oh?" Mike said. "What caused the fire?"

Otto scratched his chin. "I guess that all depends on who you talk to. Some say the fire was started by a spark landing in a pile of sawdust. Others say it was deliberately set."

"What did your father say about it?"

Otto shrugged. "He would never talk about the fire, and he flat refused to ever set foot on that property again. I guess coming so close to being burned up must have spooked him. It must have upset the other workers too, because none of them I knew would ever talk about the sawmill or what happened the night of the fire. And you couldn't pay them to go back out on that property. Even today."

"But the sawmill is long gone," Mike pointed out.

Otto nodded. "I know it. But country people don't forget bad things, or the places where they happened."

The old farmer reached into the top pocket of his overalls and pulled out a pack of unfiltered Chesterfield cigarettes. He offered a cigarette to Mike, who accepted only to be polite.

"Now, what can I do for you this morning?" Otto asked, lighting his cigarette. "This strictly a social call, or do you have business in mind?"

"A little of both," Mike replied, lighting the cigarette given him. The unfiltered cigarette was harsher than what he was used to, and it was all he could do to keep from coughing.

"Oh?" Otto said.

"I saw you out plowing, so I wanted to stop by and say hello," Mike said. "But I'm also looking for some information."

"Information I've got plenty of, free of charge," Otto replied. "Although my wife thinks I ought to charge people. She says I talk too much, and if I charged them no one would pay me so I would have to keep quiet for a spell."

Mike laughed. "My wife sometimes feels the same way about me."

"So, what kind of information are you looking for?"

"Basically I want to know about the neighborhood. I've been having a bit of trouble lately. I think someone's gotten into my house a couple of times, maybe trying to play a joke on me. I was wondering if there have been very many break-ins around here that you know of."

"Break-ins?" Otto rubbed the top of his head. "Not that I know of, at least not in the last couple of years. Something like that would have made the newspaper if reported. Not much happens around here so just about any news ends up in the paper."

"You've never had any trouble?" Mike asked.

"Not really. Somebody might swipe a watermelon or two out of the field, or a few ears of corn, but that's mostly teenagers out looking for mischief. Basically they're harmless; just trying to grab a watermelon to impress their girls, or the other guys. They never do any real damage, so I don't worry about it none.

"Heck, I used to snitch an ear or two of corn when I was a youngster. Always took field corn though, the stuff they usually feed to livestock, left the sweet corn alone. Didn't think it was right to take a man's sweet corn, even if it was only an ear or two."

"You never had anyone try to break into your house?" Mike asked.

Otto shook his head. "Nope. Never. I never even bothered to lock my doors until a couple of years ago. Saw all that stuff that was going on in the news and figured it was time I started locking up the place at night and when I was away. Still, most folks know better than to try and break into a farmer's house."

"Why's that?"

Otto smiled. "Because all of the farmers in these parts have guns. That's why. And they wouldn't hesitate to shoot someone trying to break into their home. The criminals know that, which is why they do most of their robbing in the towns and cities. I'm no exception. I've got myself a .30–.30 lever action, and a couple of shotguns. Keep them in the living room, right beside my chair.

"If someone's breaking into your house, then maybe you should think about getting yourself a gun. If you do buy one, don't just put it in a drawer, or closet, and forget about it. Take it out back and shoot the thing. Set up a few tin cans and put in a little target practice. The sound of a gunshot carries for miles; you'll let everyone around here know that you have a firearm. It might discourage unwanted visitors from coming around your place."

·Mike thought about it for a moment and then nodded. "That might not be a bad idea."

Otto grinned. "Maybe my wife was right. Maybe I should charge for my advice. Of course the first batch is always free, us being neighbors and all."

"I really appreciate the advice," Mike said. "I was starting to get worried, especially after what happened to our cat."

"Something happen to you cat?" Otto asked.

Mike nodded. "I found him dead in the basement the other morning. His throat was cut, and his eyes were gouged out. The sheriff said he probably died of old age, and that something got to him after he died, but I just don't believe that. My cat was in perfect health. I'm still trying to figure out how to tell the kids. They'll be heartbroken."

The old farmer's grin had faded as Mike told about what had happened to Pinky. He looked around, as if suddenly impatient to get back to work. Crushing out his cigarette, he shook Mike's hand again, offering a final word of advice before climbing back on his tractor. "Buying yourself a gun is still a good idea, but you might want to think about sleeping with the lights on from now on. And if I were you, I would seriously consider selling that old house and finding someplace else to live."

With those parting words, Otto climbed back on his tractor and went back to plowing the field. Mike watched him for a moment and then climbed into his van, starting back down the road toward town.

* * *

The library had just opened when Mike pulled into the parking lot. Turning off the van's engine, he reached behind the driver's seat and grabbed the briefcase he always carried with him. He had learned early as a writer to always carry pen and paper, to jot down thoughts as they came to mind. He also kept a notebook on the nightstand beside his bed, because some of the best scenes in his novels came from dreams and nightmares.

In addition to the paper and pens, he also kept a copy of his latest novel in the briefcase. His theory was that if he ever got pulled over by the police, and mistaken for a dangerous criminal, he could wave the novel to convince them he was no threat to society. So far he had not had the opportunity to test out his theory.

Grabbing the briefcase, Mike locked the van and entered the library. It was still early so he was the only patron, which was perfectly fine with him. Connie Widman was standing behind the checkout counter, straightening books on a library cart. She paused and looked his way when he entered.

"Back so soon?" She smiled. "I hadn't expected you until at least next week."

Mike smiled back. "I needed to do a little research for the novel I'm writing. Poke around in the town's history, dig up local legends, scandals, skeletons in the closet, that sort of thing." He didn't want to tell Connie exactly what it was he was looking for, because he didn't want to explain what had been happening at his house. "Do you keep back issues of the local newspaper?"

Connie nodded. "We've got the issues published within the last year; the rest are available on microfilm."

"What? Nothing on computer?" he teased.

"A library this small is lucky to have a microfilm

system, let alone a computer," Connie replied, faking a frown.

"I was just kidding," he laughed. "Microfilm is fine. How far back does it go?"

"The town's newspaper was established about one hundred forty years ago. Of course it's changed owners and names a couple of times since then. We've got most of the issues on film, except for the paper's first two years of production. There was a fire about twenty years ago and those issues were burned before they could be put on film."

"That's a shame," Mike said, shaking his head. "But that's probably farther back than I need to research anyway."

"Well, the microfilm viewer is in the reference section. There's a table next to it. Grab yourself a seat and I'll bring you the files you need. What year would you like to start with?"

"Sometime in the sixties, I guess. Sixty-eight, sixty-nine. Thank you." Mike walked over to the reference section and put his briefcase on the table beside the microfilm viewer. Connie appeared a couple of minutes later with a wooden tray filled with tiny blue boxes containing a chunk of the town's newspaper's history on spools of microfilm.

"I take it you know how to work this thing?" Connie asked.

He nodded. "I think I can manage all right."

"Okay then, I'll leave you to it," she said. "If you need anything, I'll be up front."

She set the tray down and then left him alone. Mike switched on the viewer, then started his search about thirty years ago and worked forward.

It didn't take him long to find what he was looking

for. In 1968 the town's newspaper carried three different reports saying that the sheriff's office had been
summoned to the farm of Vivian Martin in answer to a
complaint about a possible prowler. Despite thorough
searches by the deputies answering the calls, no prowlers
were ever found.

There were no more reports pertaining to the Martin
farm in the years 1969–1970, but in 1971 Mike discovered in the police reports section of the paper that the
sheriff's office had been summoned to the Martin farm
a whopping total of eleven times. Each time the call
was in the response to a possible prowler sighting.

Mike jotted down a few notes about the reports then
sat back to ponder over what he had just read. He
didn't remember much about his grandmother, but he
did remember that she was paranoid. In the year he had
lived with her, she had been afraid to leave the curtains
open for fear of someone looking in. The windows and
doors had always been kept tightly locked, even on the
warmest of summer days, and instead of sleeping like
normal people she had spent most nights wandering
from one room to the next. She only slept during the
daytime, and then only for brief periods.

He had only been five years old when he first went to
live with his grandmother, far too young to understand
the things taking place in the mind of Vivian Martin.
Still, he had sensed the old woman was terribly frightened of something. In the brief time they had lived together, her fears had affected him; he too had become
afraid of the dark. It was a phobia that took Mike years
to overcome.

As he slowly scanned through the back issues of the
town's newspaper, Mike found other police reports
pertaining to his grandmother. Twenty-seven in all. All

of them were prowler reports, and in each case no one had ever been caught, or even seen, on the property. Nothing had ever been stolen, and there were no signs of a break-in.

Although nothing was ever said in print—at least not in so many words—some of the later reports, those dating back only about ten years, hinted that Vivian Martin might be suffering from a mental condition. There were no police reports after that. Either the sheriff's office refused to answer her calls, or the newspaper got tired of printing things about her.

What Mike was looking for, and what he didn't find, was a report about mysterious faces being drawn on the floors, walls, or ceilings of Vivian's home. Jody Douglas said the previous sheriff had grown tired of Vivian calling about the faces and had painted over them, yet there was nothing about them in the papers. Surely something so strange would have been deemed newsworthy, especially in a town as small as Braddock.

Odd. Very odd.

Maybe the faces didn't appear until after Vivian had already worn out her welcome with the newspaper and sheriff's office. Perhaps by then she had been deemed an official nutcase and nothing about her was worth putting into print. There might still be a report or two about the faces on file at the sheriff's office, but Mike seriously doubted if Jody Douglas would let him take a look at them.

He leaned back in his chair and pinched the bridge of his nose, fighting off a headache that was starting to form behind his eyes. Were the painted faces and the prowler sightings related? Probably. From what he had read, it would appear someone had come up with a surefire way to terrorize a paranoid old woman.

Glancing back through his notes, Mike was astonished when he realized that the newspaper reports
about his grandmother covered a period of thirty years.

Thirty years? That's incredible. What if the prowlers
hadn't existed only in Vivian Martin's head? What if
someone had been sneaking around her house, perhaps deliberately trying to frighten her? Thirty years
was a long period of time, much too long for it to be just
one culprit. Several people had to have been involved,
at different periods of time.

Mike thought about that concept for a moment. He
knew Jody Douglas and his teenage cohorts had gone
to great lengths to make his grandmother's life a living
hell. Were there others before him, and after him, who
did the same thing? Maybe. Was tormenting Vivian
Martin a local pastime, something to be passed down
from father to son?

He stared at his notes, frustrated by the lack of information they contained. He was especially annoyed that
he hadn't come across any mention of the mysterious
faces that had been painted on his grandmother's
kitchen floor, the same faces that were now appearing
on his floor.

Maybe I'm looking in the wrong place for information.

Putting the last of the boxes back in the tray, Mike
switched off the microfilm viewer. He put his notebook
away and closed the briefcase, turning to look toward
the front of the library. Connie Widman had finished her
sorting and was now reading a paperback novel. Maybe
there was still one source of information to be searched.

Connie looked up at him and smiled as he walked up
to the counter and set down the tray of film boxes. "Did
you find what you were looking for?"

"I found some of the things I needed, but not everything. I guess I'll have to look through some of the records I have at the house." He made a motion of turning toward the door, then turned back to the librarian.

"You said you knew my grandmother pretty well?"

Connie closed the book she was reading and put it on the desk in front of her. "I knew her about as well as anyone. She used to come in here once or twice a week, regular as clockwork."

"Would you happen to remember what kind of books she enjoyed reading?" Mike asked, leaning on the counter.

Connie thought about it for a moment, then said, "At first she liked mystery novels, but later her tastes changed to books that were rather strange."

"Strange?" he asked. "How so?"

The librarian looked around as if she were afraid of being overheard, even though they were the only ones in the library. "She started reading books on the occult an awful lot. Satanism. Shamanistic studies. Myths and legends. That sort of thing."

"Do you normally carry those kinds of books here?"

"Oh no. We had to special order them through the library loan system. Created quite a stir with the regulars. They all figured she was some kind of witch. The gossip got so bad I had to hide the books when they came in."

"Do you think my grandmother was a witch?" he asked.

Connie shook her head. "Not at all. She was much too nice to be anything as terrible as that. I just think she was a lonely, frightened old woman."

"Frightened? What was she frightened of?"

Again Connie looked around. "She told me once. She said the boogers were after her."

"Boogers?" Mike asked. "My grandmother was scared of dried snot?"

She shook her head. "That's just a slang term. The actual definition of boogers goes something like this: Booger. A bogeyman. An item or thing that is unnamed or unnamable." She smiled. "The old people around here also used to call them hobgoblins."

"Hobgoblins?" Mike grinned. "My grandmother was afraid of hobgoblins?"

"Terrified of them." Connie nodded. "She said they were trying to get into her house. Poor old woman, living by herself, she must have been terribly frightened."

The grin on Mike's face faded. His grandmother was terrified of hobgoblins getting into the house. And now, all these years later, it seemed as if something was getting into the same house.

The door opened and a young boy entered the library. Mike waited for the boy to go to the children's section, before he turned back to the librarian. "Connie, I'm curious. Did my grandmother ever talk about faces appearing on the floor?"

The librarian's expression lit up. "Oh, goodness yes. Faces on the kitchen floor. On the walls. Even on the ceiling. She used to go on and on about how the faces were watching her."

"Did she ever say what those faces were supposed to be?"

Connie looked at him funny. "I just told you what they were supposed to be: they were boogers."

Chapter 20

When Tommy came home from school that afternoon, he was hoping Pinky would greet him at the front door, but the big cat was nowhere to be seen. He asked his mother if they could go looking for him, but she just said Pinky would come back in time. It was the same thing his father had said. But what if the big cat didn't come back on his own? What if Pinky was lost and couldn't find his way home? What if he was hurt?

Maybe he had stepped into a hole and broken his leg. Cats could get broken legs, just like people. Tommy had seen a cat with a broken leg once, at the veterinarian's office back in New York City. That cat had gotten run over by a car, his back leg broken with the bone sticking out all bloody and sharp. The cat's owners had brought him into the veterinarian's office in a cardboard box, carrying him right past Tommy. The cat had screamed in pain, and there had been a strong smell of ammonia because he had peed in the box. They had carried the cat into the doctor's office, but they hadn't carried him back out again. Tommy knew what that meant: they had put the cat to sleep because they couldn't fix his leg. They sometimes did that to animals, put them to sleep so they wouldn't have any more pain. They did it to animals who were in pain and couldn't be fixed, but they never did it to people. Tommy didn't understand why they did it to one and not the other.

Maybe Pinky had stepped in a hunter's trap. Tommy hoped not, because that would be terrible. Once he had watched a television show on the educational channel about hunters and trappers. It showed wolves and foxes, even rabbits, that had stepped into traps. The traps were like big mousetraps, but much, much worse. They had steel teeth that sprang shut when an animal stepped on the trap, clamping around a leg or foot, breaking the bone. He had watched the horrible pictures of animals stuck in the cruel traps, their legs mangled and broken. Sometimes the foxes and wolves would chew off their own feet to get free. Sometimes they just died in the traps, freezing to death or slowly dying from hunger. The television show had given Tommy nightmares for almost a week, nightmares far worse than any he had ever had from watching scary movies with his sister.

Pinky might also have stepped in a trap. He might be out there in the woods somewhere, slowly starving to death. Maybe he was stuck in a trap and couldn't get away, helpless to protect himself if any mean dogs came along. His father should be out looking for him, or his mother, but they weren't.

They didn't care about Pinky, not really, not the way Tommy cared. All they were interested in was fixing up the house. Tommy didn't care about the house. He cared about Pinky, cared about him so much it hurt. And if his parents wouldn't go looking for the cat, then he would.

Entering the house through the front door, he called out a greeting to his mother. He then walked into the kitchen to grab a couple of cookies out of the jar sitting on the counter, taking care not to step on any of the spooky faces staring up at him from the floor. His mother never minded if he took a couple of cookies when he got home from school, as long as he only took a couple. He wasn't very hungry at the moment, but he might get hungry before dinner, especially if he was out looking for his cat. He had just put the lid back on the cookie jar when his mother entered the kitchen.

"Hello, dear. How was school?"

Tommy turned around. "It was okay, Mom. We watched a film for science class."

"What about?"

"About spiders and how they spin their webs."

"Spiders. Yuck."

Tommy smiled. "It was really cool, especially the part that showed spiders eating flies and moths."

"Double yuck," Holly said, making a face.

"Mom, is it okay if I go out in the backyard to look for spiders?"

"As long as you don't try to pet any. Some of the spiders around here are poisonous, you know."

"I'm not that dumb," Tommy replied. "I just want to watch them. Maybe I'll get to see one eat a fly or something."

"Well, I don't care. Just don't bring any spiders home for dinner."

"I won't, Mom. I promise."

"Change your clothes first. I don't want you ruining your school clothes in your quest to study spiders."

"Okay, Mom. I will."

He crossed the kitchen, again stepping over the faces,

gave her a big hug, then went down the hallway and up the stairs. Entering his room, he tossed his book bag on his bed and then grabbed his play clothes which he kept folded on the cedar chest in front of the windows. He changed into them, and then pulled on his oldest tennis shoes. Slipping the chocolate chip cookies into the front pocket of his pants, he left the room.

Tommy wasn't really planning on looking for spiders; he had seen quite enough arachnids in the film at school to last him for the day. Instead he was going to search for Pinky.

His mother was in the living room when Tommy came back downstairs. He didn't stop to talk with her, because he was afraid she would become suspicious and not allow him out of the house. Tiptoeing past the living room, he entered the kitchen and then hurried to the back door. He felt guilty that he had lied to his mother, but not guilty enough to stop him from what he was doing. Once he was outside, that guilt quickly vanished.

There were few hiding places in the backyard, or in the front yard, so he knew Pinky couldn't be hiding anywhere close to the house. That left the barn, the orchard, and the forest as possible hiding places. Since the barn was the closest of the three, he decided to start his search there.

The old barn had once been painted red, but there was little of the original color left. The barn's paint had faded and flaked off over the years, leaving behind a mostly brown building. The roof was in better shape than the rest of the building, and he could still see portions of the large letters that had once been painted there. His dad told him the letters had once spelled out the slogan "SEE ROCK CITY," but now all that was left was "SE OCK C TY." Tommy didn't know what Rock City was, nor did he know if it was really worth seeing, but he had seen several similar signs on barns in the area, so a few people must think it was worth looking at.

Circling around to the side of the barn, he moved slowly through the tall weeds to the double doors. As he plowed a path through the weeds, he was on the lookout for snakes, fearful of stepping on one. His father had warned him to stay away from the barn because there might be snakes, but so far Tommy hadn't seen any.

The side doors had once been closed, but one of the doors had fallen to the ground and rotted away years ago. Approaching the opening, Tommy stopped dead in his tracks when a very large grasshopper suddenly took flight in front of him. It wasn't the grasshopper that startled him so much as it was the sound it had made. Kind of a rattling, hissing sound, like the sound a rattle-snake makes. He knew what a rattlesnake sounded like, because he had seen a television show about snakes. Several other grasshoppers jumped out of his way before he reached the barn doors.

Tommy's dad had told him that grasshoppers made good fishing bait. That might be true, but he could not imagine trying to put a grasshopper—especially one of the big ones—on a fishing hook. Not only were they hard to catch, and probably even harder to put on a fish hook, but they had the nasty habit of spitting a brown juice that looked like chewed tobacco. He didn't know if grasshoppers could bite, but they looked tough enough to take a chunk out of just about anyone's finger. Nope. As far as fishing went, he would stick to worms and leave the grasshoppers to someone else.

Reaching the open doorway, he stopped and poked his head inside. The interior of the barn was layered in shadows, but he could still see everything. Old farm machinery sat just inside the doorway. Beyond that the building was divided into several small rooms. He suspected the rooms were to keep horses, or maybe cows, but there were no animals there now and probably hadn't been any for a long time.

"Pinky?" he called out, stepping through the doorway. The inside of the barn smelled of old straw and dust. There were probably plenty of spiders inside the barn, maybe even a few snakes or lizards, but he wasn't interested in any of them. "Pinky, are you in here?"

Tommy wanted to turn around and leave because the barn was kind of spooky, even in the daytime, but then he wouldn't be doing a very good search. Instead he took a deep breath and stepped farther into the gloomy interior.

Pinky wasn't under the farm machinery, nor was he hiding in any of the smaller rooms. That left only the hayloft upstairs. Testing to make sure the wooden ladder would hold his weight, he slowly climbed up into the hayloft.

It was hot in the hayloft, and dark because the light spilling in from the open doorway didn't reach all of the way to the back of the barn. Crossing the loft, he had to move slowly, careful not to step in a hole or run something sharp though the bottom of his foot. Sweat trickled down his face as he searched the upstairs, the smell of old hay making him want to sneeze.

"Pinky? Are you up here, boy?"

He called twice more, but only the silence greeted him. The silence spoke of ancient things and forgotten times, as if the hayloft, and the barn itself, were inhabited by ghosts of the past. It was an eerie feeling standing there in the old barn; a building that had once been shiny and new, filled with hay bales to feed horses and cows. The horses and cows were long gone, as were the hay bales. Only the memories remained.

Tommy crossed from one end of the loft to the other, and then crossed it again. He called Pinky's name several times, but the big cat did not answer him.

He had just crossed the hayloft a second time, and was about to start back down the ladder, when he thought he saw movement in the darkness near the back wall of the loft. He stopped, one foot on the ladder, staring into the darkness to see what had moved. A minute slowly passed. Two.

"Pinky?"

Had the cat been hiding somewhere, only now coming out to answer his call? He called again, focusing his attention on the darkness at the back of the loft. Nothing moved. No cat came from the blackness to greet him with meows and a swishing of tale. There was only the darkness, and the silence. But Tommy could have sworn he saw something move, something about the same size as his beloved housecat.

Not knowing what he had seen, Tommy decided it might be a good idea to leave the barn as quickly as possible. He didn't want to have a run-in with an animal, especially one that might be mad that its afternoon nap had been disturbed. Hurrying down the ladder, he left the barn and its spooky shadows by the same way he had entered, and ran into the apple orchard. There were a lot of trees in the orchard, any one of which Pinky could be hiding behind or up in the branches of.

Moving between the rows, Tommy made sure to look to the top of each tree for the missing cat. Pinky was city-raised and had never been exposed to trees before.

Tommy wasn't sure if the cat knew how to climb a tree and get back down. He had heard of cats getting stuck in the tops of trees, had even seen it happen on one of the news shows his father liked on watch on television.

Scanning the trees for Pinky, calling his name out loud, it wasn't long before he reached the end of the orchard. Here the forest began, a place of dense foliage, more spooky shadows, and wild animals.

The boy turned around and looked back across the orchard. He could no longer see his house, because it was hidden by the rows of apple trees. Not being able to see his house made him a little uncomfortable.

In the city he never went anywhere without his parents, or his sister, except maybe to school. And even then there had been people with him that were responsible for his safety. It was a strange feeling to be alone now, one he was not at all familiar with. A strange and exciting feeling.

Tommy licked his lips.

He should go back. His mother would be mad if she knew he was out exploring by himself. His father would be mad too, especially since he had given Tommy strict orders not to wander off by himself. But he wasn't wandering, not really. He was searching for his cat, and that was important. Besides, how could they get mad at him if he never left the backyard? His father had told him that the orchard and part of the forest now belonged to them, so technically it was part of their backyard. It was a very big backyard, true, but that wasn't his fault.

He turned his attention to the forest before him. The forest was dense and mysterious, thick with foliage and shadows. It was exciting and scary all at the same time, a place that was probably not safe for an eight-year-old boy to explore by himself. But then again it also wasn't a safe place for a city-raised housecat to explore. If Pinky had gone into the forest, then he was probably lost.

"I'll only go a little ways in," Tommy said, his voice sounding oddly strained. "Just a little ways and no more. Just far enough to look for Pinky."

His mind made up, Tommy entered the forest, plunging into a world unlike any he had ever experienced before. Oh sure, he had been in the woods before. Central Park had trees, and his father had once taken him to a state park in upstate New York, but in those forests there were concrete paths, water fountains, even public rest rooms. There were also lots of other people around. Here he was alone, completely by himself, with no sidewalks, bicycle racks, or public facilities. Here the forest grew wild and untamed, touched only by nature.

Looking around, he found a path, but it was narrow and winding, not at all like the paths he used to follow in Central Park. This path had been made by animals, perhaps rabbits, not by city workers in blue jumpsuits. Still it was a path, a trail to help him navigate the deep foliage of the forest in his pursuit of Pinky.

Tommy had been following the path for several minutes when he heard sounds of movement coming from the underbrush to his left. He stopped to listen to the sounds, but they stopped when he did.

A slight quiver of fear passed through him. He wondered what had made the noise, conjuring up images of great big furry things: bears, wolves, even lions. He didn't think there were any lions in Missouri; as far as he knew all the lions lived in Africa, except maybe for the ones in zoos. He was quite certain his father would have told him if there were lions walking around, but that didn't stop his imagination from thinking about them.

What he had heard was probably a rabbit and nothing more. Or a mouse. Even a tiny field mouse could sound pretty darn big when moving through the underbrush, although the noise he had heard hadn't sounded like the rustling of leaves. Instead it had sounded like whispering, as if someone were murmuring secrets behind his back.

Tommy strained his ears to hear the sound again, but all was quiet. Too quiet. Slowly he became aware that an uncanny silence surrounded him, as if a great hush had suddenly fallen over the forest.

Why is everything so quiet?

Despite being a city boy, he knew there should be sounds. Lots of sounds. The air should have been filled with the melodies of songbirds, the barking of squirrels, even the buzzing of bees and flies. Yet he heard none of those sounds. There was only the silence.

Looking up, he studied the branches above him, searching for wildlife. He found none. The branches were empty, the trees deserted. The forest surrounding him, at least what he could see of it, was completely barren of birds and animals.

Where had they gone? Had the birds and animals been chased away by hunters? Maybe there had been a fire, like in the Disney movie *Bambi,* and the creatures of the forest had fled in terror. He looked around, but didn't see any signs that there had ever been a forest fire. The foliage around him was green and vibrant, not black and burned like a forest touched by flames.

Maybe he had scared away the forest creatures. Perhaps they had seen him coming and were hiding, waiting for him to leave again. Maybe they were frightened of him, even though he didn't have a gun and wouldn't shoot anything if he did. The pigeons and squirrels in Central Park weren't frightened of people, but country animals might be different. You might have to leave food for them before they'd let a person see them. Tommy made a mental note to bring bread crumbs with him the next time he came into the forest. He wondered if birds preferred white or whole wheat.

As he stood there looking up, he again heard a strange whispering noise. It was the same noise he had heard a few minutes earlier. Again the sound conjured up images of things best not seen in a lonely forest, sending a nervous shiver down his back. The shiver turned to fear when he realized the sound was getting rapidly closer.

Tommy turned around, trying to see what was making the noise. He couldn't see anything, however, because there were too many bushes and trees in the way. Was it a rabbit he heard? A timid bunny in search of tasty clover to munch? Did rabbits make such sounds? Did they whisper?

He cocked his head and listened. Was it whispering he heard? It sounded like whispering, as if someone were speaking very softly and very fast. But if it was words he heard, then they were being spoken in a language he didn't understand. And whatever said the words had to be quite small, because the sound came from close to the ground.

Another mental image flashed into the boy's mind: that of a strange-looking man crawling through the brush on his belly, whispering strange words as he went. A lizard man, all green and scaly, with a long, sticky tongue for eating ants between the roots of trees. The image would have been funny any other time, but coming to him while he was alone in the forest made it downright frightening.

Whatever made the noise was approaching fast. Tommy's heart thudded loudly in his chest as he realized the whispering sound was coming toward him at a dead run. Something was racing at him, something he could not see. A person or animal that cast no footsteps, and caused no brush to rustle or twigs to snap. The only sound to be heard was the whispering. Just the whispering, and nothing more.

Deciding it was a good time to call off his search for Pinky, Tommy turned around and fled from the whispering sound. A startled cry escaped his lips as he ran down the narrow path, desperate to get free of the forest.

But the forest seemed an endless tunnel of green foliage and shadows. Overhead the trees joined hands, interlocking their branches to make it even darker than it had been only moments before. Somewhere above the leafy canopy the sun still shone in a bright blue sky, but the rays of that sun no longer reached where he ran.

He couldn't see what chased him, but he could hear it. Suddenly the whispering passed him on the left, and then on the right. There were at least two of them, maybe more, moving through the underbrush, passing him, racing ahead to . . .

Racing ahead to what?

He stopped, his heart pounding madly in his chest. His throat dry. Suddenly there was no more whispering. The noise had stopped when he did. But it hadn't gone away; Tommy was sure of that. Whatever had pursued him was now ahead of him, lying in wait for him. Though he could not see anything, he could feel eyes watching him. Angry eyes. Hungry eyes.

"Oh, no you don't."

Tommy was not to be so easily fooled. He approached slowly for a few more yards, then turned and started running at a right angle. The sudden explosion of sounds told him he was right: something had been waiting for him. But he had not fallen for the trap and the chase was on again.

Reaching the end of the forest, he raced out into the orchard. He turned, certain he would now be able to see whatever it was that chased him. But nothing was there.

Stopping, his side hurting from running so hard, he watched the edge of the forest but saw nothing. A few tense seconds passed and then he spotted two very distinct shadows slip from the forest and glide along the ground.

Not animals. Not raccoons, possums, rabbits, or even dogs. Nothing but a pair of shadows, almost invisible to the eyes. They darted out of the forest and raced to the first row of apple trees, disappearing behind the trees. Just shadows, but somehow Tommy knew they were something far more than what they seemed. Something evil and very, very dangerous.

Turning once again, he ran full speed toward the house. He didn't look back, dared not look back. He only ran, arms and legs pumping, tennis shoes tearing up the ground. He didn't know if the shadows were still following him, but he didn't dare stop to take a look. He fled past the apple trees and the old brown barn, making a beeline for the back door.

Chapter 21

Holly ran her fingers gently over the kitchen floor, feeling the texture of the tiles upon which were painted the mysterious faces. Painted? If the faces had been painted, she wanted to know what the artist had used. She had majored in art in college, had been a commercial artist for several years, and knew just about everything there was to know about pigments, oils, and acrylics. If the faces had been painted, she would have been able to feel it, yet she felt nothing. The tiles with the faces were as smooth as the rest of the floor.

Nor had a paint gun been used. During her college days in New York City she had supported herself by using various air guns to paint murals on tire covers, mailboxes, and the gas tanks of motorcycles. She had gotten quite good at it, working in the evenings and on weekends. Had a paint gun been used to create the faces on the kitchen floor she would have known.

Not with a brush, air gun, charcoal, pen and ink, pencil, or even crayon. Then how had the mysterious faces been created? She was completely baffled.

Determined to get to the bottom of the mystery, she stood up and crossed the room. Opening one of the cabinet drawers, she removed a butter knife. Returning to the center of the room, she knelt again on the floor and slowly scraped the blade of the knife over one of the faces in an attempt to remove it. The wax finish came off easily, but the ebony face remained.

It's under the wax.

She leaned back, staring at the image in awe. The faces couldn't have been painted by anyone sneaking into the house last night, because they were under the wax. Not unless someone had painted the faces and then poured a fresh coat of wax over them. But that was impossible, because the wax would not have hardened in time before the faces were discovered.

Just to be sure, she set the knife aside and then leaned forward until her face almost touched the tiles, sighting along the kitchen floor. From that angle, with the overhead lights shining off the tiles, she would have been able to tell if additional wax had been poured over the area where the faces were drawn. The new wax would have been shinier, perhaps even noticeably thicker than the wax that covered the rest of the tiles. But she could detect no difference, none at all. The wax covering the floor looked the same all over.

"I just don't get it," she said, straightening back up into a sitting position.

Despite what the sheriff had suggested, or what she and Mike had previously suspected, the faces could not have been painted or drawn by someone sneaking into the house. Nor were they the result of a busted water pipe, mold, mildew, or the product of faulty tiles or workmanship. So what did that leave? What could have made them?

The supernatural.

She almost laughed out loud. Like Mike, she too was

a skeptic when it came to things unexplainable. She did not believe in ghosts, UFOs, voodoo, witchcraft, or other such nonsense. Nor had she ever been a fan of shows such as *Sightings*, *Millennium*, or *The X-Files*. Never once had she the urge to pick up a tabloid newspaper to read about alien abductions, psychic predictions, or the ghost of Elvis.

Her parents, on the other hand, believed in the supernatural, especially her mother. Despite being a devout Baptist, Holly's mother believed ghosts were quite real, claiming to have seen a couple of them during her lifetime. She also believed the devil could possess a person's body, swearing that *The Exorcist* was based on actual events.

A few days after watching *The Exorcist* together, Holly had played a prank on her mother by popping a couple of Alka-Seltzer tablets into her mouth, just enough to foam like a mad dog, and then flopping around on her bed while shouting the names of the demons she had heard mentioned in the film. Her mother had not been amused.

Holly smiled, remembering the prank she had played. Her mother believed in the supernatural, even though there were no scientific facts to support it. Looking back down at the floor, her smile faded.

Here before her, in her own home, was something that could not be rationally explained by science, something beyond the realm of normal occurrences. The faces that kept mysteriously appearing on the yellow tiles of their kitchen floor were definitely not normal. Not normal at all.

Putting the butter knife back in the drawer, she left the kitchen and entered the library. Broken shards of light bulb still lay on the carpeting, but she made no

move to pick them up. The shattered pieces were a re-
minder that something had scared Megan half out of
her wits last night, even caused her to hurt herself, and
Holly was not ready to dismiss it by cleaning up the
mess. Looking at the pieces, she wondered if the sheriff
was right. Could a raccoon have gotten into the house
and removed the light bulb from the lamp?

It only took a moment of logical scrutiny to dismiss
the sheriff's theory as ludicrous. The lamp was tall and
slender, the bulb covered by a large shade. Not only
could the bulb not be reached easily, the lamp would
have tipped over had a raccoon attempted to climb it.

Nor had any of the doors or windows been left open
last night, so there was absolutely no way an animal
could have gotten inside, even an animal as smart as a
raccoon.

If it wasn't a raccoon, then it must have been a person. Someone had come into the library, probably while
they were sleeping, and removed the bulb and shattered
it. But why? Why take the bulb out and break it when it
would have been easier to just unplug the lamp?

Turning away from the lamp, she allowed her gaze to
travel along the shelf high on the wall. In addition to
breaking the light bulb, the intruder had also turned
each and every one of the kachina dolls around to face
the wall. Again, why? Why take time to turn the statues
around? Was it all part of some elaborate joke? If so,
who was the joker?

Megan.

She shook her head. Her daughter could have been
the one who removed the bulb from the lamp, could
even have been responsible for turning the kachina
statues around backwards, but she could not possibly
have put those faces on the kitchen floor. No way. No

how. Someone else was the culprit, but she had no idea who, or why they were doing it.

Holly thought about turning the kachinas back around to face the room, but decided against it. The truth was she liked the tiny wooden figures better with their backs to her. When they were turned around the right way, it always felt as if they were staring at her. Hundreds of tiny eyes, painted or drawn, or created from shells or tiny stones. It was enough to give her the creeps.

"Well, I know of one way to keep this joke from happening again."

Instead of turning the statues back around, she grabbed the stepladder from where it stood in the art studio, and a couple of empty cardboard boxes, and began packing the kachina statues away. Each and every last one of them. Now let someone try to play a prank on her and her family. She would see who got the last laugh.

The kachinas in the library filled three boxes, and two more boxes were used to pack away the statues in the living room. She taped the boxes closed and carried them one at a time into the basement, stacking them against the wall beneath the row of windows. After all of the kachinas had been removed from the library and living room, she carried an empty box downstairs and packed away the statues lining the shelf in the basement. She had just packed away the last figure when Tommy entered the house at a dead run.

"Mom! Mom!" he yelled, racing down the hallway.

Alarmed, Holly hurried up the basement stairs and into the kitchen. She caught up with her son halfway down the hallway.

"Tommy, what is it? What's wrong?"

Tommy stopped and turned around. His chest heaved and his eyes were wide with fright. "I was in the woods and something started chasing me. I don't know what it was, Mom, but it chased after me. I had to run all the way . . ."

"Whoa. Hold on a minute, mister." Bending over, she took him by the shoulders and held him at arm's length. "What do you mean you were in the woods?"

Tommy stopped speaking and swallowed hard, suddenly realizing he was in trouble. "I was looking for Pinky. I know I'm not supposed to go in the woods by myself, but I'm worried about him, Mom. He might be hurt, or sick, maybe even dying."

The boy's eyes clouded over with tears, and she knew this was not a good time to give him a scolding. "All right, we'll talk about that later. Right now I want to know what scared you. You said something was chasing you; what was it?"

"I don't know," he answered, tossing a glance behind him. "I couldn't see them."

Holly let out a silent sigh of relief. "It was probably just a rabbit moving through the underbrush. They can sound awfully loud."

He shook his head. "It wasn't a rabbit, Mom. I know what a rabbit sounds like, and they didn't sound like rabbits. They made a funny noise, like a whole bunch of people whispering all at once. They didn't look like rabbits either."

Holly was confused. "Tommy, you just said you didn't see what was chasing you."

"I didn't see them. Not really. I stopped in the orchard to see what it was, but there was nothing there. Just shadows."

"Shadows?"

He nodded. "Two of them. I saw them come out of the forest and run behind one of the apple trees. They were just shadows. Honest. I thought it was a rabbit too, but it wasn't. I waited and saw them. They were shadows, but they weren't animals."

"Shadows have to belong to something. You know that. Something has to get in the way of the sun to make a shadow."

"I know, Mom. I learned that in school. But these shadows didn't belong to nothing. They were just shadows, and they were chasing me."

Holly started to explain to her son that all shadows belonged to something, but she stopped cold remembering what had happened to Megan the previous evening. Her daughter said a shadow had chased her down the hallway. Not an animal, or even a person. Just a shadow, and nothing more.

"How big were these shadows?" she asked.

Tommy shrugged. "Not very big. Not really." He brought his hands up to chest level and held them apart about twelve inches. "About like that. Maybe bigger. I guess they were a little smaller than Pinky. I couldn't see them very well."

"Did they look like Pinky?"

He shook his head. "They didn't look like a cat, or a dog. They looked like . . ." He fumbled for the right words. "They looked sort of like people shadows, only they were shaped wrong. All squished together. And they were fast. Real fast."

"Tommy, where did you see these shadows last?"

"They were in the orchard, hiding behind one of the apple trees."

"Okay, you wait here. Get yourself a drink. Wash

your face. I'll go have a look out back. You stay inside now. Understand?"

Tommy nodded and wiped the sweat out of his eyes.

Holly left her son standing in the hallway and entered the kitchen. Crossing the room, she opened the back door and stepped outside. The sun was shining brightly, with only a few patchy clouds dotting the sky. She wondered if one of the clouds had drifted in front of the sun, creating the shadows Tommy had been so afraid of.

But Tommy had said the shadows chased him, and they had made a noise while in the woods. A whispering sound. A shadow caused by a passing cloud certainly couldn't do that.

Closing the door behind her, she crossed the backyard and entered the orchard. As she walked between the rows of fruit trees, she focused her attention on the patches of shadows near the base of the trees, places where a small animal or two might hide during the daytime. She was quite certain what her son had mistaken for squishy people shadows was in fact nothing more than a forest dweller of some kind. To a boy who had been raised in a city, a close encounter with an otter, groundhog, or even a muskrat could be a rather frightening experience.

As far as she knew, there were no dangerous animals in the surrounding forest. All of the bears and wolves had been driven from the area long before the house she now lived in was even built. She doubted if there were any foxes left either, although she wasn't at all sure that a fox would be dangerous. Except for a stray dog, she couldn't think of any woodland creature that might possibly give chase to her son, not unless it was rabid.

Holly stopped dead in her tracks. Raccoons, otters, and other small animals were normally timid. They would have turned and run from Tommy, unless they were infected with rabies. A rabid animal didn't act like it was supposed to act. It was bold, even in the daytime, often bravely approaching humans. It was also downright dangerous. The bite of a rabid animal could easily infect a human with rabies, a deadly disease. Had Tommy been bitten by such an animal, there would have been a series of extremely painful shots, administrated into the stomach; even then he could have died.

She looked around, nervously. Suddenly the orchard didn't look so safe. The trees and the shadows they cast offered dozens of places where a rabid animal could be hiding. Even a medium-sized raccoon could become a dangerous opponent when maddened by rabies, especially to an unarmed woman.

Glancing down, she suddenly realized how little the clothes she wore offered in the way of protection. Lightweight cotton shorts, a T-shirt, and slip-on shoes did not provide much defense if she should encounter a rabid animal. Nor did she have a weapon, not even a fingernail file.

As she looked down at her ill-suited apparel, Holly caught a glimpse of movement out of the corner of her eye. Two rows over from where she stood something had darted from one apple tree to the next. The movement had been swift and as fluid as water.

Startled, she turned in the direction of the movement, trying to see what it was that had darted into the shadows beneath the apple tree. Though she had only a brief glimpse, she suddenly had the distinct impression that whatever she had seen was now hiding behind the base of the tree. Watching her.

A chill swept over her, causing her arms to break out in goose bumps. Something was watching her, watching and waiting for her to look away again so it . . .

So it could what?

So it can get closer to me.

Holly stepped back and looked around for a weapon—a rock, a stick—something she could use to ward off an attack by a rabid animal. Though she had seen nothing more than a quick blur of movement, she was now quite certain that an animal of some kind lurked in the shadows beneath the apple tree. That particular apple tree was only about fifty yards away, not a great distance if the animal could move fast.

Unfortunately there were no weapons to be had in the orchard, nothing that could be swung or thrown. Nothing but apples. Keeping her gaze locked on the apple tree two rows over, she took a few steps backward and then squatted down to pick up a couple of apples that had fallen to the ground from the tree closest to her. They weren't much of a weapon, true, but a few well-thrown apples might deter the charge of a rabid raccoon or groundhog.

Holding two apples in her left hand, and another one in her right, she slowly walked forward. She wanted to get around to the other side of the apple tree to see if there really was something hiding there in the shadows. She moved past the first row of trees and approached the second. The tree where the mysterious animal had disappeared was only four trees away. Still she could see nothing. Whatever she had caught a glimpse of must be lying flush with the ground, as Pinky had often lain when stalking something.

Stalking? Was she being stalked? If so, then three

puny apples might not be much of a defense. She wondered if there were any bobcats in Missouri. There probably were, but she didn't think that what she had seen was as big as a bobcat. Of course she had never seen any bobcats in real life.

The apple tree was less than ten yards away now. Only thirty feet separated her from what might prove to be a rabid animal. Holly stopped, considering the situation.

If what she had seen was rabid, then why was it hiding in the shadows? Rabid animals did not normally fear humans.

She let out a sigh of relief. Whatever form of animal lurked beneath the tree might not be rabid, and it was probably more scared of her than she was of it. Holly opened her left hand and let two of the apples tumble to the ground, keeping only the one she held in her right hand. She felt foolish for allowing her fear to get the best of her. No doubt Mike would openly laugh at her when she told him what had happened. What hope did she have of becoming a country girl if she let the slightest movement spook her?

She had just taken another step toward the tree when she heard a strange hissing noise coming from behind her. The noise reminded her of the sounds made by certain reptiles. It also sounded like someone talking rapidly in a very low whisper.

Spinning around, she saw a second shadow slip beneath the tree directly behind her. Not a rabid raccoon, dog, or even a groundhog. Just a shadow, almost invisible to the eye. A small patch of smoky grayness and nothing more.

The movement was so fast she only caught a glimpse of it, but there was no doubt about what she had seen.

The shadow flowed like water across the open ground, its movement totally alien to anything she had seen before. It was like the shadow of a speeding car when viewed from inside that car, all twists and turns as it flashed across the ground.

A second hissing, whispering sound suddenly erupted from behind her. Holly turned, realizing that she had turned her back on the first shadow she had seen. That shadow had moved from its hiding place beneath the apple tree and was halfway to Holly when she turned. It was nothing more than a patch of darkness on the ground, a darkness that moved under its own power.

"No you don't!" Holly yelled, throwing the apple she held in her right hand. The apple struck the ground just in front of the shadow, causing it to veer off to the left. In the blink of an eye it was two rows over and moving away from her. She watched it disappear beneath one of the apple trees in that row.

Hardly believing what she had seen, she grabbed the other two apples off the ground and threw them at the tree closest to her. The first apple missed completely. The second struck the base of the tree with a thud. As the second apple hit the tree, another shadow shot out of the darkness and raced away from her.

There are two of them. Two of what? What in the hell are they?

Neither of the shadows ran very far. Instead they slipped into the darkness beneath one of the apple trees, disappearing from sight. From where she stood Holly could not see either of them, but she knew they were there. Watching her. Waiting.

Still doubting that what she had seen could possibly be real, trying to come up with a logical explanation for it, she grabbed several more apples off of the ground.

She expected the shadows to reappear when she turned her back to gather the apples, but they remained hidden. Nor did they show themselves when she started back to the house.

At the back door Holly paused, wondering about what she had just witnessed. Had she actually come in contact with something that could not be explained within the normal realm? Were the shadows supernatural, or had she just imagined the whole thing?

If what she had just witnessed did belong in the world of the supernatural, then there was someone she needed to call—a person who would listen to her story without laughing.

Holly studied the orchard for a few more minutes. Nothing seemed out of the ordinary. Again she wondered if her imagination had played a trick on her. Dropping the apples she had gathered, she opened the back door and went inside.

Locking the door, she went into the living room to check on Tommy. He was sitting on the sofa watching television. The eight-year-old had apparently recovered from his frightening adventure in the woods. Patting him on the head, she went back into the kitchen. She looked out the back door once more, saw nothing, and then lifted the kitchen telephone from its cradle. Having dialed a number set to memory, she waited for the phone at the opposite end to ring. After three rings a voice came on the line. Holly answered.

"Hello, Mom. It's me. We need to talk."

Chapter 22

Mike arrived home just in time for dinner. He had stayed longer than he planned at the library, then he had stopped by the hardware store to pick up a couple of extra chain locks for the front and back doors. He also purchased a dozen dowel rods; wedging one of the rods in each window track would prevent anyone from sliding it open from the outside.

Carrying the dowel rods and locks into the living room, he laid them on the coffee table. He planned to start on the windows and doors right after dinner. As he turned to leave, he noticed something was different about the room. It took a moment for it to dawn on him that all of the kachina statues were missing. The shelf where they had once stood was now completely bare.

"What the hell?"

He left the living room and entered the library. The statues were also missing from that room. In place of the kachinas several lit candles had been strategically placed about the room.

"Candles in the daytime?"

Leaving the library, he walked into the kitchen. Holly was just setting the plates and silverware on the table.

On the stove was a pot of spaghetti, and he could tell by the aroma in the air that she had also made fresh garlic bread.

"You're just in time to eat," she said, flashing him a quick smile. "How did it go at the library? Did your research turn up anything?"

"I came up with a few things," he answered, crossing the room to wash his hands in the sink.

"Oh? Like what?"

"It's rather complicated. I'll tell you after we eat." He turned the water off and grabbed a paper towel to dry his hands. "By the way, what happened to the kachina dolls?"

Holly set a cutting board in the center of the table, and then set the pot of spaghetti on top of that. "I packed them away in boxes. They're in the basement."

"All of them? Why?"

She turned to look at her husband. "Because they gave me the creeps. That's why. I was getting tired of walking into a room and having a hundred hideous statues stare at me. I'm also getting tired of having to turn them back around all of the time. Someone obviously thinks it's funny to turn the statues around backward. I don't. Therefore, I stopped all of the fun and games by putting the statues away. Let's see who gets the last laugh now."

Mike thought it over and then nodded. "I can't blame you there. That joke lost its humor the first time around. It's a pity we have to pack away the statues though, because I really like them. My grandmother had a pretty nice collection going, much nicer than any I've ever seen before."

Holly smiled. "If you want to play with your grandmother's toys you can always go down in the basement."

"That's all right. I don't like the statues that much." He smiled back at her. "So, what are you going to do with all that empty shelf space?"

"I'll think of something. If nothing else we'll put books on them."

Holly called the children down to dinner. Tommy came down first, but he was sent back upstairs to wash his hands. Megan appeared a minute or so later. Though she still favored her right foot a bit, the cut had already healed enough to allow her to go back to school the next day.

After dinner, Mike helped put away the leftovers and clean the dishes. Finished with that, he went out onto the front porch to smoke a cigarette and enjoy the weather. Holly and Tommy joined him a few minutes later. The worried expression on his son's face warned him that the boy was in some kind of trouble.

Mike told Tommy to sit down, then listened as the boy told about everything that had happened to him earlier in the day. Mike was less than thrilled to learn that his son had disobeyed him by going into the woods, but there was no sense getting upset before he had heard everything. As the story progressed, he was filled less with anger than he was with concern for Tommy's safety.

When his son told about being chased by shadows, a feeling of uneasiness settled deep inside Mike's stomach. It was the second time in two days that his children had told about being chased by shadowy creatures. He didn't think Tommy or Megan was making the shadows up; at least he couldn't imagine why they would do such a thing. Maybe the shadows had been imagined, real only to them, sparked by something they had both seen on television.

When Tommy finished his story, Mike said, "Now do you see why I don't want you going into the forest by yourself?"

The boy nodded.

"It's dangerous in those woods, especially for a young person. There's poisonous snakes, spiders, God knows what else. You could also get turned around and lost very easily. It happens all of the time. How would you like to get lost in the woods and not be able to find your way back? How would you like to spend the night out there by yourself, in the dark, with no food and water, and with lots of wild animals all around you? Would you like that?"

Tommy shook his head, his eyes starting to water.

"You're damn right you wouldn't like it. And do you know why? I'll tell you why: because there's things in that forest. Scary things. Things that would just love to eat an eight-year-old boy all up. Eat him up and spit out the bones. Spit them out all shiny and clean, white as your teeth. And then where would you be, all eaten up and dead? You wouldn't have a mommy or daddy then, no big sister to play with. You would be just a bunch of bones laying on the ground. That's what you would be."

Tommy was openly crying now. Mike looked from his son to Holly and saw the anger in her face. He had overdone it, deliberately frightening the boy half out of his wits, but he wanted to make sure Tommy never ventured into the woods by himself again.

Softening his voice, he reached out and patted his son on the head. "You don't have anything to worry about as long as you stay in the yard where it's safe. You understand? And you don't have anything to worry about if I take you into the woods, because scary things are afraid of me. That's because I'm pretty scary myself. Don't you think?"

Mike made a face, pushing his nose up and pulling down on his lower eyelids. Tommy laughed and blew snot out of his nose, which made him laugh all the harder.

"Now you can go back into the house. Watch television if you want. I won't punish you as long as you promise never to go into the forest by yourself again."

"I promise," Tommy said, wiping his nose with the back of his hand.

"Tommy, use a napkin!" Holly said, too late with the warning.

Mike gave the boy a pat on the butt and sent him on his way. Holly waited for the screen door to close before turning to her husband.

"What are you trying to do, scare him to death?" She didn't disguise the anger in her voice.

"Better a frightened child than a dead one," Mike replied. "The woods are dangerous for a boy of his age. He could have gotten lost, stepped on a copperhead, any number of things. I wanted to put a scare into him so he would think twice about wandering off by himself again."

"He was already frightened enough this afternoon. I doubt if he would even think of going into the woods again by himself. What you told him will probably just give him nightmares."

"A good nightmare may be just what he needs to kill the exploring lust."

"Easy for you to say," Holly said. "You don't have to get out of bed if he wakes up screaming. Besides, he wouldn't have wandered off if you'd told him his cat was dead."

Mike looked toward the screen door. "Shhh . . . he'll hear you."

"So what if he does? He has to find out sooner or later. We can't hide it from him forever."

Mike nodded. "You're right. But he doesn't have to find out tonight. Does he? I was planning on telling him in the next day or so, when I could break the news to him gently. Now would not be a good time to tell him."

She sat on the steps and looked at him. "What if what Tommy saw wasn't his imagination? What if the shadows he said he saw were real?"

Mike almost laughed. "What? I'm supposed to believe that a couple of shadows chased my son through an apple orchard? It sounds like a really bad science fiction story."

"What if I told you I saw them too?"

"You're not serious?"

"I'm dead derious," Holly replied, looking straight at him. "When Tommy came running into the house this afternoon, I went out into the orchard to see what had frightened him. At first I didn't see anything, but then I caught a glimpse of movement out of the corner of my left eye. Just a glimpse, something moving very fast, running low to the ground.

"I didn't get a good look at it, because it disappeared in the shadows beneath one of the apple trees. But I knew it was there, watching me."

"How did you know? Could you see its eyes?" Mike asked.

She shook her head. "No. I couldn't see it. Not even the eyes. But I knew it was there. This may sound funny, but I could tell it was watching me. I could feel it. Watching. Waiting. I couldn't see a damn thing, but it was there in the darkness. I stood there and watched for several minutes, then the second one showed up."

"There were two of them?"

Holly nodded. "The second one crept up behind me while I was watching the first one. I wouldn't have known it was there if I hadn't heard it. It made a funny sound: a strange hissing, whispering noise. I turned toward the noise and saw something dart beneath the apple tree closest to me. Got a good look at it, only there wasn't much to see. Just a dark shadow gliding over the ground, a shadow no bigger than a small dog."

"Maybe the shadow was caused by a cloud passing in front of the sun."

"I thought of that," she said, "but this was too dark to be a shadow caused by a cloud. And shadows don't whisper. Nor do they run away when you throw apples at them."

"You threw an apple at it?"

"When I turned to look at the second shadow, the first one ran at me. I heard it coming, that strange whispering sound as if it were talking. I turned and threw an apple at it, and the shadow changed directions and ran away from me. It disappeared beneath one of the trees two rows from where I was standing. I threw apples at the other shadow too, and it also ran away."

"You're my wife, and I love you dearly, but I must say that I'm finding this very hard to believe."

"You think I'm making this up?" Fire flashed in her eyes.

Mike held his hands in front of him, protectively. "No. No. Not at all. I believe you. At least I believe you saw something. Tommy and Megan probably saw something too. I'm just finding it hard to believe that it was a shadow and nothing more. There has to be a logical explanation for it: a trick of the lighting, a cloud, a buzzard soaring overhead. Something."

"The shadow that followed Megan was inside," Holly countered. "No clouds or buzzards."

"I know. I know." He nodded. "But there still has to be a rational explanation."

"Maybe. Maybe not," she said.

"What do you mean?"

"I spoke with my mother this afternoon, and she said the shadows might be spirits of some kind. Ghosts. She thinks something bad may have happened to them to keep them here. She also thinks they might be evil."

Mike laughed. "I can just see the headlines now: 'Evil Spirits Attack Family of Horror Writer'."

"Well, the shadows are real, because I saw them," Holly argued. "And what my mother said makes about as much sense as anything else I can think of. You know I don't believe in ghosts. Not really. But there has been some strange stuff going on since we moved in. And you said yourself there was a Civil War battle fought on the property."

"A small skirmish. Not a battle."

"Whatever. People died."

"And what does your mother suggest we do to get rid of these bothersome spirits?"

"She suggested I light a few candles and say a prayer."

"So it was her idea to light all the candles? I should have known. Doesn't she know that it isn't safe to burn candles in a wooden house, especially one as old as this?"

"I only lit a couple of candles, and only in the library. I made sure they were in the center of the room, well away from the curtains or anything else that might catch on fire. And I won't burn them all night, or when we're gone, just while we're here to keep an eye on them."

"So, have the candles helped?"

She shrugged. "I don't know. I guess it's too early to tell."

"Did you also tell your mother about the faces?"

She shook her head. "I think the shadows were enough to talk about for one day."

Holly stood up and brushed off the back of her shorts. "You coming in?"

"I'll be there in a few minutes. I just want to sit out here for a little while more."

She nodded and left him sitting on the porch. Mike had intended to tell his wife about the things he had learned at the public library, but after her story about the shadows he was almost afraid to mention the things Connie Widman had told him about his grandmother. Now was not a good time to bring up stories about boogers and hobgoblins, when half the family was already scared of shadows. Best not make things any worse than they already were.

He was reluctant to believe the shadows could be ghosts, hoping things would soon be explained logically. Still he was going to install the extra locks on the doors before going to bed, and place the dowel rods in the window tracks to prevent the windows from being opened from the outside.

Flipping his cigarette butt onto the grass, Mike stood up. He had a lot of work to do before going to bed.

That night he was twice awakened from a sound sleep by strange noises coming from downstairs. But when he investigated the noises, he found nothing amiss. The house was quiet, but it was a strange silence that greeted him as he descended the stairs. It was as if he had interrupted someone, and they were now watching him from the darkness. There was no one there, of course, but he could not shake the feeling that something was going on behind his back. Though he found no one in any of the rooms he searched, Mike had the unshakable feeling he was not alone.

He was halfway up the stairs when an idea struck him. Turning around, he went back downstairs and entered Holly's art studio. Flipping on the light, he searched the shelves until he found what he was looking for. He removed a roll of transparent tape, a spool of black thread, and a pair of scissors. Turning off the light, he left the room.

Mike went back upstairs, taking the steps slowly to keep from making any noise. Once on the second floor, he tiptoed down the hallway until he came to Megan's room.

His daughter had gone to bed hours earlier and should have been sound asleep. Still, just to be on the safe side, he paused in front of the door listening carefully.

Standing there in the hallway he felt like a sneak. He also felt badly, for what he was about to do was to question his daughter's honesty. If she found out, it would surely drive a wedge into their relationship, a relationship that had been forged on his trusting Megan and respecting her privacy.

Since he heard no sounds coming from Megan's room, he was certain his daughter was sleeping. She rarely stayed up late on school nights, despite having her parents' permission to do so if she wanted.

Stepping to the side of the door, Mike knelt down and placed the items he had taken from the art room on the carpet. Holding the spool of black thread in his left hand, he cut a piece long enough to reach across the bottom of the doorway. He fastened the thread in place on both sides of the doorway with a couple strips of tape, making sure to keep the thread about six inches off the floor.

Standing up, he stepped back to admire his handiwork. The thread was very thin and would break easily if anyone bumped it while entering or exiting the doorway. He wouldn't have used anything thicker, because he didn't want to trip Megan. He only wanted to know if she left her room anytime during the night. Nor would Megan know a trap had been set, because the thread was all but invisible in the darkness. He would remove it in the morning, prior to getting her up for school.

You are truly a rotten bastard.

He probably was, but Mike was determined to find out who was responsible for the strange occurrences that had happened in the past couple of days. If Megan was sneaking out of her room at night to turn the kachina dolls around backwards, or to paint strange faces on the kitchen floor, then he wanted to know about it. Secretly setting up a video camera would probably have been even better, but he didn't own such a camera, so a piece of thread and a little American ingenuity would have to do.

Gathering up the tape, scissors, and thread, he crept down the hall and repeated the process at Tommy's door. He really didn't think his son had anything to do with what was going on, but he just wanted to be sure. With the black thread booby-trap, any doubts about his son's innocence would be eliminated. Finished with Tommy's door, he gathered up the items and went back to bed.

It was nearly dawn when Mike awoke again. At first he was just content to lie there, staring up at the ceiling, knowing he didn't have to get up for another hour, but then he remembered the traps he had set. He needed to remove the thread and tape before Holly or any of the kids saw the booby-traps. He didn't need to get into an argument about why he no longer trusted his children.

Climbing out of bed, he quietly slipped out of his pajamas and into lightweight pants, slip-on shoes, and a knit shirt. Holly stirred once while he was dressing, but did not fully wake up. Tiptoeing across the room, he opened the door and stepped out into the hallway.

No noise came from either of the children's rooms, so he was certain they were still asleep. Had they been up, a stereo would have been playing. Tommy liked to play one of his Disney tapes while getting dressed for school. Megan preferred listening to the top 40 on the rock-and-roll station.

Checking Tommy's room first, Mike found the thin black thread still in place, unbroken. His son had not left his room during the night. The same held true for Megan's room; the thread across her doorway was also unbroken.

Satisfied his children had not been sneaking around during the night, he removed the booby-traps and then went downstairs. He had almost an hour to kill before he had to wake the kids up, so he decided to make a pot of coffee and get in a little reading. Rubbing sleep from his eyes, he entered the kitchen and flipped on the light.

"Son of a bitch . . ." He stopped in the doorway, frozen by the sight that lay before him. The faces were still on the tile floor, staring up at him, but something new had been added since his last trip downstairs. All of the cabinet doors now stood open and a row of pots and pans sat on the floor, circling the kitchen table like Indians around a covered wagon.

Mike was furious. Someone had entered their house while he slept, opened the cabinets, and carefully arranged the pots and pans. But how in the hell had they gotten in?

He hurried across the room and checked the door leading to the basement. The door was locked with a deadbolt and two different chain locks, including the new chain lock he had just installed last night. There was no way someone could have gotten in through the basement door.

The same held true for the back door. It was still locked and could not be opened from outside. He checked the window over the kitchen sink, but found it securely fastened. The dowel rod he had wedged in the window's track was also still in place. No way someone could have opened the window from outside without breaking the glass.

Leaving the kitchen, he checked the front door and all of the other windows. They were all securely shut and locked, the chains and dowel rods still in place. Mike stopped and looked around. There was no way someone could have gotten into the house, not unless they could walk through solid walls.

Walking back into the kitchen, he stared at the pots and pans on the floor for a moment, then began to gather them up and put them back where they belonged. He didn't want Holly and the children to see the display, because he was afraid it would frighten them.

Hell, this is starting to frighten me.

He paused, a pot in each hand. Someone had been getting into their house, but nothing had ever been taken. Obviously robbery was not a motive. And except for Pinky's death, and the broken bear kachina, nothing in the house had ever been damaged. Instead faces had been drawn on the floor, statues turned around backwards, and pots and pans set out in a circle. Why? Was someone playing an elaborate joke at their expense? Or was someone going to great lengths in an attempt to frighten them?

The thought brought a chill to his heart. At first he had suspected the strange events occurring in the past few days had been a joke of some kind, but now it seemed clear that someone was deliberately trying to scare them. But why?

A smile unfolded on his face. Suddenly, everything began to make perfect sense. He and his family had not been well received by the good people of Braddock. Some were jealous that he was a successful author; others—like the good reverend and his followers—resented the kind of books he wrote. Some might even associate him with his grandmother, labeling him as equally loony. Whatever the reason, someone didn't want him around and was willing to do anything to get him and his family to leave.

"Well, it's not going to work," Mike said aloud. "I will not be scared off by a bunch of half-witted hillbillies."

He set the pans down on the counter. "This has gone on long enough. If the sheriff's office won't do anything, then I will. This time it's war."

Chapter 23

Mike had not intended to tell Holly about what he had found in the kitchen that morning, but she sensed something was bothering him. After seeing the kids off for school, she confronted him as they sat at the kitchen table. Rather than make up a story, he decided to tell her the truth. She was quite upset when he told her how he had found the pots and pans circling the table. What she said next took him by surprise.

"Mike, I think we should leave," Holly said, getting up to pour herself another cup of coffee. She filled her cup, added cream and sugar, then sat back down at the table.

"Leave?" Mike asked, as if he hadn't heard what she said.

She nodded. "Something is going on here. Something strange. I don't know what it is, but I'm frightened. If this place isn't haunted, then someone is getting into our house. There's no telling what this person might do. I'm worried about the children. What if he gets tired of playing games and decides to hurt one of them? I think we should call the police . . ."

Mike shook his head. "It won't do any good to call

the cops. The sheriff won't believe us; he'll think I did this to get free publicity."

"Then let's get out of here. Right now. Today. We'll check into a hotel for a day or two. We'll be safe there."

"Run away?" He frowned. "Let them win? Show them that we're scared?"

"I am scared," Holly said. "And so are the children. There's a lot of things going on around here that can't be explained."

"Well, I'm not scared," he said, standing up to get himself his third cup of coffee for the day. He didn't really want another cup, he just felt the need to get up and move around. Holly's words were making him angry, and it was better to move about the kitchen than verbally lash out at her.

"No. I'm not scared. Not anymore. I'm angry instead, and I refuse to be driven out of my own home. We wouldn't let this happen back in New York, and I'm not going to let it happen here."

"New York was different," she argued. "We had friends there, and the police would listen to us. Here we have no friends, no one to help us."

"We have each other, and that's all we've ever needed before."

"It's different this time, Mike."

He shook his head. "I'm not leaving. Not yet. Not without putting up a fight first. If you and the kids want to leave, then go ahead. I'm staying."

Holly looked at him for a moment in silence, then said, "I'm not leaving without you."

He walked back over to the table and sat down. "Look, so far our little intruder had done nothing to indicate that he, or she, is dangerous—"

"What about Pinky? You don't think someone who

murders helpless cats, and then cuts out their eyes, is dangerous?"

"If Pinky was murdered," he replied. "I'm not sure anymore. Maybe the sheriff was right, maybe Pinky died of natural causes and something chewed on him after he was already dead."

"You don't believe that."

"I'm not sure what to believe anymore. All I know is that, outside of Pinky, it looks like someone is playing a joke on us. Why, I'm not sure. Maybe they're trying to frighten us. The local kids around here used to do things to frighten my grandmother all the time.

"The things they did to my grandmother were mean-spirited, true, but they only did it because they knew it would frighten the old woman. Frighten her, yes, but they never did anything that could cause her any harm, never even broke a window.

"And to tell you the truth, I think my grandmother brought it on herself."

"How could you say such a thing?" Holly asked. "No one asks to be harassed, or scared."

"I don't think there was any problem until she started calling the sheriff's department on a regular basis reporting prowlers, little green men, and things that go bump in the night. Braddock is a small town, which means it's nearly impossible to keep a secret. It probably wasn't long before word got out that Vivian Martin wasn't right in the head."

"So?"

"So, you know how it is with teenage boys. They're all pumped up on hormones, just looking for a little excitement. Probably wasn't much to do back then—still isn't. Harassing an old woman, especially one deemed mentally unbalanced, would seem like just the thing to kill a little boredom. By then my grandmother had called the sheriff's office so many times nothing she said would be believed, so there was no way any of the teenagers would get into trouble."

"But why us? Why are we being harassed?"

"Terrorizing Vivian Martin has been a tradition around here, passed on from one generation to the next. Sneaking onto this property to do mischief is probably like sneaking into the local haunted houses in other towns: something done on a dare.

"And then there's the flip side."

"What's that?" she asked.

"Maybe the former sheriff was delighted that someone was harassing my grandmother. Maybe he got tried of her calling about the faces on the floor."

"Your grandmother has been dead for over six months. Why is someone still painting these damn things on the floor?"

He shrugged. "Hard to tell. Maybe whoever is doing it finds it hard to break the habit. Or maybe this is his way of expressing himself."

"Expressing himself?" She laughed. "Can't he just go tag his name on the side of a building like all the other hoodlums?"

"Seems that would be a lot easier than sneaking in here at night to do this, less chance of getting caught. But maybe sneaking into this house is the fun part. Maybe doing something like this without getting caught is what excites him."

He pulled a cigarette out of the pack lying on the table and lit it. "Or maybe this has something to do with me."

"With you?"

He nodded. "Everyone around here knows that

Vivian Martin was my grandmother. Maybe they think I'm just as crazy in the head as she was. Those who didn't like her probably don't like me either. Bloodline is taken seriously around here. Old feuds are handed down from one generation to another.

"There's also the jealousy factor to consider. I'm a successful author. Maybe one of the locals resents that fact. And then there's your friend, the reverend . . ."

"Watch that 'my friend' stuff," she warned.

Mike smiled. "I imagine the good reverend would be rather pleased if we cleared out of the neighborhood. Maybe one of his congregation is behind the faces and the statues being moved."

"It wouldn't surprise me," Holly replied.

"That's why I refuse to tuck my tail between my legs and run away," he said. "These people may have gotten away with doing things to my grandmother, but they are not going to get away with doing the same things to me. I'm going to find out who's behind all of the pranks and why."

"And the shadows?"

"Hard telling what you guys saw, or what caused them. But shadows can't hurt you. Can they? If they do turn out to be earthbound spirits, like your mother said they were, then we'll just call in an exorcist or two and whisk them back to the spirit world."

"Just where are you going to find an exorcist around here?" she teased.

"Easy." Mike grinned. "In the yellow pages."

He pushed his chair back from the table. "I want to go into town, see if I can find a home security system I can install myself. An alarm system should make our local artist think twice about sketching any more faces. You want to ride along?"

Holly shook her head. "I have plenty to do around here to keep me busy."

He frowned. "You sure you're going to be okay by yourself?"

"I'll be fine. I don't think anyone would be dumb enough to come around in the daytime." She smiled. "And Tommy's baseball bat is in the hallway closet in case they are."

He smiled back. "A wooden baseball bat planted firmly in the crotch should take the creative drive out of even the most dedicated artist."

Mike gave her a kiss on the cheek, grabbed the keys to the van, and headed out the front door. He made sure Holly locked the door after him, before he climbed into the van and started down the road.

He wasn't sure where he could buy an alarm system for the house. The town of Braddock didn't have a Radio Shack, or a Sears. Nor did they have an electronics store. But they did have a Western Auto, which sold everything from auto parts to fishing gear. If anyplace in town would have what he was looking for, then that was probably his best bet.

The Western Auto store was located on Main Street, directly across from Fran's Gift Shop. Leaving the van parked at the curb, Mike grabbed his checkbook out of the glovebox and entered the store.

He had never been in a Western Auto before, and was surprised to find it stocked with a wide variety of items. There were power tools, lawn mowers, radios, televisions, and various items for camping and hunting. They also had electrical generators, which would come in handy in case any bad storms blew through the area. He had heard that severe thunderstorms, and even tornadoes, were not uncommon in central Missouri during the springtime.

Turning away from the generators, he noticed several small satellite dish antennas on display with the televisions. He had promised to check on getting a satellite system, since there was no cable service available where they lived. He would have preferred a big satellite dish mounted in the backyard, but a smaller system would probably bring in just as many stations. Bigger was not always better when it came to modern technology and electronics.

Pocketing a couple of brochures about the satellite systems, he started searching the store for alarm systems. Unfortunately, the Western Auto store seemed to have everything but the one item he was looking for. Disappointed, Mike started to leave, but stopped when he spotted a row of glass cases in the hunting section. The cases were stocked with firearms and ammunition.

He suddenly remembered what Otto Strumberg had told him the day before, how no one broke into country homes because they knew the farmers had guns. Maybe what he needed wasn't an alarm system after all. Maybe he needed something a little louder, and with a bit more bite.

Living in New York City, he had never owned a firearm. For one thing handguns were illegal; for another he never felt the need to own such a weapon. Still, he was no stranger when it came to guns. On several occasions he had needed to research various handguns to make a particular novel he was writing that much more realistic. Readers could be the world's worst critics, willing to sacrifice a writer if he or she should get such details wrong. Not wanting to end up in a proverbial bonfire, he made sure such minor details in his book were always accurate.

Approaching the glass cases, he waited until one of the employees offered to help him. He didn't wait long.

"Can I help you, sir?" The employee's name was Rob. He was tall and thin, about Mike's age, with wavy brown hair and a thick mustache. He also had a very friendly smile, as if he was actually interested in assisting his customers.

"Yes . . . Rob," Mike said, glancing quickly at the man's name tag. "I'm interested in purchasing a handgun."

"Do you have anything particular in mind?"

"I'm pretty much open to suggestions," Mike replied, "but I would prefer an automatic."

Rob grinned. "Well then, let me show you some of our most popular models."

Rob unlocked the case and showed Mike several different makes and models of handguns, explaining the features of each. It turned out Rob was an avid gun enthusiast, and had competed in shooting competitions throughout the nation, so he really knew his firearms.

Ten minutes later Mike decided on a Glock model 23, a .40-caliber pistol with a ten-round clip. Pulling out his credit card, he was a little dismayed when Rob pushed a stack of paperwork across the counter for him to fill out.

"Jeez, it looks like I'm signing my life away."

Rob grinned. "Your life, your house, the wife, and the kids. It wasn't always this bad, but the bureaucrats in Washington gave into the demands of the anti-gun liberals. The dummies don't realize all they're doing is keeping firearms out of the hands of lawful citizens. The criminals will still have guns, no matter what the government says or does to stop them."

Mike picked up the paperwork and flipped through it. "Oh well, I guess it's a necessary evil. No use complaining."

"You won't have anything to worry about unless you've been to prison, or have been arrested for a felony."

"Nope. Never been to prison. And have never been arrested for a felony." Mike grinned. "That's because I've never been caught."

Rob laughed, and handed Mike a pen. "There's also a seven-day waiting period."

"A what?" Mike asked, shocked.

"A seven-day waiting period," the clerk repeated. "I'm sorry. I thought you knew. The law went into effect several years ago; more bureaucratic nonsense."

"No. I didn't know. I've only been living here a short time." Mike glanced down at the paperwork he held. "You mean I can't have the gun today?"

"No, sir," Rob said, apologetically. "State law makes you wait seven days. It's a cooling off period, in case you decide you don't really want a gun."

"I'm not going to change my mind," Mike argued. "I want the gun."

Rob nodded. "I would love to let you have the gun today, but it's not up to me. The government passed the law to keep people from buying handguns when they're angry."

"I'm not angry." Not yet, Mike thought. "What if I pay cash?"

"Won't make any difference."

"What if I throw in a twenty-dollar tip?"

Rob laughed. "I'd be a happy man, but you'll still have to wait seven days. You can stop by then to pick up the gun, provided your background check doesn't turn up anything against you."

Mike was frustrated. "Look, let me give it to you straight: I want to purchase a handgun for protection. Someone has been breaking into my house at night, and I'm worried about the safety of my family. I have a wife and kids."

"I would love to help, but there's nothing I can do . . . not unless you want to buy a rifle, or a shotgun."

"I'd still have to wait seven days."

Rob shook his head. "The waiting period only applies to handguns. Don't ask me why, that's just the way it is. I guess the bigwigs in Washington don't realize that you can kill someone just as easily with a rifle as you can with a pistol."

Relief surged through Mike. "You mean I can buy a shotgun, or a rifle, and take it home with me today?"

The salesman smiled. "Gift-wrapped if you like."

Mike spent the next twenty minutes examining several different rifles and shotguns, finally deciding on a Winchester 1200, pump-action, 12-gauge riot gun. The shotgun held five rounds in the magazine, and another round in the chamber, yet with a barrel measuring only 18¼ inches it was very compact. He also purchased several boxes of .00 buck magnum shells, as well as a box of .08 shot, plus a padded carrying case.

Having paid for his purchases, he carried the shotgun out to the van and laid it on the backseat. For some reason he felt different now that he was a gun owner. Stronger. More in control. As he headed for home, he almost hoped someone would break into the house again.

He looked back at the box lying on the seat behind him and smiled. "Have I got a surprise for you."

Chapter 24

Holly watched Mike pull out of the driveway and start down Sawmill Road, before turning away from the front window. She was alone in a house that now seemed terribly sinister, even in the daylight. Knowing her husband wouldn't be back for several hours, she looked around for something to occupy her time and keep her mind off of troubling thoughts. She thought about cleaning, but she had done enough cleaning in the past week to last a lifetime. Instead, she turned her attention to the vast collection of books lining the shelves in the library.

She wanted something to read that would put her in a better frame of mind; something light, a romantic comedy maybe. But the shelves were crowded with the novels her husband had written, which she had already read and which were anything but cheery and light. There were also the countless reference books Mike had used to research his novels, many of which were as scary as the fiction he wrote. Even the books Mike's grandmother had collected were not the type to be read while alone in a house where shadows slithered about, and faces appeared on the kitchen floor. Most of those were books of witchcraft, myths, legends, and folklore.

About to give up in her quest for something interesting to read, Holly discovered an old scrapbook that had belonged to Mike's grandmother. Glued to several pages of the scrapbook were newspaper articles about a local sawmill burning to the ground. The articles got her interest, because she knew a sawmill had once been located on the very property they now owned.

Carrying the scrapbook into the kitchen, she made herself a cup of instant coffee and sat down at the table to read the articles. The articles, yellowed with age, were clipped from the July 14, 1938, and July 21, 1938, issues of the *Braddock Tribune*.

According to the newspaper, a fire had broken out in the sawmill shortly after sunset on the night of July 12. The flames had spread quickly, igniting several large piles of sawdust and wood shavings. The flames from those fires had been so intense they had consumed four storage buildings, three sheds, the foreman's office, and all the cut wood stored on the property.

Flames had shot high into the night sky, visible as far as ten miles away. The glow from the flames had been seen in the town of Braddock, and the fire department had dispatched several units to fight the blaze. Unfortunately, by the time the fire department had arrived, it was already too late. Everything had been lost in the fire, but luckily no one had been killed.

Holly sipped her coffee and read the second article, trying to imagine a fire of such magnitude raging across the property they now owned. As far as she knew there was no evidence left that the sawmill had ever existed. There might have been the foundation of a building or two, hidden somewhere beneath the weeds and tall grass, but if there was, she had not seen it.

Accompanying the second article were three grainy photos of men who had worked in the sawmill prior to its burning to the ground. In the photos nearly all of the men posed with rifles.

Holly studied the pictures, wondering why on earth the men had elected to pose with rifles. For that matter, why had they brought the rifles to work with them? She wasn't all that familiar with the job requirements of a sawmill worker, but she didn't think it was necessary to carry a firearm.

So why the guns? Did the workers spend their lunch hour and break times shooting at targets and old tin cans? Was the sawmill so infested with rodents that it was necessary to shoot as many as possible to keep them under control? Or was the surrounding country-side filled with dangerous animals: wolves, bears, packs of mongrel dogs? Back in those days a lot more people walked to and from work. The sawmill was out in the country, so maybe the rifles were necessary to ensure the safety of the workers.

Another thought popped into her head. Maybe the threat wasn't from animals but from men. Maybe robbers waited along the deserted roads to hijack any unsuspecting victim that might happen by. She didn't know much about the history of the area, but maybe the men who worked at the sawmill had lived in dangerous times. She wondered if a fight between union and nonunion workers had anything to do with the need for guns, but only for a moment. It was doubtful if a union had had much influence over workers in rural Missouri. If unions even existed back then.

Holly leaned closer and studied the pictures. Even

though the photos were quite old, she couldn't help but notice the haunted looks in the eyes of the men. The looks could have been because they had just fought off a tremendous fire, had just risked their lives. They could also have been because, without the sawmill, the men were now out of a job and faced an uncertain future for themselves and their families.

Still the fire was completely out by the time the photos were taken, the men had survived, and for that they should have been grateful. Most people at such a time would not have given much thought to their sudden unemployment; they would have been happy just to be alive. While it was definitely not a time to pass around a champagne bottle, there should have been at least a smile or two on the faces of the men in the photos.

But there wasn't a smile. Not a one. All of the men were solemn, staring straight at the cameraman. And they all looked afraid. Each and every one of them.

What were they afraid of? The danger had passed.

The next dozen or so pages in the scrapbook were blank, but there were a couple more articles about the sawmill fire on the page after that. Holly read the first of those articles, finding it pretty much a repeat of what she had already read. But what was said halfway into the next article stopped her cold, causing her to go back and reread the article again from the beginning.

In the last newspaper article, an unnamed source was quoted as saying the fire had been deliberately set by employees to defend against a horde of mysterious creatures that had attacked them shortly after sunset. The creatures were not described very well, other than that "they were darker than the night around them, and about the size of a large housecat."

Deliberately set? Creatures darker than the night?

The owners of the sawmill contradicted the unnamed source, denying that the fire had been deliberately set. They said the fire was the result of a spark landing in a pile of sawdust. They also denied the existence of any mysterious creatures, claiming such reports were only local legends and folklore and nothing more.

Holly flipped back to the pictures, staring at the men in the photos. Six years ago she had been commissioned to do a painting for a VA hospital in New Jersey. As part of the research that went into the painting, she had studied hundreds of photographs of soldiers taken before, during, and after combat. She wanted to capture the essence of what it was like to be a soldier during times of war. From her research she learned what pain and sorrow looked like; she also learned the face of fear. The soldiers whose pictures she had studied had stared at the camera with tight-jawed expressions and glassy eyes.

That same expression of fear adorned the faces of the men in the pictures she now looked upon. No matter what the owners of the sawmill said, the men in the photos had encountered something which had literally scared the hell out of them. Holly doubted if the fear was due to the fire, because apparently the workers had not set aside their guns to battle the blaze. Fire could not be fought with loaded rifles, but maybe they believed something else could.

She turned back to the last article and reread it once more. The reporter who had written it finished the article by referring to local legends dating back hundreds of years, to the time of the first white settlers in the area, stories about hobgoblins and boogers.

Boogers.

Holly's mouth dropped open in surprise. She remembered the lines from the poem the children on the bus had sung about Vivian Martin—the poem they had used to tease Megan and Tommy:

> *Old lady Martin has gray hair*
> *Claims to see them everywhere*
> *Boogers in the attic, boogers in the walls*
> *Boogers under the bed nine feet tall . . .*

Apparently, Mike's grandmother had been terrified of boogers in her house. The house sat on the same spot of land where the sawmill had once stood. Vivian Martin had been scared of boogers—so had the sawmill workers.

Creatures darker than the night . . . about the size of a large housecat. Darker than night. Creatures. Shadows.

A chill suddenly passed through her body. Megan had seen something in the hallway, and in the library. She described it as a shadow darker than the rest of the darkness. Tommy had seen something in the forest, two of them. They had chased him into the orchard. Two creatures the size of a small dog. He had described them as shadows and nothing more.

She herself had seen them. They had attempted to sneak up on her, patches of blackness that glided over the ground like ebony water, moving from one apple tree to the other, hiding in the shadows beneath the trees, blending in with the darkness. She had seen them, yet what she saw was only two swiftly moving patches of darkness, about the size of a groundhog . . . about the size of a large housecat. She had seen them clearly, yet there was nothing to be seen. Not really. Just shadows.

"Boogers." She said the word aloud, as if sounding it might help her to understand what she and the children had seen.

Despite being someone who wrote imaginative works of fiction, often drawing from elements of the supernatural and the occult, Mike remained quite a skeptic when it came to things which could not be explained in a logical manner. He had dismissed what she and the children had seen as nothing more than the mistaken identity of common forest creatures, or an overactive imagination. He would not even consider, not even for a moment, that they had encountered something supernatural.

The skin at her temples pulled tight. According to the unnamed source in the newspaper article, the workers at the sawmill had been attacked by mysterious creatures. They had been unable to fend off the attack, so they had set fire to the place.

Unable to fend off the creatures, and the workers all had rifles!

That was another thing. The workers must have been under threat of attack for some time or they would not have been carrying rifles. If one worker saw a booger, then nothing would have been said. It would have been dismissed as a trick of the eyes, or a figment of the imagination. A couple more sightings would have led to a few whispered words, maybe a couple of chuckles. More sightings would have led to rumors, maybe latenight discussions over beers. Still that would not have been enough to warrant carrying guns, not unless someone had gotten hurt. Even then the supervisors and owners would not have let the employees carry guns to work unless they too had seen the shadows and felt there was a need to arm themselves.

They must have known. They must have all known. The situation must have gotten so bad that every man working the sawmill knew about the boogers, and felt there was a need to carry a gun while at work. The fire had been the final result. They had torched the sawmill in an attempt to defend themselves. It must have worked, because no one had been killed or injured that night. Nor had any more reports of boogers been filed.

Not until Vivian Martin built her house on the original site of the sawmill. She knew about the boogers, must have been fighting them off for years. The poor old woman had tried to get help from the sheriff's office, but no one would believe her. They considered her mentally unbalanced. A nutcase. Their solution to her problem was to come out and paint everything a hideous dark green. Paint over the faces.

Again a chill seeped through Holly's body. She scooted her chair back from the table and looked down at the floor beneath her feet. The mysterious faces stared up at her from the yellow tiles. Like the creatures that had attacked the sawmill workers, the faces could not be explained. But Holly now knew what the faces were, at least she thought she did.

The faces had appeared about the same time as the shadows, so there had to be a connection between them. The shadows were faceless, but the images in the floor were not. With a shudder of revulsion, Holly looked at the faces etched on her kitchen floor and knew she was gazing upon the faces of hobgoblins, the faces of boogers.

They're coming up through the floor.

Up through the kitchen floor, and through the walls, and out of the woods. Maybe even through the ceiling. The same demons that had plagued the men who worked the sawmill so many years ago, had plagued Mike's grandmother, were now plaguing Holly and her family.

"We've got to get out of here."

Holly stood up and started to leave the kitchen, but stopped and sat back down. She and Tommy had encountered the creatures during the daylight, but they had avoided the direct light by moving from shadow to shadow. That meant the creatures were probably nocturnal, and there was no need to worry about them until it got dark.

She wondered how Vivian Martin had survived so many years facing something so dangerous. What did the old woman know about the boogers that no one else did? Holly thought about the vast collection of books on the supernatural Mike's grandmother had acquired. Had she found a spell, or a charm, something that would work against the creatures? Apparently she had, otherwise she would have probably been driven from her home years ago.

She had started to go into the library to search through Vivian Martin's collection of books, when her gaze swept across the names of the men in one of the photos. The name of the young man standing to the far right seemed vaguely familiar. Holly was certain she had heard it somewhere before, but just couldn't remember where. She thought about it for a moment, and suddenly she remembered.

The name of the man in the photo was Sam Tochi. It was also the name of the crazy old Indian who had approached her in the parking lot outside of the grocery store. Were they the same man?

If it was the same man, then how had he gotten so mentally unbalanced? Was it something he had seen at the sawmill that made him crazy? Had his encounter with mysterious, shadowy creatures pushed him over the edge?

As Holly stared at the photo, she remembered the brief but bizarre conversation she had with the old man:

"What do I want? What do I want?" the old man repeated, mocking her. *"The question is what do they want?"*

"Who?" Holly asked.

"The boogers, that's who," he answered. *"What do they want? What do they always want? That's the question. It is. It is.*

"You'll see. You'll see," he said. *"You'll find out the question, but not the answer. Just ask Sam Tochi. He knows. Sam knows all about the boogers, but they won't believe me. Nope. Nope. But you'll see. You will. You have their house."*

"I have their house," Holly said quietly.

Holly felt a sick feeling in the pit of her stomach. The old Indian had been trying to warn her, but she dismissed it as nothing more than the mad ravings of a nutcase. He knew about the boogers, knew she and her family had just moved into a house where the sawmill had once stood. He was trying to warn her, but she had failed to grasp the message. But maybe it wasn't too late to do something about it.

Crossing the room, she grabbed the phone book off of the counter and began flipping through the residential listings. She didn't expect to find what she was looking for, but it was there. Sam Tochi's name, address, and phone number were listed in the book.

She grabbed the telephone and started to dial the number, but changed her mind and hung up. She hadn't been too cordial to Mr. Tochi the first time they met, threatening him with a cucumber, so it would probably be best to go see him in person. She didn't

think the old man was dangerous, just a little unbalanced. Besides, what she had to ask him was best done
face to face rather than over the phone.

But what about Mike? He'd have a fit if she told him
she was going to go talk to a crazy old man about hobgoblins and boogers. He'd absolutely forbid her to go.
She didn't even want to tell him about what she had
just read in the newspaper articles. Not yet anyway.

"So, I'll tell him I went shopping."

Her mind made up, Holly carefully removed one of
the articles about the fire from the scrapbook and
placed it in her purse. She then looked through the
phone book to see if there was a taxi company in the
town of Braddock. There was. She dialed the number
listed and requested a taxi to take her to Braddock and
back. The dispatcher took her name and address, and
promised he would have a cab pick her up in the next
twenty minutes. She thanked the dispatcher and hung
up the phone.

Grabbing her purse and house keys, Holly went out
on the front porch to wait for her ride. Her next stop
was the home of a crazy man.

Chapter 25

Sam Tochi lived in a weather-beaten, faded green house a few blocks south of the grocery store. The house sat at the end of Clara Avenue, fronted by a yard overgrown with weeds and cluttered with the rusting remains of several lawn mowers and an old pickup truck.

The taxi pulled to a stop in front of the house, the driver turning around to give Holly a questioning look. "Lady, are you sure you have the right address?"

Holly nodded. "702 Clara Avenue. That's what it said in the phone book. This is the place."

"But old Sam lives here."

Again Holly nodded. "Sam Tochi. That's who I came to see."

The driver's look went from questioning to that of surprise. "You came to see Sam? You're kidding. Right? That old Indian is crazy."

She favored the driver with a smile, then opened the door. "Maybe he's not as crazy as everyone thinks. Please wait for me; this shouldn't take long."

The driver nodded. "Anything you say. It's your money."

Holly followed a cobblestone walk up to the front door. She pushed the doorbell's button, but she didn't hear any sound from the inside and figured the bell wasn't working. Resorting to knocking, she rapped several times on the wooden door then stepped back to see if anyone was home. A few moments later the door opened a few inches and Sam Tochi eyed her suspiciously.

"Go away, Bahanna. Leave me alone!" he yelled, slamming the door on her.

Holly jumped back as the door slammed in her face. The gruffness of the old Indian startled her, making her wonder if it really was a wise decision to visit him on her own. She thought about getting back in the taxi and leaving, but decided against it. Something strange was going on at her house, something that could mean danger to her family. Sam Tochi might know the answers to a few of her questions; maybe he could even help her out. She was not leaving until she spoke to him.

Taking a deep breath, she stepped up to the door and knocked again.

Sam must have been standing just on the other side of the door, waiting for her to leave, because he yelled as soon as she knocked. "Go away, I said. I'm not buying anything!"

"I'm not selling anything!" Holly shouted back.

"I'm not filling out any forms either!"

"I'm not a salesman," she said, raising her voice to be heard through the door. "Nor do I have any forms to fill out. I only want to talk with you."

There was a moment of silence, then Sam asked, "Are you from the city? I don't want to talk to you if you're from the city."

She almost smiled. "No. I'm not from the city either."

"I still don't want to talk to you. Go away!"

Holly knocked on the door again, but there was no answer. The old Indian was obviously ignoring her, and he was probably not going to open the door again. Frustrated, she turned around and walked back down the walk to the waiting taxi.

"That didn't go very well," the driver said as she climbed back into the cab.

"Not at all," Holly said, closing the door.

"Where to now?"

"Back home, I guess. I've apparently wasted my time here."

"I told you that old man was crazy. I've given him rides a couple of times, when his truck wasn't running. Thank God, I didn't have to do it often."

They had just reached the end of the street when Holly remembered the newspaper article in her purse. If Sam Tochi wouldn't open the door for her, then perhaps what she needed was a letter of introduction.

"Wait. I've changed my mind," she said, leaning forward in the seat. "I want to go back."

The taxi driver looked at her in his rearview mirror. "What? Are you serious?"

"I'm serious," she assured him. "Turn around. I want to go back and try again."

The driver muttered something under his breath, and then turned the taxi around. "You're lucky this is one of my slow days, otherwise you would be walking right now."

Holly put on one of her sweetest smiles to make him feel better. "I really appreciate this. I promise I won't be long."

The driver brought the taxi to a stop and switched off the engine in front of Sam Tochi's house. "Take your time."

Getting out of the taxi, Holly again walked up to the house and knocked on the front door. When there was no answer, she removed the newspaper clipping from her purse and slipped it under the door. Knocking again, she said, "Please, Mr. Tochi, I need to talk with you. It's very important. My name is Holly Anthony. You probably don't remember me, but you spoke with me last week at the supermarket—in the parking lot. My husband and I live in Vivian Martin's old house. I saw your name in that newspaper article, about the fire at the sawmill, and I wanted to talk with you—"

The door inched open again. Sam stared at her for a moment, apparently trying to remember her. "I spoke to you? When was this? I don't remember you."

"Last week. In the Kroger parking lot."

"What day?"

"Er, Tuesday. I think."

He looked at her a moment, then shrugged. "Maybe I did. Maybe I didn't. I don't remember Tuesday. I ran out of my medicine that day. I don't remember much when I run out of my medicine. Sometimes I don't even remember my name.

"You said you live in Vivian Martin's old house?"

Holly nodded. "My husband is her grandson."

The old man squinted his eyes and cocked his head slightly to the side. "I remember you now," he said and nodded. "I knew you would come."

He opened the door wider and invited her in. Holly glanced back at the waiting taxi and then stepped across the threshold, wondering if she wasn't doing something foolish. Sam closed and locked the door, and then led her into the living room. The room was small, crowded with two large leather sofas, a reclining chair, a battered coffee table, and several bookcases.

Holly took the room and furniture in with a glance, her gaze locking on the collection of kachina dolls crowding the bookcases. There must have been hundreds, if not thousands, of the wooden statues, in all sizes, shapes, and colors. Some of the statues only measured an inch or so in height, while others were at least three feet tall. The taller statues stood in a row along the wall next to the bookcases. Several more of the taller statues sat atop the television set, and in the center of the coffee table.

Sam motioned for her to sit on one of the sofas while he took a seat in the reclining chair. Holly sat down on the smallest of the two sofas, but her gaze remained locked on the collection of statues.

"Keeps 'em out," Sam whispered, laying the newspaper article on his lap. He removed a pipe from the ashtray beside his chair and lit it with a butane lighter.

Holly hadn't heard what he said. "Excuse me?"

Sam put down the lighter and puffed on his pipe. "I said it keeps them out."

"Keeps what out?" she asked, eyeing the dolls.

Sam lowered his voice and looked around, as though afraid of being overheard. "Boogers. The statues keep the boogers out. But you know that. You live in Vivian Martin's house. She has kachinas too. I know she has some, because she got them from me."

"The kachina dolls in our house came from you?"

His head bobbed up and down. "I gave them to her. Told her they would keep her safe."

"I don't understand," she said.

Sam leaned back in his chair. "Most people do not understand, even when they see the truth. Nor do they believe. But I believe. I understand. I saw the truth a long time ago. Saw it when I was just a boy living on the

Hopi reservation. Saw it at the village of Hoteville, on Third Mesa. The truth was in our songs, our stories, and in our dances.

"But the Bahannas, the white people, could not see the truth. They were blind to the way of the spirits. They came to our land, built their missions, and then said our ceremonies and dances were evil. Vulgar. They took me away from my parents when I was still young, forcing me to go to the white man's school in Phoenix. There they cut my hair and told me it was wrong to speak my own language. Said it was wrong to be a Hopi.

"They took the truth away from me and I became like they were. I turned my back on the ways of my people, living as a white man would live. I left the reservation and traveled about, looking for work. I came here to live, and again I saw the truth."

"At the sawmill," Holly said.

Sam leaned forward and stared at her for a moment, then nodded. "At the sawmill. That was a long time ago. Too long. Most people around here don't even know about that old mill."

"Vivian Martin has several articles about the fire in a scrapbook."

Sam picked up the newspaper clipping Holly had slipped under the door. He looked at the picture and smiled. "I forgot all about this picture. It was very nice of Vivian to keep it for so long. I was only a teenager them. Still strong. Not old and sick like I am now. And I had many lady friends. They used to cook for me, wash my clothes . . ."

Holly was afraid the old man was about to get off the subject, and she gently steered him back. "You used to work for the sawmill when you were young. Tell me what happened. How did the fire start? And why did you carry guns to work?"

"You said you read the articles. Did it not tell you how the fire got started?"

Holly knew Sam was being coy with her. Testing her. "I read what they said in the newspapers, but now I want to hear what really happened."

Sam laughed. "I am just an old man. An Indian. Most of the people in this town think I'm crazy. They think my head is filled with old stories. Legends of my people. What makes you think I know the truth?"

"It's a chance I'm willing to take."

He laughed again. "Okay, I will tell you what happened. What I saw. I may have forgotten a few things during my lifetime—might even have forgotten a lot of things—but I will never forget working at that sawmill, or what happened the night of the fire. But it is a long story, especially the way I tell it. I had better make us something to drink first. I have coffee and iced tea, or whisky if you would like something stronger."

"Coffee would be fine," Holly said. She wasn't really thirsty, but she thought to refuse would offend the old man.

Sam nodded and started to get up, but suddenly he inhaled air sharply and sat back down. He placed both hands on the sides of his head and began to tremble, as if he were having a seizure of some kind.

"What is it? What's wrong?" Holly asked, panicked. She jumped up and hurried to the old man, but stopped short of touching him. She didn't know what was wrong, nor did she know what to do for him. She had started to look for a telephone to dial an ambulance, when Sam stopped shaking.

"Are you all right?" she asked.

Sam slowly lowered his hands. There were tears in his eyes. "Yes. I am okay now." He nodded, then looked up at her. "Sorry. I did not mean to frighten you."

Holly let out her breath. "You had me concerned. I almost called an ambulance."

"There is nothing they could have done."

"Why? What's wrong?"

"I have a brain tumor," he answered, some of the life going out of his voice. "It is only the size of a peanut, but it is getting bigger all of the time."

"Dear God. Can't they operate?"

He shook his head. "Not where it is located. And I won't let them give me chemotherapy. At my age the radiation will kill me faster than the tumor. No. There is not much anyone can do, except give me medicine for the pain.

"As long as I take my medicine it is not so bad, just a few spells like the one I just had. But if I don't take my medicine the pain is very strong. That is what happened last Tuesday. I ran out of medicine and the pain was so bad I did not know who I was, or where I was going. That is why I did not remember you at first. I did not know if I had talked with you, or if it was just something I imagined."

"What about your people?" Holly asked. "Indians are known for their traditional healing methods. Isn't there a herb someone can give you, or a ceremony they can do?"

"It is too late for such things." Sam smiled. "Now, about those coffees."

He started to stand up, but Holly put her hand on his shoulder and stopped him. "You rest. I'll get it," she said. "Just tell me where everything is."

Sam didn't try to argue. He was obviously too weak from the attack he'd just had. Instructed where to find everything, Holly returned to the living room a few minutes later carrying two cups of instant coffee. She set one cup on the table next to Sam's chair and took the other with her to the sofa.

She set the cup of coffee on the table before her. "Tell me about what happened at the sawmill."

Sam took a sip of coffee, then began telling her about the things that had happened at the Hudson County Sawmill over sixty years ago. He took his time, pausing now and then to sip his coffee. As his story progressed, Holly felt a chill settle deep in the pit of her stomach.

Sam was only fourteen when he went to work for the sawmill. He had been working at the mill for a little over two years when the boogers first appeared. No one was sure exactly what they were, or where they had come from. The area had always been rich in stories about strange creatures lurking in the deep words, and about hobgoblins, but nobody ever paid much attention to them. They were tales told around late-night campfires by old men who wanted to scare the little kids, but the stories dated all the way back to when the Osage Indians lived in the area.

Sam suspected the boogers had started showing up around the sawmill because the forest was being chopped down for lumber. Maybe something else had brought them. Anyway, at first there were only a couple of sightings: someone reporting seeing something dart behind a stack of lumber, or a sawdust pile. Those early sightings had been dismissed as imagination, or someone's eyes playing tricks on him.

As the sightings continued, they were credited to raccoons and weasels, though no animals were ever caught anywhere near the sawmill. But then the first of the faces appeared on the floor of the foreman's shack. Everyone thought the face was a joke, drawn by one of the workers. It got a big laugh from everyone until the other faces appeared.

As the number of faces increased, so did the number of shadow sightings. The workers started getting spooked, and pretty soon everyone was talking about ghosts and haints, bringing up tall tales and old legends. A couple of men got scared so bad they up and quit. That caused a lot of laughter among the others. The laughter soon died out when the boogers started attacking.

The first man to get attacked was Carl Weinmeyer. Old Carl was always sneaking off to have himself a drink when nobody was looking. You were not supposed to drink on the job, but Carl just couldn't help himself. He had been drinking for so long that he wasn't a very good worker unless he was half-drunk.

One night Carl had gone off to get a nip from the flask he always carried, hiding behind one of the wood piles where it was too dark to be seen by anyone. He was careful not to be seen, because if he got caught by the supervisor he would have been fired. He had just taken himself a little sip of whiskey when he spotted something moving in the darkness. He thought it was a possum at first, but when he looked closer he saw there was nothing there. Just a shadow. According to Carl, this shadow slipped around behind him and grabbed onto his leg. No sooner had it done that then two more shadows rushed at him.

Carl tried to break free of the thing grabbing hold of his leg, but it was real strong. The next thing he knew he was on the ground and there were things all over him. He could feel them holding him, but when he tried to pull one off there was nothing there. Carl had been drinking that night but he wasn't drunk, and he swore he could see something holding him but he couldn't grab it. His hands passed right through the thing.

And these shadows had teeth, and claws. They almost ripped him to shreds before he was able to get free and run for help. A couple of the other workers, including Sam, grabbed lanterns and searched for the creatures that had attacked Carl, but didn't find anything.

Carl's story about being attacked by shadows might not have been believed, except that it happened to another man two nights later. Happened to two more men the following week. By that time everyone knew that something strange was going on at the sawmill, so they started carrying guns. Made sure they didn't go off by themselves, not even to use the bathroom, unless they had someone else with them.

As the weeks went by, however, more and more boogers were spotted. It was like they were coming out of the ground. And that's exactly what was happening.

On the night of the fire a crack had formed in the floor of the foreman's cabin. The foreman himself was in the cabin when a black mass spilled out of the crack. The mass was hundreds of shadows pouring out of the ground like oil.

The workers were terrified, knowing they couldn't fight the things. Guns were useless, as were fists, feet, and knives. The only things the boogers seemed to be afraid of were bright lights and fire. Sam supposed they didn't like anything bright, because they were creatures of darkness. The boogers were as one with the darkness and the night; in the light they basically ceased to be.

Despite what the newspapers said, it was the foreman who ordered the sawmill to be burned. He even started the first fire himself. The fire did what it was supposed to do, driving the boogers back to wherever they came from.

Finding himself out of a job, Sam packed a bag and returned home to the Hopi reservation. He went back to Hoteville, its narrow streets and adobe houses the same reddish brown color as the barren landscape surrounding it. He lived with his parents, helping them to grow corn, beans, and other vegetables on their tiny plot of land at the base of Third Mesa.

Turning his back on what the white missionaries had taught him at the boarding school in Phoenix, he once again embraced the spiritual beliefs of the Hopi—a world of ceremonies and dances, where kachinas brought blessings from faraway mountains, and Masauwu, the god of fire and guardian of death, walked the night.

In the Puwa-Kiki, the secret cave places, Sam left prayer sticks of carved and painted cottonwood, decorated with strips of colored leather and eagle feathers. Speaking to the spirit of the rattlesnake, he offered gifts of tobacco and sacred cornmeal as he prayed for rain so the crops of his people would grow.

In the underground kivas he became reacquainted with the songs, dances, and stories of the Hopi, including the creation story which tells how the first people had climbed up through a hollow reed from the underground world, emerging through an opening in the earth known as the Sipapuni. That opening was believed to be located at the bottom of the Grand Canyon, but its passageway was now closed to all but the kachinas and the spirits of the dead returning to the underworld. In every kiva a small hole is dug in the center of the ground to represent the Sipapuni. It is placed there so the Hopi people will remember the underground world from which they came, and the spirits and creatures they left behind.

According to the ancient Hopi legends, the first humans had climbed up from the darkness of the lower levels to emerge into the light of the fourth level, the level which we all live upon today.

Sam held up his hand, displaying three fingers. "Count them . . . one, two, three. Three levels below us. There are many kinds of creatures living on those levels, living in the darkness.

"I told the elders of my village about what I had seen at the sawmill. They said maybe the boogers were from one of the lower levels, trying to get into our world. Maybe they were tired of living in the darkness and wanted to take our world away from us. Perhaps they have found a second Sipapuni to climb through. They are evil things. Things we do not want for neighbors."

"Are they spirits?" Holly asked.

"Yes and no," answered Sam. "They are like spirits, because they are not of flesh and blood like us. The world the boogers live in, the world the Hopi believe we all came from, is like a spirit land. It is the place our ancestors came from, and it is the place we go to when we die. But there are other things living there besides spirits."

Holly shook her head. "I don't understand."

Sam shrugged. "It is hard for me to find the right word to explain the beliefs of my people to an outsider. Let's just say that the boogers are something my ancestors left behind in the old world, something that very much wants to be here with us."

"But why only my house?" Holly asked. "Why aren't they everywhere?"

The old man tapped the ashes from his pipe into the ashtray, then set his pipe aside. "I think the sawmill must have been built over a second Sipapuni. It was probably once closed, but over the years the boogers have been pushing and prying at it, trying to force it open so they too can come into our world. I think they opened it a little bit, but the fire at the sawmill caused them to shut it again. When I moved back here from the reservation, I went to look for the opening, but someone had built a house where the sawmill once stood."

"Vivian Martin," Holly said.

He nodded. "She was the first one brave enough to build a house in that area. Everyone else had heard the stories and stayed away. Now those stories have been forgotten by all but a few."

"What about the faces on our kitchen floor?" asked Holly. "What are they?"

Sam smiled. "That is a booger looking at you from the world below ours. But there is no reason to be afraid. Even if the boogers open the doorway, the kachinas will keep them from getting through. One or two might come, but they are not dangerous unless there are many. As long as you have the kachinas you have nothing to worry about. The little statues are guardians. Protectors. They will move if there is any danger."

"The kachinas move?" Holly asked, astonished.

Sam nodded. "That is how you can tell if the boogers are coming; the kachinas will turn to face them. It is like they are turning to face an enemy. The kachinas are strong medicine. Very powerful. Very sacred."

Holly felt a sick feeling in her stomach. "But I took the statues down."

"You did what?" Sam asked, nearly jumping out of his chair.

"I took them off the shelves and packed them away in boxes. All of them. Even the wooden masks. I didn't like them staring at me all of the time. It gave me the creeps. I also thought someone was playing a trick on us, turning the statues around to scare us."

"Your kachinas have been moving?"

Holly nodded. "But we thought someone was sneaking into the house and doing it."

"Which way are the statues turning?"

"They kept turning to face the walls."

"How many statues are turning? One? Two?"

"All of them," Holly answered.

Sam looked around the room nervously. "Not good. Not good at all. The kachinas are strong medicine. The boogers do not like the little statues. They will not come when the kachinas are watching."

"How was I supposed to know that?"

Sam clicked his tongue and shook his head. "Did Vivian not tell you? Maybe she told your husband? Maybe she sent a letter?"

"No. Yes. I'm not sure. Maybe in a letter. Long ago. But we thought she was crazy."

"Crazy? Crazy? Everyone in this town is crazy. But not Vivian. Not her. She's seen. She believed."

"But I didn't know that. Nobody bothered to tell me."

"Not good," Sam said. "Not good at all. All of the kachinas moving means a lot of boogers are coming. Maybe even a whole army of them. The way the kachinas are facing tells you which way the boogers are coming from. The kachinas have turned around backwards; that means the evil ones are coming through the walls."

Sam snatched up his pipe, but didn't bother to refill it. "You took the masks down too? Those masks were also medicine items, made to ward off evil. They were made by the Cherokees hundreds of years ago, passed down from one medicine man to the next."

"I'm sorry. I made a mistake. I didn't know."

"You made a big mistake."

Holly stood up. She wasn't sure how much of Sam Tochi's story she believed, but the old Indian was making her very nervous. She was thinking about her children, and wanted to get back to the house. "I've got to go home. I'll put the statues and masks back where they belong. All of them. I promise."

Sam looked at her, fear etched upon his wrinkled face. "It may be too late."

Chapter 26

"**Y**ou bought a what?" Holly stood in the center of the living room, her arms folded tightly across her chest. She had had every intention of unpacking the kachinas and putting them back on the shelf, just to be on the safe side, but the sight that greeted her when she returned home made her forget all about the little wooden statues.

"I bought a shotgun," Mike answered, laying the box containing the 12-gauge on the sofa.

"Are you out of your mind?" she asked. "What in the hell did you buy that for?"

"For protection." He opened the box and removed the shotgun, holding it up for her to see. "It's a Winchester 1200 riot gun. Holds five rounds in the magazine and another one in the chamber."

She looked at him as if he had lost his mind. "Protection from what? Bears? Elephants?"

"Protection from whoever is sneaking in here at night."

"Why not buy a cannon? Or a couple of landmines?" She shook her head, obviously angry. "You said you were going into town to see about buying an alarm system. Not that."

"I did look for an alarm system, but the store didn't have any."

"So you decided to buy a gun instead?"

"It seemed like the logical choice," he replied.

"Logical by whose standards?"

"Look, a lot of people living in the country own guns; it's a way of life with them. That's why there's so few robberies and break-ins. A thief wouldn't dare bother one of the farmers around here, because he would get his butt shot off."

"And just who told you this little bit of country trivia?"

"Otto Strumberg."

"Who?"

"Otto Strumberg. He owns a farm just down the road. I stopped by and spoke with him for a few minutes yesterday when I was on my way to the library. He says there's no crime in this area, because the bad guys know the farmers own firearms. I told him about the trouble we were having, and he suggested that I get myself a gun."

"Oh, he did, did he?"

Mike nodded. "Otto told me to take the gun out back and shoot it off, put in a little target practice. He said word would get around that I was a gun owner and no one would dare come around at night to bother us."

"Remind me to send a note to dear Otto thanking him for his advice," she said, sarcastically.

"When you think about it, Otto's suggestion makes sense."

"Your grandmother owned a gun and it didn't help

her," Holly snapped. "What are you planning on doing? Shooting a few more holes in the walls?"

"No. I'm more of a shoot-up-the-ceiling sort of guy," Mike joked. His wife was not amused.

"What about the children? It's not safe having a loaded gun in the house with the kids."

"I won't load it unless I'm planning on using it."

"It still won't be safe. You know how Tommy likes to get into your things."

As if on cue, they both heard the front door open. Glancing at her watch, Holly realized the children were already home from school. "Put that thing away," she said.

Rather than argue, Mike placed the shotgun back in its cardboard box and closed the lid. They heard footsteps, voices, and then their daughter appeared in the doorway.

"Hello," Megan said. "What are you doing in here?"

"Just talking." Holly flashed her a smile. "How was school?"

"Boring as usual." She spotted the box lying on the sofa. "What's that?"

Holly glared at Mike. "Oh, your father went out and bought himself a gun."

"Oh," Megan said, obviously not the least bit interested in the contents of the box. "I'm going to go upstairs and listen to some music."

"Do you have any homework?" Holly asked.

"No. I finished it all in school." Megan stepped back out of the doorway and disappeared. She had just left when Tommy entered the living room. The boy was holding a glass of Kool-Aid and clutching an oatmeal cookie in his left hand.

"Hi, Mom. Hi, Dad. I'm home. Boy, you should have

been at school today. There was a fight on the playground between two kids. I don't know who they were, because they were both bigger. It was pretty neat. One of the kids shoved the other to the ground, and—" He stopped talking when he spotted the box lying on the sofa. "What's that?"

Again Mike received a dirty look from his wife. He ignored the look and answered his son's question. "It's a shotgun."

"Really? Wow! Can I see it?"

Removing the shotgun from its box, he held it up for his son to see. "Don't you ever touch this, Tommy. It's not for children. Do you understand?"

Tommy nodded, his gaze riveted on the gun in his father's hands. "Wow. Wait until I tell Jeff Parker about this. Jeff says he owns a .22, but this is even better. Wait until I tell him we own a shotgun."

"Whoa, hold on a minute," Mike said, stopping his son. He didn't dare look in Holly's direction. "*We* do not own a shotgun. *I* own a shotgun. Do you understand?"

The boy looked disappointed. "Can I shoot it with you?"

Mike shook his head. "I'm afraid not. A shotgun is a little too powerful. Maybe when you're bigger."

"How much bigger?" Tommy asked. "I'm growing pretty fast."

Mike smiled. "You're not growing that fast."

"Next week? Will I be big enough next week?"

"You won't even be big enough next year. I'll tell you when you're big enough, but it won't be for a long time. Until then, you are not to touch this shotgun. Do you understand?"

Tommy nodded reluctantly. "But can I touch it now,

just this once? Just this once and never again? It won't be much of a story to tell Jeff tomorrow if I never even touched it. Can I please touch it? Just once?"

Mike knew he was getting himself deeper into trouble with Holly, but he also remembered what it was like to be an excited little boy. "Okay, you can touch it. But just this once and then no more. Deal?"

"It's a deal." He set his cookie and glass of Kool-Aid down on the coffee table. "Thanks, Dad."

Mike held the gun out for Tommy to touch. The boy ran his fingers down the wooden stock and touched the metal barrel. With the touching came a dozen questions and comments.

"Wow, it's really big up close. Is this real wood? It looks heavy. Is it heavy? Is this where the bullets go? Can I see the bullets, Dad? What kind of gun is this again?"

Mike fielded the questions, then put the shotgun back in its box. "Okay, that's it. Touching time is over. Now you take your cookie and drink back into the kitchen. You mother wouldn't like it if you left crumbs all over the place."

"Okay, I will. Thanks, Dad, for letting me touch your shotgun."

He waited for Tommy to leave the room, then turned to his wife. "See? He touched it once. He's happy. He won't touch it again without my permission."

"How can you be so sure? You know how boys are."

"Tommy's a good kid. He'll leave the gun alone. Besides, it won't much matter, because I'm not going to leave it loaded."

Holly threw her hands up in exasperation. "I just don't understand what's gotten into you. How could you buy such a thing?"

"I bought it to protect you and the kids. And I bought it to protect this house and the things we own. They may have been able to frighten my grandmother, but they are not going to frighten me. Not as long as I have this for protection.

"Now, if you'll excuse me, I'm going to go make a little noise."

"What are you going to do?" she asked.

"I'm going to try out this gun, fire a few rounds, get the feel of it. Having a shotgun won't do me much good if I don't know how to use it."

"What are you going to shoot at?"

"Oh, I don't know. Tin cans. Old records." He grinned. "Maybe even a shadow or two."

"That's not funny."

His grin faded. "Sorry. I couldn't resist. I'll probably set up a target in the apple orchard. I just want to make some noise, let anybody know who might be listening that the Anthony family is no longer putting up with shit from anyone."

Holly looked at the gun and frowned. "Just make sure you go *way* out in the apple orchard, and aim away from the house. I don't want anyone getting shot."

"I'm not stupid. I have no intention of aiming toward the house. Even if I did, a shotgun doesn't have much range. That's why I picked this gun instead of a rifle."

"Whatever," she said, still annoyed that he had purchased any kind of firearm at all. "Just make sure Tommy doesn't follow you."

"He went upstairs. I'll slip out the front door." Transferring the shotgun to the padded carrying case, Mike grabbed the box of .08 shells and started to leave the living room. He stopped in the doorway and turned back to his wife. "By the way, where did you go today?"

"What do you mean?" Holly asked, still angry about the shotgun. "How do you know I went anywhere?"

"I passed a taxi on Sawmill Road when I was coming home. Since we don't have any neighbors on this road, I figured you might have gone somewhere."

Holly nodded. "I took a ride into town. I just got back before you did."

"Shopping?" he asked.

"No. I went to see Sam Tochi."

Mike gave her a funny look. "The old Indian? What on earth did you go see him for? And how did you even know where he lived?"

Holly crossed the room and lifted her purse from the coffee table. Removing her cigarettes from the purse, she turned back to face Mike. "His address was in the phone book. I went to see him because everyone says he's an expert on local history. I thought maybe he might know something about the strange things that have been going on here."

Mike chuckled. "Everyone also says that old man is crazy in the head."

"He may not be as crazy as people think."

"Why? What did he tell you?"

She lit a cigarette then told Mike about her visit with Sam Tochi. He listened without talking, shaking his head when she finished telling her story.

"That old man is a nutcase." Mike laughed. "Surely you don't believe anything he had to say. Do you?"

Holly's jaw muscles clenched. "A lot of things he said made sense. Why shouldn't I believe him?"

Not waiting for an answer, she left the room and entered the library, grabbing Vivian Martin's scrapbook off the shelf. Returning to the living room, she opened the scrapbook to the newspaper clippings about the sawmill.

"Here. Read these, and then tell me there isn't something strange going on around here."

Mike set the shotgun and box of shells on the coffee table, and then took the scrapbook from her. Holly sat on the sofa, waiting for him to read the articles. He read the first two and started to hand the book back to her, but she pointed out that there were more articles in the back.

"So?" Mike said, looking up from the book. "It sounds like the reporter who wrote the last article was prone to repeating gossip and local lore. He would make a great tabloid writer."

Holly opened her purse and took out the newspaper article she had shown Sam Tochi. "Look at this picture, the one on the bottom. Look at the names of the men in that picture. Sam Tochi was one of the men in the photo. He used to work at the sawmill. He was there the night the fire was set. He said everything in that last article was true: the workers were attacked by shadowy creatures. Some of the men got hurt pretty badly."

"Working in a sawmill is a dangerous job," Mike said. "Someone falls down, gets hurt, and then blames it on a shadow. Probably used that excuse to keep from getting fired for being clumsy. Or because they were drunk at the time."

"Then how do you explain why the men were carrying guns. Sam said they carried them for protection against the boogers."

Mike laughed. "If they were certain evil shadows were attacking them, then they would have known guns would not be of any help. They probably took guns to work with them to shoot rats."

He picked up the shotgun and shells. "That crazy Indian is probably the source for all the stories about spooky shadows. I bet he makes up the stories, and then gets rich selling his magical kachinas to anyone foolish enough to believe him. No doubt he made a fortune off my grandmother."

"Then how do you explain the kachinas turning around by themselves?"

"By themselves? We actually haven't seen them turning. Have we? Sam probably pays some teenager to sneak in here at night and turn the statues. Probably figures if he scares us he'll be able to sell a few more kachinas."

"You have an answer for everything, don't you?" she said.

"Pretty much," he nodded.

Holly was not amused. "What about the kids? What about me? We all saw the shadows."

Mike smiled. "No doubt you saw something, or you think you saw something. I still say there has to be a logical explanation for everything that is going on around here."

"You had better hope you're right," Holly said, standing up. "Because if anything happens to the children I'm going to stick that shotgun up your butt."

Mike thought about making a comment, but decided to let the conversation end with his wife having the last word. Instead he left the living room, stopping by the kitchen to fish an empty milk carton out of the trash.

Carrying the protective gun case containing the Winchester in his right hand, and the empty milk carton and box of shells in his left, he left the house by way of the front door and circled around to the apple orchard. He was almost to the forest before he decided he was far enough away from the house to safely shoot the shotgun.

He placed the milk carton near the base of an apple tree, then walked about fifty feet away and set the protective case down on the ground. Mike flipped the latches and carefully took out the shotgun. A twinge of nervous excitement danced through him as he lifted the gun. Although he had handled several firearms during his lifetime, he had never actually fired one, something Holly didn't know. His wife would have had a fit had she known he had purchased a firearm without ever firing one before.

"But we'll just keep that our little secret. Won't we?"

Opening the box of shells, he fed five bright red shells into the belly of the shotgun. There was a noticeable click as he worked the slide, chambering one of the shells into the firing position. What he held was no longer just a shotgun. Now it was a loaded firearm. A weapon. And what a weapon it was: a police 12-gauge riot gun, with an 18¼ barrel and a full choke. A firearm that could blow a melon-sized hole through the chest of even the toughest opponent.

As he loaded the Winchester, Mike realized something very dear and precious had been taken from American men in society's attempt to become civilized. Holding the shotgun he felt different, stronger, more centered than he had for a long, long time. The gun felt like it was a natural part of him, like a severed limb that had been miraculously reattached.

He imagined how it must have been two hundred years ago: a man and his gun providing for his family by putting fresh meat on the table, warding off outlaws and Indians, and protecting his home and the things he held dear. It felt so good. So right. How could anyone ever say that owning a firearm was wrong?

He wondered where things had gone so terribly wrong. When had the politicians and the feminists convinced the men of this country that owning a firearm was a bad thing? When had the weapons been taken out of the hands of innocent, law-abiding people and put into the hands of the criminals? When had the dark ages of this country actually begun?

In many places the right to own and bear arms was little more than a dim memory, nothing but meaningless words handwritten on crumbling sheets of ancient parchment. The right to bear arms, as provided by the United States Constitution, was now illegal in many places, as was the right to life, liberty, and the pursuit of happiness.

He fed the last shell into the magazine and then took a deep breath, raised the shotgun to his shoulder, and switched off the safety. He aimed at the plastic milk carton and slowly squeezed the trigger.

The shotgun roared and kicked violently, nearly knocking him on his butt. Mike had underestimated the 12-gauge's explosive power. He had also underestimated how loud the blast would be, had not bothered to wear hearing protection of any kind, and would be lucky if he hadn't damaged his eardrums.

Lowering the shotgun, he rubbed his right shoulder and shook his head to clear the ringing from his ears. He also became painfully aware that the empty milk carton still sat in the same position it had moments earlier, completely void of any pellet holes.

"I missed?" Mike walked forward to get a better look at the milk carton, not believing what he was seeing.

"How in the hell could I miss with a 12-gauge? It's impossible."

It may have been impossible, but he had in fact completely missed the milk carton. Rapidly fading were the images of pioneer Mike Anthony standing with his trusty gun in hand, facing down grizzly bears, stampeding buffaloes, and attacks by wild Indians.

"Son of a bitch. I missed."

He stopped about ten feet away from the empty carton and worked the shotgun's slide, ejecting the empty shell on the ground and slipping a new one into place. The air around him was now scented with the sharp odor of gunpowder. Not wanting to inflict any more damage on his shoulders, he held the gun at waist level, pointed the business end toward the carton, and pulled the trigger.

Mike's second shot also missed the milk carton, tearing a whole in the ground about eighteen inches to the left. Working the slide quickly, he fired again, finally hitting his target.

The milk carton launched into the air as a cloud of pellets punched holes in its front side, tearing out its back side completely. He fired again, and again, hitting the carton twice more with the remaining two shells.

"That's it. That's it," he laughed. "Who's the man now?" He turned toward the house, wondering if Holly had witnessed his impressive display of shooting skills. Unfortunately, he was too far away to tell if anyone watched him from the windows. If nothing else she had heard him. Hell, the whole neighborhood had heard him. He hoped that whoever had been sneaking into their house at night had also been listening.

"Maybe this will convince them not to come around here anymore."

He thought about doing a little more shooting, but decided against it. It wouldn't do to use up all of his ammo, especially when he wasn't planning on going back into town that day. An empty gun wasn't much of a threat to anyone.

Putting the shotgun back in its protective case, he gathered up the pieces of the milk carton and started back for the house. Despite having missed a couple of times, he felt good about his shooting ability. He also felt better prepared to protect his family and belongings.

He dared anyone to try sneaking into their house now. Just dared them.

Part III

Only the unknown frightens men. But once a
man has faced the unknown, that terror becomes
the known.

—Antoine de Saint-Exupéry

Chapter 27

Mike's mouth was dry; his hands wet with sweat. He sat in one of the oversized chairs in the library, his back to the wall, facing the open doorway. Cradled in his lap was the Winchester riot gun he had purchased earlier in the day at the Western Auto store. The shotgun was loaded with five rounds of .00 buck shells. For safety's sake, he had not chambered a round. Not yet.

The house was dark and spooky, quiet except for the occasional creak of settling. Holly and the kids had gone to bed hours earlier. She had tried to get him to go upstairs too, but he had refused. Someone was getting into their house, attempting to terrorize them, and he was going to put a stop to it. If the sheriff's department wouldn't do anything about it, then he would.

Allowing the gun to rest fully on his lap, he wiped his hand across his forehead. It was a humid night, and his skin was damp with sweat. The heat made it hard to stay awake, caused him to fight to keep from going to sleep. He would have opened a window to let in the night air, but if someone was getting into the house, he wanted to find out how they were doing it.

Opening the windows would just make things easier for the intruder.

Nor could he watch television in the living room to relieve the boredom. Even with the sound turned all of the way down, the screen's flickering light would warn anyone outside the house that someone was still up. Listening to the radio was also out of the question, even with headphones, because he had to be able to hear any sounds that might warn him an intruder was present.

No television. No radio. He wanted nothing to be different from any other night, lest the invader suspect a trap.

A trap. That's exactly what it was. Mike had given strict instructions for Holly and the children to stay upstairs tonight. To make doubly sure those instructions would be obeyed, Tommy would be sleeping with his mother. Now it was just a matter of waiting to see who showed up that did not belong.

Suppressing a yawn, Mike allowed his eyes to close momentarily. The house was dark; there was no point in straining his eyesight in the darkness. He would be able to hear if anyone broke into the house: the jiggle of a door latch; the squeak of a window being slid up; footsteps coming down the hall. All he had to do was relax and wait for them.

He must have dozed off. The heat must have taken its toll on him and he had fallen asleep. He wasn't sure how long he had slept, but when he opened his eyes the shadows in the room had changed position. They were also darker and deeper than they had been earlier.

Mike glanced at his watch. A little over an hour had passed since he last checked the time, so he hadn't slept long. Still there was enough of a difference in the room to make him suspect the moon had traveled halfway across the sky and was now on the opposite side of the house. It was dark in the library, much darker than it had been before.

Where it had been humid and hot earlier, it was now quite cool in the room. Raising his right hand, he detected a slight breeze blowing from behind him. Carried upon the wind was a foul, loathsome, odor, like the smell of something dead.

He sat up straight in the chair, the last of his nocturnal fogginess leaving him. How could there be a breeze when all of the windows were closed?

Turning his head slowly, he sought out the source of the wind. It came from behind him, but there was nothing there but the wall.

"This is impossible," he said, standing up. Still holding the shotgun, he slowly approached the back wall. It was the same library wall where the wooden masks had once hung, now marred by the large cracks running from floor to ceiling.

Stepping closer, he realized the wind was coming out of the cracks. At first he thought the cracks must go all the way through to the outside of the house, and what he felt was nothing more than the night breeze, but the wind was icy cold, leaving him chilled where it blew across his bare skin. While it was probably cooler outside, it could not possibly be that cold.

With the wind came a faint whispering sound, as though something spoke deep within the walls. The sound reminded him of scurrying insects. For a moment he imagined thousands of cockroaches moving about in the walls on spiny legs, carrying on whispered conversations with one another. It was not a particularly pleasing image to imagine.

The whispering sound grew louder, causing him to take a cautious step back from the wall. As he stepped back, he caught a glimpse of movement out the corner of his left eye. Someone, or something, was in the library with him.

Mike spun around as a shadowy shape slipped beneath a coffee table. Another shadow scurried along the wall on the opposite side of the room. The room was dark, but the shadows were darker.

What the hell is that?

He thought at first they were raccoons, but they did not move like raccoons. In fact they didn't move like any animal he was familiar with. They glided rather than walked. They were also shapeless, nothing more than patches of black against a dark background.

Mike heard a sound behind him and turned, startled by what he saw. Shadows were squeezing out of the crack in the wall, flowing into the room like blobs of liquid mercury. Four, five, six of them, they glided over the wall and raced along the baseboard.

Shadows. Just shadows. Pools of darkness attached to no animal, person, or any living thing that he could see. Yet they were alive, and aware of his presence in the room.

More whispers came from behind him. He turned as the shadow hiding beneath the coffee table rushed toward him. Though it was just a shadow, he felt something solid collide against his ankles, knocking his feet out from under him. He fell and struck the floor hard, the shotgun flying out of his hand. As he fell, he was aware of other shapes racing at him.

Knowing he was in danger from things unknown, Mike hit the floor and rolled. Getting to his knees, he started to stand back up, but suddenly a weight landed on the back of his left leg. Fiery pain shot through the calf of that leg, causing him to cry out. He had been bitten by something he could feel but not see.

Rolling to his right, he kicked the invisible attacker off of him. He staggered to his feet and started to pick up the shotgun, but he knew the gun would be useless against things he could not see in the dark. Despite its deadly firepower, the shotgun did have its limitations. Instead of grabbing the Winchester, he hurried across the room and turned on the light.

Switching on the lamp, he caught a glimpse of a dozen shadowy shapes racing across the room after him. He saw them for only a brief instant, for the shadows abruptly changed direction and ran away from him, apparently fleeing from the light.

"Jesus Christ," he whispered, freezing dead in his tracks at the sight before him. Though liquid in movement, the shadows did have identifiable features when viewed in the light. They were tiny dwarfish creatures, no bigger than a weasel, with horribly grotesque faces that appeared to be almost human. He recognized the faces of the shadowy beings, for he had seen portraits of similar creatures displayed upon his kitchen floor. His grandmother had also seen the faces, might even have seen the creatures themselves, but no one had believed her.

Mike stood there, watching in horror as the shadows raced around the edges of the room. What he was seeing could not possibly be real, but it was. They were nothing more than shadows, but these shadows had teeth and claws that were all too real. Glancing down, he saw that the left leg of his blue jeans had been ripped by the shadow that attacked him.

In that instance all of his doubts and disbeliefs in the

supernatural were tossed aside like dried leaves on a windy day. He had refused to believed his wife and children, passing off what they had seen as nothing more than overactive imaginations. But the things he saw now were definately not figments of anyone's imagination.

Holly suddenly appeared in the doorway behind him. "Mike, what's going on? I heard you scream."

"Stay back!" he shouted. "Don't come in here!"

Holly didn't listen. She entered the room, stopping just behind her husband.

Never taking his eyes off the far wall, Mike crossed the room and grabbed his shotgun off the floor. As he did, he stepped in front of the lamp, causing a shadow to be cast across the room. In that patch of darkness several creatures could be seen.

Holly cried out in terror. "Dear God, Mike, what are those things?"

"Boogers," he answered, sliding a shell into the shotgun's chamber. Aiming quickly, he pulled the trigger and fired. A flash of flame leaped from the barrel as the 12-gauge roared. The buckshot ripped through one of the boogers, tearing a hole in the opposite wall. The creature was unhurt by the gun, for it was, after all, nothing more than a shadow. And you could not hurt a shadow. Or could you?

"Light. We need more light!" Mike shouted. He grabbed the lamp, fumbling to remove the lamp shade. The lamp had originally been fitted with a hundred-watt bulb, but that bulb had been broken. Now it only had a forty-watt bulb, which was obviously not bright enough to ward off the boogers.

"Quick, grab the lamp off of my desk. It's brighter."

Holly didn't move, frozen with terror by the things she saw.

"Hurry!"

She stumbled back, tearing herself away from the sight before her. She raced across the room and into Mike's office. Unplugging the lamp's cord from the wall, she snatched it off the desk and ran back into the library.

"Here," she shouted, entering the room.

With some reluctance, Mike turned his back on the shadows. Handing Holly the shotgun, he grabbed the lamp and plugged it into the wall. Flipping it on, he aimed the bright beam of light at the boogers.

As it swept over them, the shadowy creatures fled across the room. They flowed up the wall like an ebony waterfall in reverse, disappearing into the cracks.

"They can't stand the light," Mike said, triumphantly. "It's driving them back."

A shadow darted out from under the coffee table. Racing along the baseboard, it fled out into the hallway.

"Mike, one of them is getting away!"

He handed Holly the desk lamp. "Keep the light on them and you'll be safe. I'm going after that one."

He ran out into the hallway, unsure whether to turn right or left. There was no light in the hallway, so everything was still completely dark. Turning left, he ran into the living room and flipped on the light.

Mike thought he saw something dart beneath the sofa but he couldn't be sure. Perhaps it was only a trick of the lighting. Perhaps he was just seeing things. Still he needed to check beneath the sofa to be certain.

Starting across the room, he was suddenly aware he had left the shotgun with Holly. Not that the gun would have done him much good; the last thing he

needed was to shoot holes in the furniture. Still he
could have used the shotgun's barrel to poke beneath
the sofa in an attempt to flush out anything that might
be hiding there. He looked around the room to see if
there was anything else he could use—a broom or a
mop—but there was nothing to be had.

Not wanting to drop to his knees to look beneath the
sofa, afraid something might lunge at him with sharp
teeth and claws, he decided the best course of action
would be to move the sofa out of the way. Grabbing one
end of it, Mike shoved the sofa several feet to the right.

Nothing was revealed when he moved the furniture,
nor did anything come running out. Determined something had to be hiding underneath the sofa, he grabbed
the other end of it and shoved. This time he got results.

A blur of blackness shot past his feet, causing him to
jump back with a yell. He turned to follow the path of
the creature, but it was already racing out of the room.
Again wishing he had not given up his shotgun, he
hurried after the fleeing booger.

As he ran into the hallway, he caught a glimpse of
the mysterious creature entering the kitchen. He entered the kitchen just a scant second behind it, flipping
on the lights. As he flipped on the fluorescent lights set
in the ceiling, Mike caught a glimpse of movement beneath the kitchen table. The area directly beneath the
table appeared to be covered with a swirling mass of
blackness, but as the lights were turned on, that blackness disappeared, as though it was sucked down
through the crack in the floor.

Mike stopped, his hand still on the light switch,
staring in disbelief at the floor beneath the table. There
was nothing there, nothing at all.

Crossing the room, he slowly approached the table

and slid the chairs back out of the way. The faces on the floor stared up at him, mocking him in silence. He ignored them. The night had already been too strange, without giving thought to what was drawn on the floor.

Kneeling, he examined the crack beneath the table. As his fingers slid along the crack marring the tiles, he was aware of a coldness seeping up from the floor. It was a chill equal to what he had felt in the library, making him think of underground caverns and passageways. Nameless places where blind things slithered and crawled.

A shiver of fear crept up Mike's back, strong enough to cause his teeth to chatter. As he touched the crack, feeling the coldness numbing his fingertips, he could almost imagine there was something down in the darkness, deep below the basement, staring up at him. Dozens of tiny creatures that looked up from their world of blackness, seeing the light that spilled into the narrow crack in the kitchen floor. Seeing him.

Snatching his hand back from the crack, he stood up and looked around. There was nothing in the kitchen. No nocturnal predators of any kind. He was quite alone. The boogers had gone, driven away by the bright lights.

"But what happens if the lights go out?" he whispered, again feeling a shiver of fear march down his spine. It was a question he did not want answered.

Chapter 28

Though Mike had stayed on guard duty for the rest of the night, the boogers had not come back. But it didn't matter. They were getting out, leaving just as fast as they could get packed. Enough was enough. He was a horror writer; he got paid to write nightmares for a living. He was not about to live one.

Breathing a sigh of relief as the day dawned bright and clear, he opened the curtains in the library and living room, allowing the sunlight to enter. Apparently the boogers didn't like bright lights, preferring instead to lurk in darkness and in shadows, so they probably would not be much of a threat in the daytime. He and his family were safe for the time being, at least as long as the sun shone and as long as they avoided places of darkness.

Shortly after the booger attack, Holly had gathered the children together in one bedroom for safety. They were both awake now and, not wanting to panic either one of them, she was helping them to pack in an orderly, calm manner. All they would be taking were a few suitcases of clothes, and a couple of items they could not bear to leave behind. The rest they would come back to get later, or send someone else to get.

Mike stood in the front yard and looked up at the house. His new home had lost all of its appeal and charm. It was no longer a quaint old country house, a place of tranquil days and lazy summer nights. It was now a place of deadly secrets where darkness reigned. Neither he nor Holly wanted to spend another night in the house.

Since they made a conscious effort not to upset the children by hurrying, it was already late afternoon by the time they had the van loaded and were ready to leave. Mike locked the front door of the house and then climbed in the van. He waited for everyone to get seated and then attempted to start the vehicle, but the engine was dead. He tried several times, even pumped the accelerator a few times, but without any luck.

"Son of a bitch," he whispered, switching off the ignition.

"What's wrong, Daddy?" Tommy asked, leaning forward in his seat.

"Nothing's wrong. Just a little delay." Mike glanced at the dash to see if he had accidentally left the lights on, draining the battery, but they were turned off. The radio was also switched off. He had never been much of a mechanic, so Mike hated it when he had car troubles. Even the simplest of problems gave him a headache and sent his blood pressure soaring.

Expecting the worst, he pressed the button to release the hood catch and climbed out of the van. He was thinking that maybe he had a dead battery, or a loose cable, but when he lifted the hood he found out that his mechanical troubles were far worse than that. Much to his horror he discovered that most of the engine's electrical wiring had been torn loose.

"What the hell?" He propped up the hood with a rod and stuck his head closer to the engine, as if he had not really seen the problem. "I don't believe it."

He heard Holly telling the kids to sit still. A few moments later she joined him in front of the van. "What's wrong? Did you find the problem?"

He stepped back so she could see. "I found the problem easy enough. Fixing it may be a little harder."

Holly looked at the engine and saw the pieces of broken wiring hanging down. Her eyes widened in surprise. "Who did this to us?"

"Good question. It must have happened last night while we were sleeping. It looks like someone doesn't like our van."

She turned toward him, her eyes bright with fear. "Mike, those things we saw last night must have done this. They don't want us to leave."

He looked at Holly then turned again to study the engine, a feeling of dread forming deep in the pit of his stomach. If the boogers knew enough to rip out the van's wiring, then that brought up a problem altogether unexpected: the shadowy creatures were intelligent.

"Dear God, they're intelligent," he said, keeping his voice low so the children wouldn't hear him.

"What?" asked Holly.

"The damn things are intelligent." He turned to her. "Think about it. If what you're saying is true, if the boogers did rip out the wiring to keep us here, that means they're smart. They have to be smart to know we use the van for transportation, even smarter to know what to tear up to keep it from running."

"But why do they want to keep us here?"

He shrugged. "I don't know. Maybe they're planning on doing the same thing to us that they did to Pinky."

The color drained out of Holly's face. "Mike, we can't stay here. The children."

"What's wrong, Daddy?" Tommy called.

Mike closed the hood, not wanting anyone else to see the torn wiring. He flashed a smile in Tommy's direction. "Just a dead battery. That's all. No big deal."

"What do we do now?" Holly asked, still keeping her voice low.

"I'll just go back inside and call a taxi," he said, loud enough to be heard by everyone. "It shouldn't take too long for one to get out here. In the meantime, you kids give your mom a hand unloading the luggage."

Going back into the house, Mike looked up the number for the local cab company and started to make the call. But the phone in the kitchen was dead. The phones in the living room and his office were also dead. There was another phone upstairs in his bedroom, but he didn't want to go up there to use it. There was something about the house that made him nervous. It seemed to be closing in on him, and with the sun now on the backside of the house it was far too dark and shadowy. He kept catching movement out of the corner of his eye; real or imagined he couldn't be sure.

Trying to put on a happy face for the children, he stepped back outside. "Just my luck. The phone doesn't seem to be working either."

"What are you going to do, Daddy?" Tommy asked, starting to worry as only an eight-year-old could.

Mike saw the concern in Holly's eyes. "I'll tell you what, let's just leave our things here and walk."

"Walk?" Megan was shocked. "It's five miles to town."

Equally anxious to get away from the house, Holly said, "Honey, it's probably only three or four miles at the most. And our closest neighbor is less than half that distance; we'll stop and ask to use their phone to call a taxi."

"But if you're going to use the neighbor's phone, why do we all have to go?" Megan asked. "Why can't you or Dad go, and the rest of us stay here?"

"Because we're a family, and families stick together," Holly answered, saying the only thing she could think of to say. "Besides, a good walk will do us good. It will be fun. You'll see."

"What about our things?" Megan asked. "What if someone comes along and steals them?"

"They'll be safe until we get back," Mike replied. "No one ever comes out here."

Megan refused to give in to the idea of leaving the suitcases just lying on the ground, so they had to load everything back into the van. More time wasted. Mike debated about whether or not to bring the shotgun, but then decided to leave it in the van. It wouldn't look good walking through town toting a firearm, and it might frighten the neighbors if he did stop to use someone's phone.

"Okay, everything's loaded. Let's get started." He closed the rear doors on the van and locked them. Megan was still less than pleased with the idea of walking, but she kept quiet as they started down the driveway. As they reached the road, Mike turned and looked back at the house. He didn't see anything, but he had the distinct feeling that he was being watched. That all of them were being watched.

* * *

Sam Tochi paced in the center of his living room, growing more agitated by the minute. What he had learned yesterday upset him, bringing forth a fear he had not felt in years. He had slept little that night, despite taking twice his normal dosage of pain medicine and burning enough sage and sweetgrass to choke a horse.

The woman who had come to see him, Holly Anthony, had said that the kachina statues in her house had been moving. Not just one or two of them, but all of them. This was not good, not good at all. It could only mean that the Sipapuni was again open, or partially open, and the boogers were pushing their way through from the other side. To make matters worse, the stupid woman had taken down all the kachinas and wooden masks, leaving no medicine at all to guard the entrance into this world.

Stupid woman. Stupid Bahanna. Sam had warned her that the kachina statues contained powerful medicine, and they must be put back in their proper places to keep the boogers from coming through in force, but he wasn't sure the woman had believed him. She had hurried from his home, saying that she would put the statues back, but perhaps she was only anxious to get away from him. Maybe she too thought that he was nothing more than a crazy old man.

It would not be the first time that a white person had closed his or her ears to the things he had to say. He had tried to tell the people of Braddock about the Sipapuni and the boogers for many years, but they only laughed at him. Vivian Martin had been the only person to ever listen to him, but that was because she had seen the boogers with her own eyes and was willing to listen to anyone who could help her. She had listened to him, but she too had been called crazy.

Sam grabbed his pipe out of the ashtray beside his chair, but he did not light it. He was tired of people calling him crazy, tired of them laughing at him. He should pack his things and move back to the reservation, leave all these stupid Bahannas to their own problems, but he couldn't. The boogers were not just a threat to the people of Braddock and the surrounding countryside. If they opened the Sipapuni, then they would be a problem for every living thing on the planet. A very serious problem.

No. He could not turn his back and walk away. That would be wrong. He had to do something to help, even if his help was not appreciated.

Crossing the room, he picked up the telephone and dialed information. The woman who'd come to visit was new in town, so her number would not be listed in the phone book, but he might be able to get it from the operator. Unfortunately, the operator told him that there was no listing for a Holly or Michael Anthony, so their number must have been unlisted. Sam was trying to think of what to do next, when movement caught his eye.

Turning, he saw one of the kachina statues sitting on top of his bookcase begin to shake. It was only a slight movement at first, barely noticeable, but as he watched, the shaking began to increase as if the statue was beginning to vibrate. Sam held his breath, fearful of what was about to happen next.

A second statue, sitting atop the same bookcase, also begin to vibrate. Like the first, the movement was barely noticeable to start but rapidly increased. And then, as Sam watched, both statues slowly turned to face in a new direction. They both turned to face the west, looking in the direction of Vivian Martin's old house. The kachinas had turned toward the Sipapuni, ready to do battle with the evil that was attempting to enter the world.

Sam stood with mouth open, watching the tiny statues that sat on the bookcases in his living room. He stood motionless and watched them for several minutes, but the statues had stopped moving. Nor did any of the other kachina statues vibrate or turn. It didn't matter, however, for he had gotten the message. The kachinas were warning him that the Sipapuni was opening, and that time was running out.

Grabbing the telephone, he made another call. He needed to tell someone about what was happening, warn them about the dangers. He knew he probably would not be believed, but he had to try. Maybe just this once someone would listen to what he had to say, instead of dismissing his advice as nothing more than the ranting of a crazy old man.

He waited for his phone call to be answered, then quickly said what he had to say. He hung up the phone then looked around the room for the keys to his pickup truck, finding them under an old hat. He rarely drove his truck because it usually wouldn't start for him, but maybe this time he would have better luck.

Pocketing the truck keys, he went into the bedroom and removed his medicine bundle from where it was hidden in the back of his closet. He also removed a loaded .22 revolver from his dresser drawer, tucking it into the waistband of his jeans. Sam knew that the pistol would be of little use, but it made him feel better bringing it along.

Leaving the house, he locked the door behind him

and then climbed into his rusting Ford pickup truck. He inserted the key into the ignition and tapped the accelerator pedal a few times, praying that the truck would start without giving him any problem. His prayer must have been heard, because the old truck fired right up.

"Thank you," he said aloud as he backed out into the street.

His kachina statues moving could only mean that Holly Anthony had not done what she'd promised to do—she had not put the kachinas in her house back in their proper places. Therefore, Sam was going to pay a visit to the Anthony family. He was going to try to convince them to put the statues back before it was too late.

Leaving the town of Braddock, he followed State Road #315 west toward Sawmill Road. He wasn't planning on going all the way to Sawmill, however, because he knew of an abandoned logging road that would shave a couple of miles off the trip. The road was in bad shape so it was rarely used by anyone, but Sam's truck was four-wheel drive so he had no problem with ruts and potholes. The logging road ended at Bloodrock Creek, just on the backside of Vivian Martin's property. There used to be a bridge across the creek at that spot, so trucks could haul logs to and from the old sawmill, but that bridge had washed out years ago. It didn't matter that the bridge was gone; Sam could walk to the house once he reached the creek.

He turned off of #315 onto the old logging road, concentrating on avoiding the larger potholes. The truck bucked and bounced, and threatened to fall apart at any moment, but he finally made it to Bloodrock Creek. He thought about trying to drive across the creek, but only for a moment. Though the water wasn't deep, he would probably bury his truck in the soft creek bottom if he tried to cross.

Switching off the engine, he grabbed his medicine bundle and climbed out of the pickup. He started to take the pistol, but then decided to leave it in the truck. Showing up with a gun could make things worse. Instead of listening to him, Holly and her husband might just call the police.

As Sam stepped out of the pickup, he was instantly aware that something was wrong. The forest surrounding him was quiet. Too quiet. He studied the treetops above him, but there wasn't a bird to be seen. Not one. Nor did he hear any in the distance. The forest was completely silent, as if every bird and animal had decided to pack up and leave. He had heard a similar silence once before, in this very forest. It was the hush that fell over the area when the boogers started appearing, many years ago.

"This is not good," he said, shaking his head. "Not good at all. I may be too late."

Clutching his medicine bundle tightly to his chest, he slowly waded across Bloodrock Creek. The water was less than a foot deep where he crossed, but he had to go slowly to keep from losing his footing on the slippery rocks. Once he reached the other side, he again paused to listen to the silence that surrounded him. It was an eerie quiet, one that spoke of unseen dangers.

Sam pushed onward, following rabbit trails that twisted between the trees and underbrush. He paused twice more to listen to the sounds around him, but nothing had changed. The only noises he heard were those he made. A few minutes later he broke free of the forest, emerging into the apple orchard behind Vivian

Martin's old house. He was greatly relieved to be out in the open once more.

He crossed the orchard to the house, circling around to the front door. Stepping up onto the porch, he knocked on the door but no one answered. He looked around and noticed a van parked in the driveway, so someone must be home. Unless they owned a second vehicle. He knocked again, but there was still no answer.

Knowing time was running out, Sam tried the door, hoping to find it unlocked. The door was locked, but only the lock in the knob had been engaged; the two deadbolts had been left unlatched.

"It looks like they left in a hurry," he said to himself, studying the door. "Maybe they are only gone for a short time."

He removed his billfold from his back pocket and took out a plastic phone calling card. Slipping the card between the door and its frame, he wiggled it beneath the latch and unlocked the door. Putting the phone card in his back pocket, he opened the door and entered the house.

"Hello?" he called, stepping across the threshold. "Hello? Is there anyone home?" There was no answer.

Sam had only visited Vivian Martin a few times, but it was enough for him to remember the general layout of the house. Still, he was surprised to see the change that had taken place since his last visit. Gone was the clutter and mess that had covered almost every inch of free space. Where he used to have to squeeze between boxes and bags, he was now able to move easily from room to room.

Closing and locking the door behind him, he made his way down the hallway to the living room. The room was clean and neat, with furniture that spoke of practical good taste. But Sam wasn't interested in the interior decorations, and he gave the furnishings only a quick glance. Instead he focused his attention on the far wall, looking with dread at the empty wooden shelf that ran the length of the room—a shelf that had once been the resting place for hundreds of kachina statues.

"She did not put them back," he said, a wave of anger flowing over him. "She said she would, but she lied. Stupid woman. Stupid. Stupid. Stupid."

He left the living room and hurried into the library, again finding a shelf barren of kachinas. In addition to the empty shelf, he spotted a long vertical crack running down the wall. He crossed the room and placed the palm of his right hand against the crack. He held his palm there for only a moment, because the cold he felt caused him to snatch his hand back in fear. It was a cold not of this world, but of someplace dark and evil.

The crack extended from ceiling to floor, and he wondered if it continued down into the basement. And if it did, was it the same size in the basement or was it larger? He needed to know, for the size of the cracks might tell him how far the Sipapuni had been opened. If the doorway to the underworld was only partially opened, then maybe there was a chance that it could be closed again before it was too late.

Leaving the library, he crossed the hallway and entered the kitchen. He was halfway across the kitchen when he spotted the faces on the floor. It was a long time since he had seen such faces, but there was no mistaking what they were. They were the faces of evil creatures that inhabited the world below ours. The faces of boogers.

Sam stopped and stared at the faces for a moment,

suddenly feeling as if he were being watched. He turned and looked around the room, but saw nothing out of the ordinary. Except for the faces on the tile floor, it looked to be just a normal kitchen. And he looked to be the room's only occupant, but he knew that things were not always as they seemed.

Opening his medicine bundle, he reached in and removed a tiny leather pouch containing sacred yellow cornmeal. He opened the pouch and took a pinch of cornmeal between his thumb and forefinger, and then, whispering a prayer for cleansing, he slowly walked a clockwise circle around the faces in the center of the room. As he walked the circle, he sprinkled the sacred cornmeal, hoping to keep the evil ones from coming up through the floor.

He walked the circle four times, four being a sacred number, then closed the pouch and put it back into his medicine bundle. Turning away from the faces on the floor, he crossed the room and opened the door leading to the basement. It was dark in the basement, and he had not thought to bring a flashlight, but luckily he was able to locate the switch to turn on the lights. Switching them on, he started down the wooden stairs to the basement.

He almost expected to find a Sipapuni in the basement floor, but no such opening was visible. It might still be there, somewhere, but he could not see it. Maybe such things were only visible to spirits and the kachinas. Maybe he had to die first before he could see the doorway to the underworld.

Sam didn't find any opening in the floor, but he did find six cardboard boxes filled with kachina statues. Again his anger flared. "Stupid woman. She lied to me. She said she would put them back, but she lied. No matter. I am here now. I will put them back where they belong."

Picking up one of the cardboard boxes, he walked back across the basement floor. He had just reached the steps when the door leading to the kitchen slammed shut with a bang. He stopped and looked up at the door, wondering who had closed it. Did one of the homeowners come home, find the door open, and shut it. No. He would have heard had anyone entered the kitchen. He would have heard them walk across the floor above his head. If not a member of the Anthony family, then who had slammed the door?

He was still wondering who had shut the door, when suddenly the lights went out, casting him into total darkness. Sam started to call out, but changed his mind. Had someone been in the kitchen, he would have heard them. But he had heard no one. Except for the banging of the door, and the sound of his breathing, only silence surrounded him.

Maybe the wind had caused the door to slam shut. That was possible, but he doubted if the wind could also turn out the lights. And how could there be a wind when the house was locked tight? That was a good question, but there was a wind. He felt it. Standing at the bottom of the steps, he felt an icy wind blowing on the back of his neck. Second question: how could there be a wind in a basement?

Fear touched Sam Tochi's heart and squeezed it tight. It was not a fear of the unknown, for he suddenly knew who, or what, had slammed the door leading to the kitchen. And he knew why the lights had gone out. Standing there in the darkness, feeling an icy wind upon him, he realized that the Sipapuni was opened far wider than he had suspected. He also realized that he had just walked into a trap—a trap set by creatures far more intelligent than he'd ever imagined.

"So, little brothers, you like to play, do you?" Sam smiled and set down the box of kachinas. "That is okay. I like to play too." He reached into his pocket and removed his butane lighter, thumbing its tiny wheel.

The flame produced by the lighter wasn't very bright, but it was enough for him to see that he was in big trouble. Very big trouble. Around him the floor seemed to ripple and roll as shadows scurried about in the darkness, staying just beyond the circle of light cast by the lighter's tiny flame. Circling him like sharks at a feeding frenzy, the boogers waited for their chance to rush in at the old Indian.

Sam was terrified, but he knew as long as he held the lighter there was still a chance that he might make it out of the basement alive. He thought about climbing the stairs to see if he could get back into the kitchen, but his instinct told him that the basement door was probably locked. All was not lost, however, for he still had his medicine bundle, and he still had the boxes containing the kachinas. If he could keep a circle of medicine items around him, then he might be safe until the Anthony family came home and found him in their basement.

A strange whispering sound came from behind him. Sam turned in time to see a booger dart within the circle of light and then dart back out again. That was not good. Not good at all. Obviously, the glow cast by the lighter's flame was not bright enough to keep them away. It was only a matter of time, maybe only minutes, before the boogers overcame their fear of the lighter's glow and charged him in force. He had to do something, and he had to do it quickly.

Tearing open the cardboard box, Sam started dropping kachina statues on the floor around him. He didn't have time to place the statues properly, and only hoped that the medicine of the kachinas might buy him a few more minutes of time. A few more minutes to think of some way to fend off the boogers.

He had to close the Sipapuni, he had to close the opening to the underworld, but he didn't know where that opening was. He could not see it, and he could not feel it. Wait. Maybe he could feel it. Sam felt an icy wind blowing in the basement, a wind that carried with it the smell of death. The wind must come from the opening, blowing from a place where evil things lived. Looking at the flickering flame of his lighter, he knew from which way that wind blew.

Praying that his lighter would last a few minutes longer, Sam hurried across the basement. He used the flame to guide him, arriving at one of the far walls. Like the wall in the library above, this wall also had a crack in it. And from that crack a strange wind blew, carrying with it the smell of death and the sounds of things whispering.

"This cannot be the Sipapuni," he said, placing his hand against the crack. "It is too small. But maybe it leads to the opening."

Not knowing whether he had found the opening or not, Sam pulled his hand away from the crack. Still keeping a firm grip on his lighter, he opened his medicine bundle with his teeth and removed one of the pouches containing cornmeal. Allowing the medicine bundle to drop to the ground, he opened the pouch with his teeth and hurried to take out a pinch of cornmeal. Stepping closer to the wall, he shoved the sacred cornmeal into the crack.

He had just placed the pinch of cornmeal in the wall,

when a patch of darkness flowed from the crack and seized his hand. Sam cried out and tried to step back, but it was too late. One of the boogers had him, dragging his fingers deep into the crack. There was a loud snapping sound as the first two fingers of his left hand broke like dried pieces of chalk.

"No!" Sam screamed, pain shooting up his left arm. He tried to pull away from the wall, but the boogers had him. More patches of blackness flowed from the crack to grab him, dragging his hand even deeper into the wall. He thrust his other hand toward the crack, hoping the flame of his lighter would drive off the boogers. But the shadowy creatures were not afraid, for the lighter was low on fuel and the flame weak.

Instead of being frightened off, the boogers grabbed his right hand and dragged it too into the wall. Again several sharp cracks sounded as the finger bones in Sam's right hand snapped like pretzel sticks.

Sam screamed in pain and kicked at the wall, but he could not get loose. He was as helpless as a fish on a hook, the bones in his hands being broken and crushed as the boogers slowly dragged him into the wall. Blood spurted from his broken hands, but he could not see it for he had dropped the lighter and was now in complete darkness. He could only feel the blood, wet and warm, flowing from his injured hands and running down the undersides of his wrists.

Inch by inch the boogers dragged the old man's hands, and then his wrists and arms, into the crack, crushing bones and smashing flesh until his chest was flat against the wall. Sam Tochi was still alive, but he no longer screamed or thrashed about. He only stood there, eyes staring but not seeing, mouth moving but no words escaping his lips.

His body was still alive, but his mind and spirit had gone to a place where it was warm and safe. Sam did not see the wall before his face, or the blackness reaching out to pull his head, and the rest of his body, into the crack, carrying his crushed bones and flesh down into a world that was dark and cold.

He saw instead the desert country of Third Mesa, and the town of adobe buildings that was Hoteville. A place of warm sunshine and simple pleasures, where ceremonial music filled the kivas and kachinas walked the night. These were the sights he saw as the boogers slowly dragged his body inch by inch into the narrow crack, for the spirit of Sam Tochi had gone home.

Mike and his family had only gone a mile or so down the road when he heard a strange noise coming from the forest to his left. Slowing his pace enough to drop back from the others, he listened carefully to the sounds around him. Almost immediately he realized that the local songbirds, so boisterous only moments before, had hushed their melodies. And in that unfamiliar silence he could clearly her a queer whispering sound, as if a dozen or so people were quitely having a rapid conversation beneath the leafy canopy of the trees. It was the same whispering he had heard coming from the crack in his library wall, right before he was attacked by the boogers.

He stopped and turned in the direction of the sound. Though he couldn't see anything, he could clearly hear the strange noise as it moved through the forest. The sound seemed to be following them, moving at a rate that paced their steps. More whispering came from the forest on the opposite side of the road. Again, he saw nothing.

We're being followed.

There was no doubt in his mind that the boogers had followed them from the house. He couldn't see them, but he could plainly hear the noise they made. Like tiny voices. Excited, hungry voices. He didn't know how many of the shadowy things were following them, but as long as they stayed on the road, protected by the sunlight, they should be safe.

Not wanting to alarm his family, he started walking again, hurrying his pace to catch up with the rest of them. Holly and the kids were engaged in a lively conversation and hadn't noticed he had stopped. It was just as well; no sense panicking them unless it was necessary.

Rounding a bend in the road, he stopped again. Up ahead Sawmill Road narrowed to little more than a bumpy path running through a very dense section of old growth forest. Here it was always dark, no matter what time of day it was, the towering oak trees blocking out any and all sunlight. Mike saw nothing to indicate danger, yet he knew something waited for them in the darkness covering that narrow stretch of road.

He turned quickly and looked behind him. There was nothing to be seen, but he could still hear the whispering sounds that followed, pacing them. No. Not pacing. Stalking. The boogers had been stalking them, herding Mike and his family into a trap. He was certain now that more of the shadowy creatures waited up ahead in the darkness that covered the road. It was a perfect trap, one he had almost foolishly led his family into.

"Wait! Stop!" Mike said, his mouth going dry with fear. The others stopped, Holly turning to give him a concerned look.

"What's wrong, Daddy? Why are we stopping?"

"Shhhh . . ." Mike studied the darkness ahead of him, and then turned and looked at the road they had just traveled. Standing there, he became aware of how late it had gotten. The sun hadn't set yet, but all around them the forest was already growing dark.

Suddenly he realized the mistake he had made, placing his family in danger. This was exactly what the boogers wanted, this is why they had sabotaged the van. They wanted them out in the open, alone in the forest. In the shadowy darkness that covered the road they could attack from all directions. Five miles to town? It might as well have been five hundred miles. They would never make it.

I've got to do something, and do it quick. But what? What can we do? Think, man. Think. You're a fucking writer, use your damn imagination.

Standing there in the middle of the road, his family watching him, he quickly thought up and dismissed a dozen different plans of action. He was unarmed, so he couldn't fight the boogers. Not that having a gun would have been of much help. That left only one option open: they had to make a run for it. But they couldn't continue forward; they would never make it in the darkness that lay just up the road. Their only defense was to retreat.

He tried to keep his voice calm, but it wasn't easy. "Tommy, remember the games we used to play in the park? Remember how we used to have races and you would always win? Well, I bet you're even faster now. Let's say we all have a race back to the house to see who is the fastest?"

"Back to the house?" Tommy asked. "You said we were leaving."

"We can leave later, but let's have a race back to the house now."

Mike turned to look at Holly and Megan. He thought his daughter would give him an argument, but she remained silent. Apparently she too had been listening to the sounds following them and knew something was wrong. Fear showed in her eyes.

"You guys up for a race?" Mike asked.

Holly and Megan both nodded.

"Okay then, it will be a family race." Mike smiled, his gaze gliding over the forest beyond the road. "Everyone line up. No cheating."

He stepped up to where Holly and the kids stood, lining up to face in the direction from which they had just come. His wife took his hand and gave it a quick squeeze, letting him know that she understood what was going on. He looked at her and smiled. A weak smile, one chiseled from fear rather than happiness.

"Okay. Everyone get ready." Tommy leaned forward in his best imitation of a sprinter's stance. Apparently he was the only one who had not heard the whispers and didn't realize the danger surrounding them. Megan also leaned forward slightly, but she knew the race was for anything other than fun. "On your mark. Get set. Go!"

They took off running back toward the house. No sooner had they started than the forest around them exploded in a barrage of sounds. There must have been dozens of the unseen creatures, maybe even hundreds. They were completely surrounded.

"Hurry!" Holly yelled, keeping the children before her. "Don't stop."

"Faster, Tommy. Don't let me beat you," Mike yelled, spurring his son on to greater speed. He threw a glance over his shoulder and saw a sight that nearly took his breath away. Back behind them where the road narrowed and the towering trees created eternal darkness, the forest floor seemed to be rippling and boiling. But it was no natural phenomenon that he saw. Instead it was hundreds, if not thousands, of shadowy creatures scurrying from their hiding places along that stretch of road, to give pursuit to Mike and his fleeing family.

Oh, dear God.

Like cockroaches spilling from an open sewer, the boogers poured from that darkened patch of forest to give chase. They moved like ebony liquid, flowing over the ground and around trees and brush. With them came the maddening whispering sound they made, growing in volume until all other noises perished beneath it.

Mike could no longer hear his footfalls, could barely hear himself when he shouted encouragement to his son and daughter. The whispering filled his ears like the shrill cadence of a million hungry locusts, bringing fear and madness with it.

Tommy looked back at his father. A smile was no longer pasted on the boy's face. He heard the noise too and knew what it represented. Instead of a smile, his eyes had grown large with fear. Mike wanted to tell his son that there was nothing to be afraid of, but he could no longer find his voice.

They reached the driveway and raced into the yard, stopping when they reached the van. Turning, Mike expected to see an army of shadows chasing after them, but there was nothing there. The boogers had stayed in the forest, not daring to venture out into the open where sunlight still caressed the land. The hideous whispering had also stopped, replaced by a heavy silence that was every bit as terrifying.

"We're safe," Holly whispered, embracing her husband. "They don't like the light."

"Safe?" Mike glanced up at the sky. There were only a couple more hours of daylight left until it got dark. They were safe for now, as long as they remained outside in the open, in the daylight. But night would be coming soon, and with the night would come the boogers.

Chapter 29

Night was coming. The sun had already dipped below the tree line to the west, casting long shadows across the front lawn. With the darkness would come the boogers. Mike didn't want to go back inside the house, preferring instead to stay outside in the open. But he no longer had any choice. Inside there were lights to keep the dangerous shadows at bay. As long as there were lights they would be safe.

Unlocking the front door, he led his family back inside the house. Holly started flipping on lights as soon as she entered, not waiting to be told to do so. She paused, however, just inside the kitchen doorway, her finger on the light switch. Even in the darkness she could see that something had changed. When she switched on the light, what she saw horrified her.

The hideous faces on the floor had doubled in number, maybe even tripled. And they were no longer just on the floor. They were also on the walls and ceiling, staring out at her from their world, trying to get through. The sight was so startling, so terrifying, she almost screamed. Along with the faces, there was a strange circle of yellow powder on the kitchen floor.

"Mike. Mike. Come in here, quick!" She heard footsteps coming down the hallway. Her husband entered the kitchen.

"What is it? What's wrong?" He froze, seeing the faces scattered across the kitchen. "Dear God. There's twice as many as before."

Holly turned and pushed past him, fleeing into the library. But the faces weren't just confined to the kitchen. Not anymore. They were in the hallway, library, living room, and in Mike's office. Dozens of them, on the walls, ceilings and floors—even on the carpeting—staring out from their world, seeking entrance into a world they wished to claim as their own.

"They're trying to come through," Holly said, fear choking her voice to little more than a whisper.

"Well, they're not through yet," Mike replied, looking around him. "And they aren't going to get through either, not as long as we keep the lights on."

He turned to Holly. "See if you can find some more candles, anything that will cast extra light. I'm going to go upstairs and turn on all the lights up there. Have the children stay in the living room. The lighting is good in there: they should be safe."

The house was lit as brightly as they could make it, but it did little to dispel the fear clenching Mike's heart in an icy grasp. Holly had found an extra case of candles; lighting them, she had positioned the candles throughout the rooms on the first floor of the house, with most of them forming a large circle in the living room. In the middle of that circle of tiny glowing flames the family now gathered, huddled together on the larger of the two sofas. They waited for night to fall fully upon their home, hoping they would survive it.

As the hours slowly passed, Mike and Holly both became aware of a feeling of being watched. There was also an uncanny calm that fell over the room, every bit as electric as the calm before an August thunderstorm. Taking his shotgun with him, Mike stood up and slowly crossed the living room. Stepping outside of the circle of candles, he paused to offer his wife and children a smile of reassurance. None of them returned his smile, their eyes bright and shiny with fear and nervous anticipation.

Leaving the living room, he stepped into the hallway and stopped. He stood listening for sounds that might alert him that danger was present, but he heard nothing out of the ordinary. Other than the quiet hum of the refrigerator's motor, there was only silence. He had just stepped into the kitchen when the lights went out.

"Mike!" Holly screamed from the living room. "What happened to the lights?"

"We must have blown a fuse," he yelled back, knowing in his heart that what he said was not true. The fuses were all new; he had replaced them when they first moved in. "The fuse box is in the basement; I'll go down and take a look."

Setting his shotgun on the kitchen table, he picked up one of the candles and started toward the basement door. He had only taken a few steps, however, when he became aware of movement around him.

Turning, he watched in horror as the faces on the floor, ceiling, and walls began to move. With blinking eyes, and mouths screaming silent cries, they glided across the tile floor and up the walls, circling him like sharks. The floor seemed to rise up with their passing; the walls bowed toward him.

They're trying to push through. The candlelight isn't bright enough to keep them out.

"Mike, they're coming!" Holly screamed.

He grabbed the shotgun and ran back into the hallway. Holly had left the living room and now stood just outside the library door, pointing into the room. The walls in the library were also bowing inward, as though invisible hands were pushing against them from the other side.

A sharp popping echoed through the room as the cracks lining the opposite wall lengthened and grew wider. From the cracks blew an icy wind that stirred the flames of the candles on the tables, threatening to blow them out. If those candles blew out, the room would be cast into total darkness, and the boogers would enter by the hundreds.

A child's scream rent the night. Mike and Holly raced back into the living room. Megan and Tommy stood on the sofa in the middle of the room, staring in wide-eyed terror at what was going on around them. As in the library and kitchen, the walls in the living room were rippling and bowing inward. Demonic faces appeared in the white walls, staring at the children, mocking them with silent laughter. Cracks were also forming in the living room, in the walls and in the ceiling above their heads. Plaster rained down like tiny hailstones as the cracks spread from one corner of the ceiling to the other.

Mike watched as a shadowy shape wriggled free from one of the cracks. It fell to the floor and quickly slithered beneath the hutch. A second shadow appeared in the same crack. Frustrated, not knowing what else to do, he raised the shotgun to his shoulder and fired at the shadow. The wall exploded but the shadow was still there. It too fell to the floor and scurried beneath the hutch.

Holly yelled, "Damnit, Mike. Don't shoot. You might hit one of the children."

"I'm not aiming in their direction," Mike yelled back, angry that the shotgun had had no effect on the shadows.

Suddenly there was a loud crash from the front of the house, and the sound of something large coming down the hallway. Mike spun around and chambered another round into the shotgun. He brought the weapon to his shoulder just as a large shadow fell across the threshold into the room. He started to squeeze the trigger, but paused when he realized there was something familiar about the shape of the approaching shadow.

Sheriff Jody Douglas stepped into the doorway, freezing when he spotted the shotgun in Mike's hand. "I heard a gunshot. What the hell is going on in here?"

Mike quickly lowered the shotgun. "There's no time to explain. We have to get out of here."

The sheriff didn't move. "No one is going anywhere until I find out what's happening here. The station received a phone call from Sam Tochi about an hour ago; he said I needed to get out here ASAP. Now, what the hell is going on?"

"They're coming through," Mike said, pointing at the far wall.

"Who's coming through?" Sheriff Douglas asked, mesmerized by the images floating across the walls and ceiling.

"The boogers," Mike said, nearly screaming. "They're coming through from the other side. You wouldn't believe my grandmother, but maybe you'll believe your own eyes. Look for yourself, but do it quickly because we're leaving."

Mike grabbed the children and herded them across the room. He was almost to the door when Holly stopped him.

"Mike, it's dark outside," she said. "We'll never make it to his car."

Mike stopped and pointed at Jody Douglas. "If he can get into the house, then we can get out. Let's go."

Holly didn't move. "They stopped us from leaving before."

"So what do you suggest we do? Stay here forever?"

She turned and pointed at the empty shelf on the far wall. "What about the kachinas? Sam Tochi was right. He said the statues kept the boogers from coming through the opening. We have to put them back. If we don't, millions of those things might come into this world. They'll destroy everything.

"Please, Mike. It might be our only chance to safely get away. Think of the children."

Mike stopped, his shoulders slumping. "All right, I'll get the fucking statues." He handed Holly the shotgun. "I can't carry boxes and this too."

"I'll give you a hand," Jody Douglas said. He tore his gaze away from the animated faces on the opposite wall and looked at Mike. "I don't know what's going on here. Sure as hell don't know what those things are. But if the old Indian knows how to fight them, then I think maybe we had better listen to him."

Mike started to tell the sheriff to stay there and protect Holly and the children, but he knew the sheriff's pistol would have little, if any, effect on the boogers. Besides, the sheriff had a flashlight.

"All right." Mike nodded. "Let's go."

Hurrying through the kitchen, they opened the door leading to the basement and started down the stairs. Mike went first, the sheriff right behind him. Even with the flashlight, the basement was much too dark for comfort. Crossing the room, they reached the spot where Holly had put the statues. Five of the boxes were sealed, but the sixth box had been opened. Several statues had been taken from the box and scattered about on the floor.

Mike wondered for a moment why the statues had been taken out of the box, but only for a moment. Grabbing two full boxes of statues each, the two men hurried to get back upstairs. Neither of them wanted to stay in the basement any longer than necessary, for the darkness surrounding them seemed to be moving as if alive. From that darkness came an evil wind and strange hissing sound.

They had just started back for the stairs when the basement floor rose up beneath their feet like a giant bubble. It rose and fell, the concrete slabs breaking apart and giving way beneath them. The pieces of concrete disappeared, as if by magic, falling into a large circular shaft that had suddenly opened up in the middle of the room. The shaft appeared to lead straight down into the very bowels of the earth. The Sipapuni was opening.

Mike was in the lead. Feeling the floor giving way under his feet he threw himself forward and rolled. Sheriff Jody Douglas wasn't so lucky. As the floor gave way, he fell into the shaft.

"Help me!"

Getting to his knees, Mike turned and saw the opening that had appeared in the middle of the basement floor. The darkness within the opening appeared to be vibrating, throbbing, as if it were filled with millions of scurrying cockroaches. But it was boogers and not bugs that filled the shaft, jostling each other as they clawed their way out of the darkness in an attempt to enter this world.

Sweet Jesus. It's too late. They're coming. Millions of them.

Mike was paralyzed with fear, unable to look away or flee to safety. Something else was in that opening. Holding on by little more than his fingertips, Sheriff Jody Douglas clutched the broken edge of the basement floor in an effort to keep from falling into the shaft.

"Help me! Please!" the sheriff cried. There was fear in his eyes. Real fear. For maybe the first time in his life Jody Douglas had become the victim.

Please? Did he say please?

Looking at the sheriff, Mike suddenly felt his heart grow cold. Was the sheriff begging for his help? Did he actually say "please"? Wasn't that what Vivian Martin had said when she begged Jody Douglas and his friends to leave her alone and quit tormenting her? Had he listened to her? Had he shown compassion, or mercy? No. He had continued to torment her, making her life a living hell.

Nor had the sheriff shown much compassion toward Mike and his family. They had asked for his help on several occasions, but instead of help they had gotten sarcasm and ridicule.

"Please?" Mike said the word aloud, letting it roll slowly off his tongue and lips. Why should he help the sheriff after all the nasty things he had done to him and his family? Let him fall. He deserved whatever hideous fate awaited him at the other end of that shaft. Why should he help him?

Because it's the right thing to do.

Mike felt the anger slowly leaving his body, and knew he had no other choice than to help the sheriff. It wouldn't be right to leave him. Not right at all. And he had always done the right thing in life, something taught to him by his parents and his grandmother.

Still on his hands and knees, Mike hurried across the basement. Reaching the edge of the pit, he threw himself on his stomach and stretched his hand out toward the sheriff. "Give me your hand."

The sheriff wriggled and squirmed, trying to pull himself farther out of the shaft. "I can't. I'm slipping."

"Give me your hand," Mike repeated. "Hurry, before the whole floor caves in."

Jody Douglas tried again. Pulling himself up with little more than his fingertips, he thrust his right hand forward for Mike to grab.

Mike grabbed the sheriff's hand and started to pull him from the shaft. But it was too late. The swirling mass of darkness in the shaft surged and rose upward as thousands of boogers spilled through the opening from their world. They swarmed over the sheriff like ants, attacking him, dragging him down. Mike tried to hold on, but he couldn't and the sheriff was torn from his grasp. A scream echoed through the basement as Jody Douglas was dragged down by the boogers, a scream that spoke of terrors unimaginable.

Pushing away from the opening, Mike got quickly to his feet. The sheriff's flashlight lay on the floor where it had fallen. Next to the flashlight was a set of keys. He grabbed both and then raced across the room, pausing only long enough to pick up two boxes of kachinas. He had just reached the top of the stairs when the rest of the basement's floor disappeared into the pit.

Racing back into the living room, he opened one of the boxes and hurried to put the kachinas back on the shelves. Holly grabbed the other box to help.

"Where's the sheriff?" she asked, pulling a handful of statues out of the box.

"He didn't make it," Mike answered. "The boogers got him."

She looked at him in horror for a moment, then re-doubled her efforts at getting the kachinas back on the shelves.

"It's too late!" Mike cried, feeling the floor tremble beneath his feet.

The others felt the trembling too. His eyes wide with fear, Tommy backed away from the center of the room, bumping into the wall. Instantly dozens of shadows poured out of the cracks, swarming over the boy. Tommy screamed and tried to get away from the wall, but the boogers had him.

"Tommy!" Holly yelled.

Mike dropped his box of kachinas and raced to help his son. He had only taken three steps, however, when Tommy was lifted off the floor by the boogers and dragged to the top of the wall. He hung suspended in the air, legs kicking, head pressed tightly against the ceiling, as the boogers attempted to drag him through the crack into their world.

Mike jumped up and grabbed his son's left ankle, trying to pull him down off the ceiling. But the boogers held Tommy tight, and all that came loose was the boy's tennis shoe. Dropping the shoe, Mike jumped and grabbed Tommy's ankle again.

Tommy screamed as the top of his head banged against the ceiling. He screamed again as his father grabbed his ankle and pulled. They were long, high-pitched screams. Screams of fear. Screams of pain.

"Help him, Mike. Help him!" Holly cried. "Don't let him go."

Mike gripped Tommy's ankle and pulled, praying that he wouldn't dislocate his son's knee or tear the leg out of its socket. He knew he was hurting the boy, but he had no other choice. If he let go, the boogers might drag Tommy higher up the wall, breaking the boy's neck as his head pressed against the ceiling. Or they might somehow be able to drag him through the crack, carrying him down into their world as they had done to the sheriff.

"The flashlight!" Mike yelled to Megan. "Get the flashlight and shine it at your brother. We have to get those things off of him!"

Megan stood frozen with fear, looking at her father but making no move to obey his command.

"Megan, for god's sake hurry!" Mike yelled.

Megan blinked and shook her head. Sprinting across the room, she snatched up the flashlight and aimed it at her brother. As the bright beam of the flashlight swept across Tommy, several of the boogers released their grip and fled back into the wall.

"That's it. That's it," Mike said, feeling his son slip down the wall a few inches. "Aim it right at him. Aim it at the wall around him. Get closer. They don't like the light."

Holding the flashlight like a sword in front of her, Megan advanced across the room toward her brother. As she approached, several more boogers released their grip on the boy and fled into the cracks.

Tommy slipped a couple more inches down the wall, enough that Mike could jump up and grab him by the waist. Knowing he might not get a second chance, he grabbed his son tight and jerked as hard as he could.

There was a groan of pain from Tommy, followed by the sound of fabric ripping, and then he was free. Mike tore Tommy from the grasp of the boogers with enough force that he fell backward with his son landing on top of him.

Rolling to his side, Mike quickly got back to his feet. He lifted Tommy off the floor, checking to make sure that his son was not hurt. Except for a torn shirt, the boy appeared to be uninjured.

No sooner had he gotten Tommy off the wall than a terrible trembling rumbled through the house. With the trembling came the sound of whispering, growing louder with each passing second. The whispering came from the basement below them. The doorway was fully open now and the boogers were entering by the thousands.

Mike spun around, trying to think of what to do, looking for a weapon, or a way out for him and his family. But his mind was so filled with terror by the things he had witnessed that it would no longer work for him. He had no plan. No plan at all.

"Burn it!"

He turned toward the sound of the voice, not hearing what had been said. "What?"

"Burn it!" Holly screamed. "Burn the house. The fire stopped the boogers at the sawmill. The workers set fire to it. Burn it, Mike. They don't like the light. It's our only chance to seal the opening."

Pulling his lighter from his pocket, he crossed the room and touched a flame to one of the curtains. The curtain began to burn, but slowly. Too slow. "This isn't going to work. I need gasoline, or something flammable."

"Get the cleaning solvents in my studio," Holly shouted. "They're flammable."

"Good idea." He dropped the lighter back in his pocket. "You wait here with the kids. Don't move."

He grabbed the flashlight and ran out of the living room, trying to ignore the faces on the wall that seemed to race down the hallway with him. Entering Holly's studio, he grabbed several one-gallon cans of cleaning solvent off of the shelves. He didn't bother to read the labels, because just about everything she used was flammable.

Opening one of the cans, he splashed the liquid around the studio, and then stepped back into the hallway. He poured the contents of the second can along the hallway, forming a liquid path from the hallway, to his office, and back to Holly's studio. Tossing the empty can aside, he pulled his lighter from his pocket.

"This had better work." He flipped open the Zippo and struck the wheel, but nothing happened. He tried again. Nothing.

"Come on. Come on. This is no time to be difficult. Work, you son of a bitch."

He struck the wheel again. This time the lighter worked. "Thank you. Thank you."

Holding the flame to the puddle at his feet, Mike barely had time to jump back as the cleaning solvent he had splattered about burst into flames. The flames climbed the walls, and roared down the hallway to his office.

Grabbing the remaining full cans, he ran back into the living room. "Everybody out. Now. Holly, take the kids and get by the front door. Only don't go outside until I tell you."

"What about you?" she asked.

"I'll be there in a minute." Mike waited for his family to get out of the way, then entered the living room and began splashing everything with flammable liquid. He doused the carpeting and the walls, the curtains and the furniture. He repeated the process in the library, and in the kitchen, and then set fire to all three rooms. As the rooms ignited in flames, an eerie hissing, screaming sound filled the air around him.

It's working. They don't like the fire.

Mike watched in delight as dozens of boogers ran from the fire, disappearing back into the cracks from which they had come. As the flames spread, the faces adorning the walls, ceilings, and floors began to fade and disappear, and the cracks in the ceilings and walls closed.

Knowing he had to be sure the opening was closing, Mike reentered the burning kitchen and hurried to the basement door. Opening the door, he stepped onto the stairs and aimed his flashlight at the room below. The shaft leading down to the world below was still there, but it was smaller now than it had been earlier. As he watched, the opening grew even smaller until it was no more. The boogers had returned to their world, closing the door after them.

"Mike!"

He turned away and started back up the stairs, panicked by the sight that lay before him. The fire had spread faster than anticipated. A wall of flames nearly separated him from the rest of the house. He had to hurry, because in a few minutes the whole house was going to come crashing down on top of them.

Dodging the flames, he raced across the kitchen and out into the hallway. Turning right, he hurried along the hallway toward the front door. The smoke was so thick, the heat so intense, Mike thought it might already be too late. He thought he wasn't going to make it. But then he was at the front door, hugging Holly and the kids.

"It's working. The fire is driving them away." He fumbled to open the door. "Hurry. We've got to get out of here."

"What about the boogers outside?" Holly asked.

"Let's hope they aren't there anymore." He pulled the door open and ushered his family outside. They crossed the front porch at a dead run, stopping when they were far enough from the burning house to be safe. Mike almost expected to be attacked when he stepped outside, but nothing rushed at them from the darkness.

Reaching into his pants pocket, he pulled out the set of keys that had once belonged to the sheriff. He tried several of the keys until he found the one that unlocked the patrol car. Mike waited until Holly and the children were safely seated, then started the patrol car and pulled away from the house.

At the edge of the driveway he paused, watching as their new home went up in flames. He should have been upset, saddened by the loss of the house and everything they owned, but he wasn't. They still had each other, and that was far more precious than material items. Nor was he upset about the prospect of moving back to New York City, which is exactly what they would do. There were dangers to living in a big city, any big city, but at least those dangers were of the known variety. Besides, anything the Big Apple could throw at him now paled in comparison to the challenges he had faced in the less than peaceful countryside.

Mike pulled out of the driveway and started slowly down Sawmill Road. Behind them the house continued to burn, the shadows dancing around it nothing more than those caused by the flickering flames. The boogers were gone, returning to their world. Baptized by flames, the doorway to the lower level was once again closed.

Author's Note

In August 1971 in the village of Belmez, not far from the city of Cordoba, in southern Spain, an image of a human face appeared on the kitchen floor of an elderly woman's home. No recognizable pigment of any kind had formed the strange image which appeared in the pink tiles.

Upset and bewildered, the owner of the house tore up the floor and replaced the tiles with concrete. But three weeks later a second face emerged.

A third face appeared, then a fourth, then a series of faces all together. The local authorities were called in, and the kitchen was locked and sealed. Four more faces, including that of a woman, appeared in another part of the house. But they were the last, for the phenomenon melted away as inexplicably as it had begun.

To this day no one yet has come forward with a satisfying explanation for what happened. The Faces of Belmez remain a mystery.

ONYX

BORIS STARLING
Messiah

"The killer's good...The best I've ever seen."

The first victim was found hanging from a rope. The second, beaten
to death in a pool of blood. The third, decapitated. Their backgrounds
were as strikingly different as the methods of their murders. But one
chilling detail links all three crimes. The local police had enough evidence to believe they were witnessing a rare—and disturbing—
phenomenon: the making of a serial killer...

"He'll kill again."

Investigator Red Metcalfe has made national headlines with his uncanny gift for tracking killers. Getting inside their heads. Feeling what
they feel. He's interviewed the most notorious serial killers in the
world. He knows what makes them tick. *But not this time.*

"Pray."

❑ 0-451-40900-0/$6.99